Fate of Smoke

Fate of Smoke

The Soulfire Series

Book One

Alisar Eido

The Unlikely Spark
Austin MMXVII

More Information at:

www.alisareido.com

www.alisareido.com/the-unlikely-spark

Cover by Amanda Cavazos-Weems

Logo by Logan Kees

ISBN-978-0-9989741-0-1

First Print Edition, Paperback, June 2017

10 9 8 7 6 5 4 3 2 1

Acknowledgments

Thank you to each and every person
who has spent time believing in this work.
Because of people like you, everything is possible.

A special thanks to the Beta Readers:

Natasha Reneau

Corissa Chopelas

Charlotte Griesel

Janet Hancock

Dedicated to 21st.

It is often through chaos that we find our finest order.

Chapter 1

Mortimer paced the study, soaked to the skin and shaking. The water from his tracks darkened the rug creating a grey path he marched over and over. He paused at the window to peer into the gloomy afternoon. The road to the abbey was clear, not even a figure in the distance. No motion at all, except the silver green flickering of the rain on the surrounding woods. The man strained his gaze towards the ground three stories below, trying to pick up recent hoof prints in the mud. The rain was too heavy to be sure.

He tore himself from the window and continued his dogged route. He did his best to keep his eyes off of the many specimens gleaming on the shelves. Most appeared to be plants, though he knew from experience that it was a mistake to look closely. There were tiny, pickled horrors hidden among the jars of greenery. Insects, the teeth of various creatures, the skulls of beasts, of men; the most gruesome of which were pieces of past patients, preserved forever for the study of their faults. All cunningly disguised with a layer of botany. To keep his mind off the morbid collection, Mortimer turned his attention to the enormous bookcases lining half of the room's walls. Medical histories and folk tales sat side by side with no obvious system to organize them. Knowing the man they belonged to there was surely some order to it, though the pattern would likely be lost on outsiders due to sheer complexity.

He ran his finger along the leather bindings, feeling their likeness to his own hands. He too was browning with age and wrapped with a dusty coat. He'd filled out the jacket in his prime, though it would have been hard to tell by how loose it hung now.

It made his already lean frame seem even more insubstantial. He might have once been handsome, too. But the dregs of middle age and something like sorrow had withered him; hollowing his cheeks and chasing gray paths through his wild-hanging hair, ragged like the edge of old pages.

Just as he began to lose himself in the shelves a sound pierced the quiet pattering of rain. He whirled to face the door, pressing his back to the bookcase. His eyes searched manically for a form in the dim light. It was only the tarnished grandfather clock chiming three. Mortimer let out a huge huff of relief. The man he waited for was known for stealthy entrances. Thankfully this had not been one of them.

The ease was short lived, however. Each moment held the same potential for a sudden appearance. A shiver ran down his spine, a mix of nerves and the chill of the drafty room seeping through wet clothes. He slid along the bookcase for a few steps allowing the shelves to guard his back until he could be sure the shadows were empty. As Mortimer's hand found the end of the case he turned to continue his pacing, for warmth if nothing else. But as he went to take his first step his eyes met the empty sockets of another creature.

He let out a scream and threw himself back from the beast. Colliding hard with a desk, he crumpled to the floor in a flurry of papers. His heart beat out of his chest as he looked up at the massive rearing form. His throat gulped in dry desperation for the air to cry for help. But before he could find words, the tide of panic began to drain away. He'd forgotten about the pelt.

The hide of this particular beast was a prized possession to the man who kept the study. The skin lay listlessly over several stands like a rag on a fence. The structure supported it in a strangely upright slouch inside a glass display. In its current state, it was a gigantic wolf, perhaps eight or nine feet from nose to tail. On one unfortunate occasion, Mortimer had discovered that it spent the majority of the month as the skin of a human; a period in which its owner covered it with a deep purple drape. It had to be over a hundred years old, though it still made the change with the full moon, a quality that endlessly fascinated its keeper.

Mortimer struggled to his feet on shaking legs. His stomach turned over as he noticed the numerous papers strewn about the floor. He gathered them hurriedly, trying to shuffle them into some sort of order. He stacked them on the desk as neatly as he could manage with trembling fingers and realized to his horror he'd dripped water across them. Frantically he began blowing, praying they'd dry by the time the man he waited for came home. As he fanned them a few words caught his attention. The graceful script read:

Possibility of Plague- Slim to None
Possibility of Pox - None
Possibility of Malaria - None
Possibility of Consumption - Slim to None
Possibility of Undiscovered Ailment - High

A trickle of recollection told him he'd read something about this in the paper. Something of a mystery sickness that had been cropping up in the next town over. No one had been able to make sense of it as of yet. Every doctor in the region was baffled and scurrying for their medical books. He read on, though the writing became increasingly harder to decipher. The letters scratched onto the page grew haphazard and crooked as if scrawled in a rush.

Patients tend to fall ill over a period of three to twenty-four hours.
First signs include mild fever, dizziness and disorientation, often

followed by fainting. If the victim remains conscious, they may report a feeling of chest constriction with bouts of severe coughing, in most cases yielding a black tar-like substance from the lungs. Patients begin to sweat profusely as with extreme fever, though bitterly cold to the touch. If not properly warmed, sweat may freeze to the skin, cause frostbite. Final stages, body takes on extremely pale hue, shedding tar substance form lacrimal glands of the eye. Black substance overflowing the mouth. Patient convulses. Sickness is contagious. All attendants removed at once. Go immediately. Peak of danger at moment of death.

The passage stopped as if the writing itself were out of breath. At the very bottom of the page the handwriting returned to its original grace in a single, lacy line.

No known cure. Few preventative measures. All observed cases fatal. Possible causes:

Mortimer shuffled through the disordered stack burningly curious for the list promised on the next page. He was so absorbed in his search, he hadn't noticed his new company.

"Didn't bother to hang your coat? Put those back."

A shiver startled down the sides of Mortimer's neck. He looked up to the door where lurked a lanky shadow with a voice he'd know anywhere; smooth like the strike of a knife. A young man, perhaps twenty-five, stepped forward. He was tall, well dressed, and gaunt, carrying a bulging medical bag. His dark brown hair was neatly tied back, framing the rather sickly structure of his face.

"Well?" The young man snapped. Mortimer recalled the papers in his hands and rushed them onto the desk.

"Darius, I..."

"Unless you are about to give me an unimaginably good reason why you left your post last night I'd suggest you say nothing."

Mortimer stopped to consider what the doctor might describe as a proper excuse. The truth wouldn't do.

He'd sat on guard outside the house for hours, which gave him plenty of time to watch the sun set and start fearing his own faults again. Something primitive seethed in him on nights like that, something vengeful, hateful. Feeling it rise, he'd gone to the pub to immobilize himself. Better passed out than violent. But Darius had heard that story before. He would have no sympathy for it again. Fumbling, he chose to be vague.

"I couldn't do it. Something came over me and I just couldn't."

"Drunk?"

"I wasn't. Not then. I kept my word. Sober as day. But you know what goes on with nights like these. You know what happens. I could never forgive myself if something happened to the girl on my account. So I left. I'm not the one for this, Darius."

"Nice of you to tell me after I've paid you," the doctor said taking a few measured steps forward.

"Here, then. I don't want it." Mortimer pulled a bag from his pocket and dropped it on the desk. No noise followed, except for the slight shifting of the doctor's perfectly white sleeve as he set his bag on a nearby armchair. It sloshed. It sickened Mortimer that he recognized the sound. Darius must have bled a patient while on his last call. On such occasions the doctor would collect the blood in bladders and bring it back with him. Certain tenants of the abbey needed to be kept fed.

Darius chuckled at the small bundle of coins the old man had cast on the table, a dark growling sound that held no amusement. "Am I supposed to take that back?"

Words bubbled in Mortimer's mouth but he was uncertain if

the question had been meant for him to answer. "I had hoped..." he ventured quietly.

Darius silenced him by slamming a fist onto the desk. "I couldn't care less what you hoped. You take it. You keep it. And you do your damned job," Darius snarled. The young man recoiled slowly, settling back into his previous poise. It seemed he'd rattled himself with the sudden outburst just as much as Mortimer. "Under these circumstances, I will not entertain negotiations." He tugged his vest to tidy it and went to stir up the embers of the previous night's fire.

"Then why me? You know I'm not cut out to do this type of thing. You have the money to pay anyone you like."

Darius shrugged. "The people I like can't be paid to sleep in gutters. You, however, are there so often no one thinks twice. I suppose that makes you a bit special this once."

Mortimer couldn't argue. He fell silent and sipped the air, still able to feel the heat of last night's spirits on his tongue lighting little fires in the sores on the inside of his cheek. There was no way out from under an insult that factual. Eager to move off the topic of his habits, he choked down his shame and changed the subject.

"Who is she?" he asked. Darius continued his task as if he hadn't heard. The white noise of the storm filled the space between them, punctuated by the careless clink of the fire poker striking brick.

The old man took a gamble and pressed the doctor further. "I'm serious, Darius. I'm not doing this unless you tell me more. I'm supposed to guard the girl's house but you haven't told me from what. How am I supposed to do it without knowing what I'm looking for?" To his surprise, the doctor turned to reply.

"You're right." Mortimer's eyebrows climbed high with surprise at the uncharacteristically docile reaction. "You should know more. Especially because your role is about to change. I made a call to that house just this morning, expecting to see you outside of it I might add. The girl's mother is sick. And since you were nosing into my things, let me assure you. She does not have the disease I've written about in those notes you so kindly reorganized for me. It's likely a cold. But they are in the house."

"Who?"

"Oh, of course you don't know. You weren't there. Demons. Demons are living under the house. They come out at night to search for the girl. There's no doubt they're there. Take one look at the candles in the place and they point to their routes as clear as day. They burn down faster on the side the bastards pass.

"They can sense her in the house, but not where. They're likely a rather low order without much intelligence. Regardless, they are not to be taken lightly. I suspect it's creatures like that that are causing the sickness. People are being eaten from the inside out. Soul first. Seeing as that's what I've been dealing with lately, I'm sure you'll forgive me for not giving a damn about your hesitations."

Mortimer braced himself on the desk and sank into the chair in a stupor. It sounded absurd. If the words had come from anyone less studied in the matter he might have laughed. "Sounds like The Prophecy if I didn't know better."

"Pity you don't. The only child, of an only child, and so on for generations? A girl whose hair is 'red with the blood unjustly spilled into Death's kingdom'? Demon's cropping up out of nowhere? She's the descendant of Merlin that The Prophecy talks about. That's exactly what's happening."

The old man's fingers wrapped the wooden arms of the chair like clinging vines as the color fled his face. He'd always thought something would have put an end to him before this day came. "It wasn't supposed to be for another hundred years or so. H-how can you be sure?"

"Are you questioning my intelligence or my study of the subject? The latter would be stupid, and the former...I highly doubt you want to take the conversation there," Darius warned. "More than anything, I'm sure because I met her. She radiates it. Some power you can't explain. It's jarring. Hell has been torn open, Mortimer. And that girl is our key to sewing it back up again."

Darius leaned back and crossed his arms, letting the old man take in what he'd just heard. He watched him scratch his oily, graying hair, sweat rolling down his brow, finding a certain satisfaction in the man's distress. Turning back to tend the small flame in the fireplace, the doctor continued. "You will tell no one. Creatures like that are drawn to panic. It helps them find a host. People who fear for their life shine like beacons to them. The last thing we need is mass hysteria because you decided to open your drunk mouth at the pub."

He let a scathing look fly over his shoulder, catching the guilt on Mortimer's downcast face. "Now for the best part. Your new role. In the case that you do see something unusual, and my guess is you soon will, you may not have time to seek me out. In that case, you will take the girl."

Darius jumped and whirled around at the sound of his desk chair toppling over. Mortimer had shot up out of his seat. "I will do no such thing," he said through gritted teeth.

"Good God! Sit down, man!" Darius hissed, trying to turn his startled jolt into something more threatening. But the old man stood firm.

"I am no kidnapper. I will not steal some poor, young thing from her family. And after she serves our purposes? What then? She'll never be able to go home. If she lives. I cannot wish that on anyone, force it on anyone, or allow you to inflict it upon them. I won't stand for it!"

"It doesn't matter what becomes of her. The Prophecy doesn't account for it and neither should we. If we fail in this she'll suffer the same fate as the rest, which will be merciful compared to our own, might I add. If we succeed I'm sure that problem will take care of itself. Find some hapless idiot dumb enough to marry the brat, or something. Who cares?"

A vein pulsed on Mortimer's forehead where the beads of sweat once grew. He was preparing to storm out of the room when Darius caught him with a final blow. "If she stays in that houses she will die." Mortimer shut his eyes against the news but Darius only poured forth more. "That death...you've never seen a thing like that. And no amount of note reading will ever let you understand. There are no words for it yet. There hasn't had to be...for how people contort when...how their faces..." The doctor fell silent, forcing down the memory before he could continue. "Next to that, kidnapping would be a mercy. Besides, she's a smart little thing. Too smart, even. If she realizes what's inside the house she may go willingly. If not however, you must take her. If you don't you will find out exactly what my notes could not tell you. Her blood will be on your hands. And we both know how long that takes to wash off, don't we?"

In the following quiet Mortimer found himself empty. His chest was hollow, holding no more of the courage he'd found in rage. It had steamed away and vanished like smoke as all the breath went out of him. He looked away, watching the fire gaining life in the hearth. "It never does," he murmured.

"That is something you should consider," Darius replied. Something insidious rang through his comforting tone. "Just think about the opportunity you have. Vengeance for your sister, it's not. But it is a second chance. Those are hard to come by." He slithered closer. "All you have to do is take the money, watch the house," Darius paused to relocate the bag of coins from the desk back to Mortimer's hand. "And save a girl's life. Yes?"

Mortimer looked at the bag in his hand, his joints aching with the urge to toss it into the fire. "Yes," he whispered.

"Good. Oh, before you go, some advice," Darius crooned. Mortimer glanced up at him, cautious of the offer of help. The young man's face held nothing of the calm comfort his words had pretended. His features sharpened with anger, he seized the old man by his ragged coat, jerking him violently around to face the beast in the glass. Darius pressed him hard against the case, forcing him to look again into the empty eye sockets of the wolf just inches from his own. Mortimer's shallow, frantic breaths fogged the glass before the animal's nose as if the skin itself might be breathing too.

"Defy me again, and that will be you."

Darius released the man with a push, making Mortimer stumble to keep from the ground. He caught himself on an armchair and turned as fast as he could to defend himself from the next attack. The doctor had not moved.

He stood in cold, impossible stillness next to the ghastly shell of the beast. The newly dancing fire sent their shadows leaping up the sanguine wallpaper behind them. Darius growled a final order.

"Get out."

Chapter 2

Misty white halos bloomed from five dainty fingertips pressed against the parlor room window. A brilliantly autumn-haired girl in a soft blue dress stared out past the rain soaked hedges lining the front walk. She watched a thread of smoke rising from the distant woods, her freckled nose a hairsbreadth from the window pane.

The fog of her breath on the glass grew and shrank hypnotically. The cacophony of party guests being gathered inside from the garden rang down the hall, but did nothing to break her focus. Her ears were already full with the washing sound of rain, the hesitant tick of the grandfather clock in the corner, and the tap of her father's approaching steps.

"Ah, there you are, dear. I was wondering where you'd gone off to." Mr. Dellins stepped in from the hall. She made no reply, continuing her silent gaze into the grey. The click of his best shoes drew close, his voice sounding over her shoulder.

"...Verenna?"

"He's late. The doctor. He should be here by now."

"That's hardly something to be troubling yourself with on your birthday."

"It's been hours!"

"Two hours. Only two hours since your party started and half of it you've been pressed up against this window waiting. You should get back to your guests."

"They're not *my* guests. How is it even my party if there's hardly anyone I like invited?" she whined, slumping down into a flowery cream armchair.

"Well dear, you don't like very many people," he ventured against his daughter's glare.

"Mum's sick. Do you expect me to just go about my day like nothing's the matter?"

"It's just another little head cold. She'll be over it within the week. She always is. Besides, she worked so hard to plan tea for you. She insists…"

"But what if she has it?" Verenna cut in.

"Has what? Half the time I swear I don't know what you're talking about."

"The *Mystery Illness*, Daddy! It was the headline in yesterday's paper. You must have seen it. *Whispers of Mystery Illness In Bronwell.* They say there's no cure."

"Kitten, Bronwell is far away. A hundred miles at least. And how the devil do you keep getting hold of the paper? It's no good for you when you take everything you read to heart this way. They make up half the hubbub they write about to sell more copies."

The papers had described the simmering worry in the walled city. They told of streets packed with the rich leaving for their summer homes in case the situation worsened and churches overflowing with the poor come to pray for deliverance. But Verenna's ever ready imagination painted chaos; clots of evacuees clogging the roads, thieves fighting for what they'd left behind, people falling dead in the streets to fatten the invading rats. Yet the main concern of everyone she knew was convincing themselves of how distant that problem was. They called it 'the problem to the north', if they spoke of it at all. Something about it curdled her mood.

Verenna sighed and returned to the window, again pondering the thread of remaining smoke. The fire must have gone out in the rain. With the weight of disappointment in her voice, she warned, "I don't think it's as far away as we all want it to be."

"Let it go." Her father groaned, pushing his glasses up and giving a weary rub to the bridge of his nose.

"You know the old abbey on the way out of town?"

"Honestly, dear. You have the most gruesome obsession with that place. I'll never understand the appeal of a rundown abbey turned hospital."

"Hospital for?"

"The incurably ill," he sighed.

"Exactly. It has to be the disease from the paper."

"You of all people know that that place was a hospital far before this new disease turned up in Bronwell. You're making this more troubling than it needs to be."

"Don't you think it's the slightest bit odd that suddenly everyone is seeing the doctor from the abbey? He never comes to town and now he's all anyone talks about. They say he lives out there and tries to cure the dying. What I don't understand is why no one calls Dr. Carter anymore."

"I was told he was ill when I sent for him. But he seems to think that your mysterious abbey doctor is a suitable replacement. From the way he wrote it, he's sending his own personal god. He said the man saved his daughter from Consumption last year, if you can believe it..." Mr. Dellins trailed off. "I'm sure Dr. Carter will be well soon."

As per usual, Verenna had heard only what she needed to continue arguing. "See? Even the doctors are getting sick. And the smoke. I've watched it for weeks," she said, turning to him with a clever gleam. "I think I've worked out what it is. They take all the cases of the illness from here in Canterford to the abbey. Then, when they die, they burn them so..."

"Stop it this instant. There are young men present," he whispered and pointed towards the noise of the party.

She scowled at the thought of the guests she'd abandoned. "I don't like any of them. Why weren't any of the good ones invited?"

"If you want the truth, you've scared the rest away. This outspokenness, and the subjects you bring up! It's a touch off putting. These men want to talk of marriage, not burning bodies."

"What's this party for, then, my birthday or my engagement?" Verenna shot out of her seat, her ears growing pink with indignation at the thought that she might have been tricked.

"Verenna…" Mr. Dellins began in a consoling tone. She looked back to the window, searching for a biting reply. "Vivie," he placed his hands gently on her shoulders. She dared a peek at him from the corner of her eye. "Look at me, will you?"

Grudgingly, she did. His kindly eyes smiled at her from behind his thin spectacles, shining like the silver buttons down his well pressed vest. The wisps of grey in his hair reminded her of snow clouds carrying winter onto his temples. But the lines around his eyes were her favorite. They'd come from laughter and squinting at books and business ledgers. She watched them deepen and shallow as he spoke.

"Do you know what this party is really about? Hmm?"

Looking down at her tiny shoes with a pouting lip, she shook her head.

"Your happiness," he finished, lifting her chin. "We want the best for you, your mother and I. We want you to smile. That's all we ask of you today. If you meet a few gentlemen, wonderful. If you meet no one, there's always tomorrow. Give them a chance, but first and foremost, be happy. Do you think you could?"

The corners of the girl's mouth began to twitch skywards though she fought valiantly against it. Her father beamed at the sight. "Now, you've spent long enough out here. And if I'm not mistaken, it's almost time to open your gifts. There's one on its way that I think you'll particularly like." He put his arm about her and guided her down the hall towards the commotion at the back of the house.

The great room was consumed with chatter and the tinkling sounds of cups and polite exchanges. With her father's hands on her shoulders to prevent escape, Verenna was forced to scan the room for a seat with the least objectionable neighbor.

One of the lacy garden chairs had been pulled inside still stood empty. She moved for the seat until a plump hand reached out and patted it; the stumpy fingers of Willoughby Porter.

"Right here." The tenor of his voice reminded her of a whining violin. Willoughby was boring, foppish, and had been slowly balding for at least a decade. He had come dressed in his finest, mostly silk, with a cravat so large it hid what little neck he'd managed to grow. On his lap sat a picnic basket with a massive blue ribbon around it.

"I've saved a place for you."

"Oh, I see that." The slightest push from her father urged her forward, her flaring nostrils giving away her distaste.

"Thank you, Mr. Porter," her father said as he turned her loose to join Willoughby.

"Yes. Thank you, Mr. Porter," Verenna parroted with just barely enough sincerity to appease the both of them.

"If you two will excuse me. Must make sure everyone's comfortable before gifts." Mr. Dellins bobbed the slightest bow.

"Of course. Wouldn't dream of keeping you." Willoughby bowed his head as if he were about to be knighted. Her father ignored the show and stepped away, leaving Verenna to flounder through a conversation with the man. Willoughby wasted no time starting things off.

"This rain is a shock. It might even be the same storm that had us arriving late."

"Just might be," Verenna said with no attention. She was busy searching over each shoulder for another place to take.

"Look at someone when you're talking to them, girl." Verenna jumped as she noticed Willoughby's mother perched on the other side of him. She had a pinched mouth, wiry black hair, and wore a sickly, parrot green dress, likely to distract from her features. "With the glowing reviews my son gives you, I thought you'd have some mastery of conversation at the very least."

"Naturally," Verenna said, meeting their eyes and pressing the edges of her teeth together into a grimacing smile.

"Well? Sit, why don't you?"

"Mother, we are guests," Willoughby attempted under his breath.

"I am aware. I am also aware of how rude it would be not to take a seat that was specifically saved for you." The old woman leered at her. Verenna gripped the back of the chair, dragging it ever so slightly away from the duo while giving one last look around for anywhere else to be. She'd nearly given up when a soft "yoo-hoo" rose above the din. Her twin cousins; a dim, heavily-perfumed light at the end of the tunnel. Any other day she would have sooner sat outside in the mud, but compared to the bleak option before her, she'd give relatives a chance.

"Oh hello!" Verenna called. She moved to join them with the chair in tow, letting Mrs. Porter's clucking fade behind her.

"I've warned you, girl. It's very rude. Didn't I warn her, Willoughby? No son of mine will come calling again."

"Mother, don't be silly. Tea next week Verenna! Don't forget!" Willoughby called.

Verenna held up a hand to acknowledge him, though she didn't hear his words. She was already preoccupied by her cousin's sly smiles. The both of them were covered in frills to the point of looking like a pair of iced cakes. In the past, they'd proven snide on good days, and hazardous to her health on bad ones. Verenna wound her way through the maze of other guests and placed her chair in the treacherous area between the twins.

"Martha...Gisselle..."

"Late," Martha teased. Both had tinkling giggles that reminded Verenna of plates breaking.

"Where were you? The rain started and you vanished. Honestly, we thought you'd melted." Again, they laughed. Verenna lowered herself onto the very edge of her seat, primed to jump up.

"No such luck. Here I am," Verenna said with false gusto.

"And we couldn't be happier for it." Gisselle's blue eyes glimmered as she patted Verenna's knee.

Martha joined in her sister's fun. "I'm just thankful you didn't turn out sickly like your mother. No one thought you'd make it this far. But here you are! A full seventeen years later. No prospective husband, but, you know, alive."

"You're setting some example. You're three years older than me and I haven't gotten any wedding invitations." Engagements tended to be stylishly long in Canterford. The build up to a wedding was a drug for the public. But four years was excess.

"Good heavens, we were promised the Anson boys at sixteen. It's only proper to wait a few years."

"Is that what they told you?" Verenna looked wryly from one shocked face to the other as the chime of her father's glass called the room to attention. When the sisters leaned in to listen she stared at the backs of their heads, imagining how satisfying it would be to yank the tiny bows from their perfect blond curls and wondering how their fiancés had resisted the same urge.

"Everyone! Over here, yes, attention please. I believe it's time we let the birthday girl open her gifts. What do you say?" There was a light shower of encouraging applause as Martha passed her a palm sized wooden box. Still outraged at Verenna's comment she practically slapped it into her hand.

Verenna looked skeptically down at the gift. It could be anything. They could have wrapped up another dead spider like they did when she turned eleven. The spite on their rosy faces indicated she might not be far off. But a room full of expectant eyes made her pull up the lid. She looked away and listened to the crowd's reactions. No one screamed. There were even a few oo's and ah's. She risked a peek at the contents.

"It's...beautiful?" Verenna couldn't help her confusion. It was a garnet necklace. A rather elegant one at that.

"Isn't it just?" Gisselle's grin told her the real surprise was on its way.

"It really is. I, it's...thank you. You know it's just like the one I lost all those years…"

Verenna paused and looked at the two sisters who were barely controlling their giggling. "That's how we knew you'd like it so much. It does look just like it, doesn't it?" Martha blurted, looking as if she might pop for holding her breath. "Just like it," Gisselle agreed.

"Thanks," she repeated, clasping the jewelry about her neck. Who knew how many years it would disappear for if it were left on the table. Before she had even finished straightening the necklace the blue ribboned basket was thrust in her face. Willoughby had wound his way through the chairs and practically launched himself at her to be next in queue.

"Here you are! Happy birthday!"

Undoing the latch that held it shut, she reached into the darkness of the basket. Her hand met something soft. She looked up warily but Willoughby who nodded reassurance. When her hand emerged, she held a little, white kitten with a bow on its neck. Its fur puffed out on all sides like a cloud, except for a clearing around its face, which was pushed in and frowning.

"It reminded me of you. Sweet and small and lovely." Willoughby beamed.

"Ohhh, how…" She looked back at the kitten's ill-tempered scowl. It hissed. "Thoughtful," she finished. Luckily, she was spared having to come up with any more words for the prissy little thing as her father called her name from the hall. She hadn't even seen him leave the room. But when she looked over she saw only a mountain of tea roses. The explosion of deep green and pale pink jutted from a massive sienna pot. All together the plant must have been three feet tall.

"Happy birthday, Vivie."

"How wonderful!" she said, jumping from her seat. She nearly tripped over her cousin's skirts but managed to flounder around them to throw her arms around her father.

"From mother and myself with love. We'll have them planted in the garden for you. You'll have them every year now."

"They're my favorite! Thank you!" She whirled and took a deep breath of the blossoms as if she'd wash her face in them. It was only after her face was planted in the blooms that she realized there was still someone holding them. She hurried back as a mischievous laugh issued from behind the enormous bouquet.

"Might want to wait until I'm out of here, Miss. I'm afraid I don't smell quite as nice as one of your flowers." The flower shop boy. In her excitement Verenna had forgotten who made their deliveries.

"Fabien!" she squeaked and clapped hands to her face to cover the growing blush on her cheeks.

"My lady. And where would you like these, Sir?"

"I think that corner there should be fine for now, thank you," Mr. Dellins instructed.

With the arrangement, out of his arms he turned to the room.

His height was noteworthy, as well as his untamable blond hair and wild green eyes. He managed to be striking even as the most underdressed person present. Verenna could swear she felt the parlor cool from all the newly fluttering fans.

"A very happy birthday to you, Miss Verenna."

"And to you. I mean…" Verenna had rushed the response and paid the price. She could feel the red of her face traveling to her ears. Thankfully he ignored the blunder.

"I hope it's been lovely thus far."

"It has."

There was a pause that left them simply smiling at each other as the room watched. It wasn't allowed to carry on long. Mr. Dellins broke in with a stern, fatherly, "Right then. You must have other deliveries, my boy, wouldn't want to keep anyone waiting."

"Very right, Sir. I should be going. Enjoy your flowers, Miss."

"You can stay if you like," Verenna blurted despite her father's disapproving gaze. "There's plenty of room." The offer was kind, but a lie. The parlor was packed tight.

Fabien lit up as if to say yes, but Mr. Dellins narrow-eyed stare corrected him.

"I'll, eh, actually be going. I do have to make a few more deliveries. But thank you for your invitation Miss Verenna. Very nice of you." He turned again to the room. "Gentlemen," he said with a respectful nod. There was no reply. "Ladies," he acknowledged with a slight bow. The breeze from the fans picked up to a full-on wind. And finally, with a full bow, "Miss Verenna."

One of the maids stepped forward to escort him to the door. Dreamlike, Verenna gazed after him until the sound of her own name woke her.

"Vivie, back to your seat, dear. There are more presents to open." Her father had come forward to usher her out of the middle of the room. "We got you the flowers, not the delivery boy," he whispered as she took her seat. "Now, which gift goes next?

Verenna was still distracted. She leaned in her chair and peered down the hallway. Fabien's height seemed even more impressive backlit by the open door. He paused and put his hat on before sliding out into the rain, carefully skirting a dark outline blocking his path. The shape did not move as he made an awkward edged around it. This new figure of a man stepped over the threshold, slow and deliberate, his limbs long, seeming stretched by the grey light behind him. Something heavy swung at his side. Verenna watched the servant nod, curtsy, and escorted him into the front room. It had to be the doctor.

Her mind rummaged for a way to get back to the front room while he waited there. If her father had his way she'd be opening gifts the whole time the doctor was there. Verenna was on fire with questions, she had been for weeks, ever since she saw the smoke coming from the abbey. She barely acknowledged that another box had been placed in her hands. The maid had come down the hall to whisper to her father. They both promptly headed for the front room. She could feel opportunity draining away. Could she run after them? No, they'd just drag her back.

"Well, go on then. Open it," a voice called from the corner. It brought Verenna back from thought, making it uncomfortably clear that the whole room was waiting. There was no excuse not to go on opening gifts, no reason they'd accept for her to go charging off.

Without anything close to a plan, Verenna shot up out of her chair, the next gift dangling from her hand by its ribbon. "Wait!" she yelled after them. Everyone froze including her father and the maid. Of course, she hadn't thought of anything to say afterwards. "Wait," she repeated a little quieter to give herself time to think.

"I wanted to say, um, that is, I want to tell you…" She could feel the flustered red of her ears on the rise once more. Thankfully, inspiration struck.

"Gratitude. Before we go any further, I'd like to express my deepest gratitude to you all. For being here today..." She paused and took a loud breath. "For such lovely gifts…" thus commenced the expert wobble at the knees. "I'm just so...overcome...I...." With that she wilted to the floor, even allowing a limp hand to knock the cutlery off of a small tea table nearby for that extra touch of realism. She was after all, a master of well-timed fainting. The rush of gasps and worried exclamations told her it had played perfectly. Except of course for Martha's squawking.

"She's faking. She always does. I know it. Honestly, it's the silliest thing."

Verenna wouldn't have anyone spoiling this. As her cousin ranted on, she managed to peek through her lashes just enough to spot the fork that had fallen with her. With the confusion and stress still fresh, she snatched it and gave Martha's foot a good jab, delighting at her shriek. Verenna immediately shut her eyes again and dropped the utensil, just in time for her father to reach her and lift her from the ground.

"Give her air!" he called, dispersing the crowd to the edges of the room. "Everything will be fine. A doctor's just arrived for her mother. He can easily have a look at her too. Please, everyone stay calm, I'll be back in just a moment."

Verenna felt herself being hurried away and knew they were headed to the front room. She took the short trip there to congratulate herself on a job well done. In a few moment's her father was placing her on the chaise next to the parlor windows.

"She seems to have fainted," she heard him say. She could picture him wringing his hands the way he did when he worried about her. The voice that answered him set her shivering.

"How endearingly typical," it sneered. The sarcasm was velveteen and poisonous. Slow, deliberate footsteps marked the doctors approached. Her eyelids trembled, fighting not to peek despite overwhelming curiosity. Verenna could feel the stranger kneel beside her and draw close to examine her. Just as she thought she would be able to keep her eyes shut, the shock of cool fingers on her neck broke them wide open. Without thinking she grabbed his wrist to pry away the source of the chill.

The doctor was not at all what she expected. He was much younger, perhaps twenty-five. Also thinner, meaner looking, with shadows playing in the strange hollows of his face. It looked as if he hadn't eaten in weeks. Though his clothing suggested he could afford a king's feast every night.

They were deeply colored, rich materials from the blue of his vest to the red silk cord that held back his sleek, dark hair. Such dark colors made his skin seem unusually fair. But by far his most noteworthy quality was the intensity of his stare. She was afraid to move. He'd fixed her like a snake. Verenna lay there clutching his wrist completely paralyzed. Stranger still than his pallid face was the look of terror that hung on it. He too was afraid. Of what she could not imagine. By his expression he might have been watching a city up in flames. He tore his wrist away from her. Before she could give his reaction too much thought his manner shifted. A smirk drew up one side of his mouth.

"How is she?" Mr. Dellins pressed as he hovered above them.

"Her pulse is certainly fine."

It was then she realized she'd given herself away. She'd woken up too quickly from the faint. Both she and the doctor knew it. Verenna cursed herself internally for getting sloppy just as she reached the finish line of an otherwise exquisite performance. The important part was that her father believed the act.

"Thank God," he sighed seeing Verenna spring awake. "My

dear, are you alright?"

"Yes, it's just my head," she placed a dramatic hand on her forehead and let out a moan.

Wringing his hands just as expected, her father said exactly the words she was after. "You'd best look her over Doctor…"

"Doctor Darius Defoe," the young man finished.

It was him. She'd have time for her questions yet.

"It's good to meet you. I'm afraid I must go reassure our guests. Vivie darling, you're in good hands. I've never heard anyone come so highly recommended by their peers."

"What peers?" the doctor inquired with a cold, dry look over one shoulder.

"Erm, yes, quite," Mr. Dellins stammered. The young man's arrogance had set him off balance. "I'll check in on you in just a bit dear."

As soon as her father's footsteps faded Verenna launched into the interrogation. "Are you that doctor from the abbey?"

The young man seemed vaguely surprise. "You certainly don't waste any time, do you?" he muttered. "One moment you've fainted, the next you're full of questions." His wintry fingers wrapped her wrist to take her pulse.

"Well, aren't you?"

The young man paused to count the rhythm. "Perhaps."

The girl's face crunched up in frustration. "I know you are."

"Then why bother asking?"

The two went quiet, a challenge coming to life in the silence. The smugness of an assumed victory crept back across the doctor's face. Verenna's determination redoubled.

He began to examine the girl's head for bumps or cuts from her fall.

"You're in town because that mystery disease has reached us, hasn't it?"

The doctor paused to take her in, his eye the only moving bit of him, shifting in search of how much she knew. Reminding himself that she couldn't possibly know more than what had been in the papers, he continued his exam.

The slight break in his calm demeanor gave Verenna hope. She'd hit on something and it only served to encourage her.

"It must have. In all the times we've called a doctor it's never been you. And my mother gets head colds all the time."

"Is that all the evidence you have?" he raised an eyebrow to dismiss the whole discussion.

"Everyone says there is a doctor that lives at the abbey in the woods, with all the extreme cases. The ones no one knows how to cure. He takes them in to study them, hardly ever comes to town…They call it Falseman Inn, you know? Most agree it's a hospital. But others, they say that some of people who live there aren't really people at all. They're something else that only the doctor knows. You do know, don't you?"

"Ridiculous," he muttered. The young man swallowed hard but kept himself collected, holding up a finger for her eyes to follow. It did not distract her.

"Of course you know. That's the reason you won't answer me."

"Watch my hand, please."

Her eyes swung with the motion like two copper pendulums, bright and sure. "I just don't think it's a coincidence that you've suddenly started coming to town. Bronwell is only a week's ride from here at best. There have surely been cases in Canterford."

"Cases?"

"You're the doctor to the incurable. What cases do you think I'm talking about? Whatever's in Bronwell, we have it here too."

"That is completely untrue. Even if it was, what would you personally do with the information? Save them all?"

She swatted his hand out of the air. The fierce russet

pendulums fixated on him, prying him for secrets.

"My mother's got it, hasn't she?"

"I haven't seen your mother yet, but I highly doubt it. I told you. It hasn't reached this region."

"Then what's the smoke?"

"Good God, you're dramatic."

"And you are a liar. It has reached us. You're treating the people who have it out there at the abbey. And when they die, you're the one having them burned. Maybe to stop it from spreading. Maybe to hide how many have been taken."

To her surprise the doctor said nothing. He stood, shaking his head, and shut his medical bag with a snap.

"Well, say something!" Verenna snarled, shooting to her feet to meet him eye to eye, though she fell at least six inches shorter than him.

The doctor sighed. "As a physician," he began, pausing to toying with her. The girl was so desperate for the next word she could hardly stand still. "My recommendation is that you drop this kind of nonsense all together. And to avoid further *fainting spells,* drink more water, loosen those corset strings a bit and try to find a hobby other than watching the smoke from your neighbor's chimneys."

He watched delightedly as Verenna's ears went scarlet on either side of her furious face. Rouge flooded her cheeks as well. If it carried on, she'd be as red as her hair within the minute.

Verenna stared up at him as if sheer ferocity and willpower might make her grow to match his height. His every feature made her stomach turn. Her hands itched to slap him, each joint electric with the urge. Just as she thought she might give in, the doctor shifted, cleared his throat and looked away.

With one thin hand he reached inside his vest. She leaned away, unsure of what he'd produce from it.

Her startle set him smirking. Out fluttered a delicate white handkerchief. "Your nose…" He extended the well-pressed cloth.

"What about it?" she blustered.

"It's bleeding."

Verenna snatched the handkerchief and dabbed above her lip. A perfect ruby blot stood in stark contrast to the crisp fabric.

"I...is that...blood?" she stammered. The world went hazy.

"Unless you have another red liquid you tend to store inside yourself." He would have continued, but the girl had gone suddenly pale. "Good God, you're not *actually* going to faint, are

you?"

"No....of course…no." Her knees buckled and she toppled towards the floor.

Chapter 3

"But how do you know he was telling the truth?" Verenna demanded, throwing herself face down at the foot of her mother's bed. She'd never forgive herself for fainting. The doctor's whole visit had gone by and she had next to no information to show for it.

"He's a doctor, Vivie. He'd make more money telling me I did have it than telling me I didn't. He had no reason to lie."

Verenna groaned a few muffled words into the bed covers.

"What's that?"

"There's something wrong about him. There's something he's hiding."

"Now you're just being judgmental. He was a perfectly polite young man. A little mysterious, I'll grant you, but more than competent."

Verenna made a languid roll onto her back and looked up at her mother. Her face was only beginning to show the creases of her age. For her years, poor health, and having had such a terror of a child, she had come through it remarkably well preserved. Only a few grey strands dared to creep amongst the oak brown braids of her hair. Verenna hoped she'd look the same when she got older. Though her hair blazed ruby, both had the same copper-brown eyes.

"It's ridiculous, really. He's only done good for me and yet here you are moaning," her mother said with a playful smile. "It's going to be alright."

"But what if it isn't? And what if the smoke…" She never

finished the sentence.

"And what if it floods and the sun doesn't rise? Vivie. Everything is fine. I'm going to be fine. In a day or two that is. Would you pass me my knitting? It's on the chair."

The girl rose, sighed and fetched the soft, bluish bundle with shuffling steps. She passed it to her mother and would have plopped back down on the bed again, but a sliver of night peaking in between the curtains brought her towards the window. Verenna pulled the drapes aside. Under the full moon the street below seemed splashed with milk, it's glossy spill interrupted only by the sleeping mass of a beggar on the cobblestones. From the chimneys streamed ashen ribbons. They stretched to feed the low bellied clouds that threatened to swallow the night up in rain. One stream in particular, the finest thread of smoke in the distant woods, had all of the girl's attention. It came from the abbey.

Verenna let herself imagine what might be happening at the source. She saw warped faces gazing down at a pyre from darkened windows like a hundred beetle eyes. They wavered behind the haze of heat from the fire. The doctor would be there. He'd stand back from the flames directing whatever assistants he kept as they trudged their weighty bundles to the flames. Each mass cast into the blaze with an earthen thud

The sound of her own name tugged her from her wondering. "Verenna? You're dreaming again. You shouldn't worry about that abbey so much. It's a good thing they do there. Those people would have nowhere to go otherwise."

"But there's a fire every night! A big one if I can see it this far away."

"Old buildings are drafty things. Of course they have a fire at night. Most likely many. It's nothing."

"I doubt it," Verenna muttered.

She looked to the lamp flickering beside her on a lace draped table. Hard to imagine that butter colored spark was the same substance as the roaring red she pictured at the abbey. With the right conditions, they were the same thing. Verenna watched the flame move, noting that it pulled towards the window, burning one side of the wick faster than the other. Assuming it was a draft she shut the curtains and returned to the bed, drooping her head onto her mother's shoulder.

"Do you wish I was like other girls?"

"Absolutely not." Her mother dropped her knitting to her lap. "Without your temper and odd interests, your father and I would have been bored to death by now. There's never a dull day with you. I started calling you Vivie because of how vivid your hair was. I had no idea at the time it would apply to your imagination too. What I can't figure out is where you got either, the imagination or that shade of hair. But I wouldn't change it."

Verenna closed her eyes as the click of her mother's needles resumed. "Even when I upset the Porters?"

"Between us dear, especially when you upset the Porters. Everyone needs to be shaken up once in a while. You have an active mind. That's always a good thing. Even when it's getting you into trouble. Minds like yours are what the world needs."

The rhythmic tap of the knitting needles set Verenna's mind drifting back to thoughts of the abbey and its smoke. "What if there is something wrong, though? What if that disease..."

"Darling, get some rest. I think it's sweet you're so worried for me, but there is really no need. It's been a long and exciting day for you. It'll all make more sense tomorrow."

Groaning she rose limp-limbed from her mother's bed. "You always say that."

"Because it's always true."

Verenna shuffled to the door.

"Vivie?"

The girl spun around. Hope caught in her throat. Maybe her mother would say she believed her; about the abbey smoke, the disease, the doctor. Any of it would do.

"Happy birthday, love. Remember. You are exactly what the world needs."

A nice enough sentiment, but the weight of disappointment sagged her shoulders. Verenna put on a weak smile. "I'll try. Good night, Mum."

"Good night."

Verenna took up her candle at the door and slipped into the hallway. The familiar creak of the boards could have told her where she was even without the light. Her bedroom door hung open at the end of the hall like a welcoming hand. The maid had already turned down the sheets and gone, knowing she'd be up late talking with her mother. The fireplace snapped politely in greeting. Its low flames cast the room in amber.

The fresh linens and lace edged pillows held no appeal. She wasn't at all tired. Instead she padded to the window, set the candle on her writing desk, and threw the drapes carelessly aside. The distant line of smoke was barely visible now.

Verenna flopped into her desk chair and leaned her cheek to her fist. She was almost lost in thought when something soft bumped against her leg. She startled and looked down to find the kitten from Willoughby's basket playing with the hem of her night dress. The bow that had dwarfed it at the party had been removed which seemed to have improved the creature's attitude considerably. She scooped it up by its fuzzy white middle. The little thing curled itself in her lap and gazed out the window as if joining in her vigil. It purred when she pet it's ears but did not move it's pale green gaze from the night outside the window.

Her heel tapped in a vain attempt to rock worry to sleep. Despite the soothing hum of the kitten she couldn't rest easy. She produced her latest stolen newspaper from the desk drawer with the false bottom. With a headline like 'Mystery Illness' how could anyone sleep? She let the flimsy pages drop to the table and leaned back to watch the last whispers of smoke peter out above the trees.

❧

Verenna awoke to the sting of hot wax on her hand. The cat had upset the candle she'd left on the desk. It rolled dripping across the table, the wobbling flame still alive to melt it. Her head whipped around just in time to see the kittens tail vanish under the bed.

Grumbling, she swatted the candle off the table. It extinguished the instant it hit the floor, leaving only the struggling embers in the fireplace and the saucer of the full moon to light the room. The flakes of white tallow Verenna peeled from her skin uncovered red stamps of heat. She shook the hand to free it of the prickling feeling. Then with a huff she snatched the candle and knelt to light it from smoldering wood in the hearth.

She had no idea how long she'd been asleep or what time it might be. It certainly wasn't morning. The sky was too dark and moody. The growling clouds she'd seen earlier had lumbered to the very edges of the moon and started shedding their watery burden.

As the candle sparked to life she heard something downstairs. Not a boom like thunder, but several, like books falling. For a moment she wondered if it was her tired ears making things out of the weather. It happened again.

She pressed an ear against her door listening. Perhaps it was the maid, or her father up for a late night read in the study. Curiosity got the better of her and she cracked the door. She watched the flame of her candle follow the draft, leaning towards the hallway beyond. Verenna followed it's pointing.

It could be her mother. She did hate to trouble the maids in the middle of the night. "Ridiculous," Verenna muttered to herself. How did her mother expect to get better wandering around on the cold floors in the dark? She marched for the stairs with the kitten chasing her skirt.

Rain tapped harder at the glass as she passed the windows on the stairs. It seemed to get darker as she descended, and darker still as she approached the study. Crediting it to the storm finally consuming the moon, she ignored it and pressed on. Verenna squinted her eyes, widened them, then squinted again, trying to force them to see into the shadows. As they adjusted she could see several large volumes had fallen from the shelf. That accounted for the noise. But who had knocked them down?

"Father?" There was no reply. She tried again. "Mother? Are you making that racket?" Still, all quiet. Shrugging she seated the books neatly back where they came from. "Come on," she urged the kitten. "Back to bed." To her surprise it had stopped playing. It stood frozen, staring the same way it had on her lap at the window. It seemed mesmerized by the spot on the shelf where she'd replaced the books.

Another drip of wax pricked her hand. The candle flickered madly, making the shadow of the volumes waver on the wall.

She nudged the kitten gently with her foot to break its focus. "Nothing to play with," she chided. "Off we go."

Finally, the little creature shifted to follow her. She reached stairs with a few muted steps and looked up, grasping her heart and jumping back as she caught sight of a form on the steps above her. "Father!" she panted. "You scared me!"

Silence greeted her.

The hair on the back of her neck prickled. Out of nerves she swallowed and continued. "Angry I'm out of bed? Say something at least."

Nothing came in return.

As Verenna watched the shape, she started to doubt it was her father. Perhaps it was the shadow of the trees moving in the wind outside; a cluster of shadows undulating against the wall. The longer she stared, the stranger it became. It was more devoid of light than anything she'd ever seen. Liquid night, suspended, weightlessly tumbling like ink dropped into water.

The cat hissed from his hiding spot behind her ankle as the figure rolled one step forward. The shape began melting towards the stair it rested on, pooling there, congealing its lightlessness. It swayed on the step, left to right and back again, searching, smelling.

The candle flared, devouring one side of the wax at an alarming rate, tumbling over its dish, spattering her hand and dripping to the floor. The flame strained away from her as if drawn to the form on the stairs. Verenna managed a last whisper.

"Hello?"

The creature charged. The dark of its body poured down the steps, surging to reach her. The kitten bolted as Verenna stumbled backwards. She scrambled to the front door. Her hands fumbled with the lock as the creature gained momentum, rushing past the last step of the stairs. Throwing the door wide she burst into the front garden at a run. The cold rain shocked her skin, spurring her on faster. She reached the garden gate. Daring a look back Verenna saw the creature overflow the entryway to pursue her. It rolled along the ground like swift moving fog devouring all the light before it, gaining size, swelling its darkness into a frenzy.

The hinges of the garden gate screamed as Verenna flung them open and took off down the street. Her bare, sprinting feet slapped the forming puddles on the cobbled street. It followed just as swiftly, tugging at the flames in the streetlamps, threatening to leave her with only moonlight to escape by.

"Anybody!" she shrieked between panting. "Help anybody!"

She had no sense of where she was or where she might go. Nothing seemed familiar anymore.

The creature gained on her. She could feel it in her spine. Her throat was raked raw with screaming by the time she flew around the corner onto Main Street. There had to be some shopkeeper up late enough to hear her.

"Anyone, help! I'm here! Help!"

Tears streamed down her face seamless with the downpour. She was running out of breath. Terror burned in her lungs and legs, forcing her further against the demands of exhaustion. The creature closed in. Verenna could feel it's pull at her back, drinking away her will to run just like it drank the candle flame.

Something slammed into her side. The force tossed her against the brick wall of a shop, her head striking brick with a nauseating crack.

Verenna sank to the ground in a spinning daze. Surely this was the end. Her eyes refused to focus as she tried to glimpse her attacker. It might have been a trick of her rattled mind, but there appeared to be two dark shapes before her now.

The forms circled each other in the street. One, the tumbling blot that had chased her from her home, the second, a bizarre shape of a man. He stooped low with his shoulders hunched forward as if standing were painful. Now and again he'd place his hands on the ground and shift himself along on all fours. The two beasts circled each other. She lay there half conscious, their forgotten prey.

Seeing their distraction Verenna forced herself up on one elbow and tried to crawl for the alley without the creature's notice. Her eyes never left their blurred dance as she inched towards escape.

The shapes stopped circling, coming to an impasse mere inches from each other. Then, out of the nothingness, erupted a riot of primal snarling as the two toppled to tear at each other on the ground. All manner of unholy sound gushed from the violence. The creatures rolled closer. The man shaped fighter emerged on top of the pile. He ripped the other beast from the cobblestones and threw it to the other side of the street. Then on all fours, the outlandishly bent figure turned to her.

Verenna let her body go slack in the hopes that whoever or whatever this shape in the dark was it would mistake her for dead. With her eyes closed she had only the soft shuffling sound of the beast's footsteps to know it's approach. A hand came down on her shoulder as if pawing to wake her. She flinched at the touch but kept quiet, holding her breath as the creature sniffed for life.

A sudden wash of cold passed over her, forcing a gasp into her ragged lungs. The ink-like entity had returned and pounced on the beast. The fight began again on top of her. The forms grappled a hairs breath from her wide eyes. She shrieked and covered her head, balling up as they stepped around and on her. In the melee of yelping and growling she could hear the strike of metal on stone. The clink and scrape of missed blows with a knife inched closer and closer until one of the misfires landed. An icy plunge between her ribs that sent a curl of agony through her body. Clutching her stomach she watched her blood run with the rain into the cracks of the street.

She rolled to her back. The fighting had stopped. The creature from the house had gone and the other hurried to her once more. Verenna knew as it knelt beside her that it was not human. She raised a weak hand to ward off blows. None came and it fell back to earth useless. The beast paced around her in quick, worried loops, resting now and again by her side to whimper. Its hovering blocked the rain from her open mouth as she gaped like a fish in shock and pain.

A haze pushed in from the sides of her vision. Numbness seeped into her limbs; a cold, insidious lullaby that insisted she sleep. The gash in her side pulsed as it gushed her life onto the ground. Verenna tried to form words with her twitching throat but stumbled over them, coughing. She tasted iron.

Her heart could no longer keep up with the pounding of the rain. Verenna felt herself sinking into the ground, the smell of wet earth overwhelming her senses. A few last, muffled sounds drifted to her ears before she washed away with the water; running steps, the clack of shoes. Someone was coming for her.

The urgency in the newcomer's voice rang clear through her failing senses. "Get back! You've done enough!"

Such a familiar tone; velveteen even in anger. The shout hurried the creature away and a new shadow took its place. Her eyes closed as a cool hand slid behind her head to lift it from the stones. A last whisper reached her before oblivion.

"I'm so sorry."

Chapter 4

Acrid smoke filled Verenna's nostrils making her lurch out of sleep. Her fists clenched around white bundles of sheet. Feeling trickled back to her arms and legs as the sour taste of unclean teeth overwhelmed her mouth. A room swam into focus. There were faces here, watching her. Dread bloomed fresh in her stomach, urging her to get to her feet, to brace herself for a fight. She flailed to escape the blankets only to have two shackle-like hands wrap her upper arms and press her down. She kicked and spat, encouraged by the "oomph" she heard as her knee collided with what felt like a stomach. Curling her body to one side she tried to bite her assailant's arm. Finally, the sound of her own name put an end to her violent writhing.

"Miss Verenna! Verenna Dellins!"

In the pause, a pair of deep green eyes appeared out of her sleep hazed vision, framed by disheveled blond hair. "Fabien?" she creaked, throat weak from lack of use. His grip on her arms loosened as she recognized him. "Where? How long...?"

"Don't worry. Lay back and we'll explain what happened."

"No. No," Verenna muttered attempting to sit up again. He pressed her back.

"Miss, you're going to have to trust me a moment. I promise it'll all make sense soon."

Despite her confusion she was glad to see him. A friendly face after such an awful dream was a relief to say the least. It had to have been a nightmare. The shadow in the house, the chase, her blood running in the cracks of the street; if it had been real she'd surely be dead. Then again, if she'd imagined it all, how had she come to this strange new place.

The room was unfamiliar but not at all frightening; tidy and dim, with daylight trickling around the edges of the curtains. To her right stood a rivet studded oak door. Beside it a lamp and an armchair worn flimsy with age. To her left, the light of an oil lamp gleamed off of a collection of bottles and medical tools laid out across a table. And next to it stood the doctor. A shiver danced down her spine. He looked considerably less gaunt than when they'd met in the front room of her house, though not an ounce more pleasant. In his fingers he held what looked like a smoldering stick of incense.

"You?" The word stumbled from her mouth without her permission.

"You?" he replied raising a mocking eyebrow. He pulled a bit of leather from his pocket and extinguished the smoking end of the stick.

He nodded to Fabien who released his hold on her arms and seated himself at the foot of the bed. Verenna waited expectantly for one of them to launch into some kind of explanation. But Darius turned back to the instruments on the table, and Fabien's encouraging stare told her nothing. "Well, talk. How did I get here? Where *is* here?" she croaked.

Darius answered while pouring the contents of a ruby bottle into a suspicious looking jar and swirling it. "Where do you think you are? Last we met you were full of theories. Take a guess."

The hair on the back of her neck prickled as she said the words, "Am I dead?" Fabien broke out laughing as Darius spat out an indignant reply.

"Absolutely not! I saw to that personally."

Verenna's mind whirred as her second guess took shape. For some reason it chilled her more than the first. Her stomach squeezed in on itself as she whispered the name. "Falseman Inn."

"Correct. I knew you were smarter than you looked. Now," Darius set down his concoctions and took a place next to her on the edge of the bed. Something somber reverberated in the depths of his voice as he spoke. "Do you remember what happened?"

Verenna glared down at the white sheets and tried to focus on the last thing she knew was not part of a dream. Reality and sleep wound together in a mangled knot. "I don't know. I woke up because there were sounds coming from downstairs, books had been pushed off the shelf. I put them back, I think, and...I must have gone back to bed because I had the most horrible dream I've ever..." She looked up.

All the humor had left Fabien's face. He glanced to Darius who stared down at his folded hands.

"What?"

"Did the dream have to do anything with you being chased out of your house and ending up dead on Main Street?"

Her head swam. Each detail of the night came spinning back in sharp, horrific contrast. "Yes," she whispered, hoping the word wouldn't set free her welling tears. The sounds of the brawling creatures echoed back to her like the ring of metal. She tried to shake them from her ears. "It can't be true," she muttered. What about the knife? She'd been stabbed in the dream. If any of this were real there had to be some trace of where the blade had slid between her ribs. She grasped at her side. Her hand met a distinct lump of bandages hidden under her night dress. Frantic, she searched the dress for a tear, for blood.

"It's not yours. The gown. One of the women here was kind enough to give you one of hers."

Darius' words meant nothing. Her hands hurried along the gauzy belt encircling her body. Judging by its thickness, it hid a devastating injury. "No, no, no, no." Verenna hardly heard herself. Fabien took her hands to stop her undoing her bandages.

"Miss, you'll make it worse."

"Worse? I've been stabbed! How could it get worse?"

"You'll tear the stitches," Darius scolded. "Now, relax and behave. Don't be a brat about it."

Fabien rushed to her defense. "I'd expect you to have better bedside manner after being a doctor as long as you have. She's been through a lot. Give it a rest."

"I did. A week of it. In which time I've saved her life and tended to her every need. I'm the one who needs the rest." Darius rose and went back to the jar he'd been mixing, swilling the dull, greenish liquid around the sides and holding it up to the lamp light.

"Saved?" Fabien grumbled.

"Don't start," Darius growled without turning. "I certainly didn't see you being a hero."

"Oh, and you were? I don't think it counts as real 'saving' when it's also self-serving."

"What's self-serving?" Verenna's initial shock had cleared enough for her to join in the conversation.

The tension settled between the two as they grudgingly quit the argument. "Personal disagreement. Think nothing of it." Darius dismissed.

"He's right. It's nothing. Just lay back now and relax."

She took Fabien's advice and lowered her head to the pillow. Staring at the ceiling, her jumbled thoughts came into better order. "Did you say I'd been here a week?"

"I did," Darius hesitated.

"My parent's will be looking for me."

"The whole town's looking for you," Fabien added under his breath, "And then some."

"They don't know I'm here?"

A pause set in and Darius stopped stirring. "No."

"Why not!?" Verenna shot up again, this time feeling a tug in her skin as she strained her stitches. A tingling line awoke under the wrappings.

"We can't let just everyone know you're here," Fabien said in an attempt to calm her.

"You kidnapped me. Don't deny it. How else would you know what happened?"

"Firstly, no one is holding you hostage, you just haven't been well enough to get up and leave. Secondly, there was a man who saw you running out of the house. He followed you to help and saw the whole thing. The luckiest part of it all is that I ran across the situation while leaving my last patient."

"Then tell my parents. Tell them where I am or you're both kidnappers."

"Miss, it's not that simple. If they know, they'll come here with police. It's just not safe for them to be here. The abbey's got to be as private as possible for the sake of those being treated." Fabien reached for her hands but she yanked them away.

"So, it's not safe for my parents to come, but it's perfectly safe for me to stay here?"

"Well, in a way..."

"That makes no sense. And what are *you* doing here anyway? Isn't this place for dying people?"

The question seemed to fluster Fabien. Darius turned from his work with a mixture of warning and expectation on his face.

"I...It's not glamorous, mind you," Fabien struggled.

"I'm listening." Verenna crossed her arms, unable to imagine a decent reason for his presence.

"Flowers," he finally regurgitated. "The shop I work for sends their old flowers here when patients die. I deliver them. Then I heard you were here, so I've been around a lot."

He'd escaped her, though all of it seemed entirely too convenient. Verenna shook her head. "I don't belong here. I'm not dying. I'm not even sick."

Darius scoffed and added the contents of another mysterious vial to his concoction. "Not anymore. Believe me, when you were found you more than qualified. If I hadn't taken a few drastic steps to save you on the spot you wouldn't have made it to this room."

Verenna ran a hand over her newly throbbing side. "None of this makes any sense."

"It doesn't have to. Now drink this." Darius extended the jar he'd been swirling. She peaked over its rim at the sloping greenish liquid, shrinking from the sour stink of it.

"I want to go home." She turned away with a huff, refusing to acknowledge how it hurt her side to do so.

"We'll see to that later. First, drink this," the doctor insisted.

"Later as in today?"

"A month if you don't do as you're told."

"I want to go home now!" Verenna shrieked, a biting pain stirring in her injury.

"And there's nothing I'd like more than to send you packing. But you are not well enough, and you are my responsibility. So you will stay, and you will drink this." Darius inched the glass closer. She twisted even farther to avoid it. Tears gathering in the corners of her eyes as the motions tugged her stitches near to breaking.

"She's a lady, Darius. Watch your tone," Fabien stood to meet him, though the doctor ignored the confrontation entirely and pressed on.

"That hurts your side doesn't it, pouting like that?"

"No. Why?" she sniffled.

Darius smirked. "That's a lie if I've ever heard one. I haven't given you anything for the pain since last night. You'll need this soon if you don't already."

"What I need is my own bed in my own house."

"Maybe so. Or maybe you need answers."

She felt the bed shift as he alighted on its edge. "What do you mean?" Everything in her wanted to defy him, but curiosity demanded she hear him out.

"You were so curious about this place you faked fainting just to get a private audience with me. I know you have questions about what goes on here. If you stay, I can promise they will be answered. I can also promise you the best treatment money can buy, all for free, if you just stay put."

Verenna scanned him for signs of a trap, but even Fabien seemed confident in the proposal. She couldn't imagine anything more fascinating than exploring the abbey. There was the risk that if she saw too much they might try to keep her. Still, the lure dangled. With a creak of uncertainty, she said, "Dr. Carter will help me at home. He can..."

"No, he can't. That man dreams of being able to do what I'm capable of. He'd try, bless him, but he couldn't keep infection from something that deep," the doctor bragged, gesturing to her side with the sloshing jar.

"He's right," Fabien confirmed. "I hate admitting it, but you won't find a better doctor."

Verenna counted the years she'd known Fabien. Three perhaps. They'd never been close, her father hadn't allowed it, but still she'd never caught the young man lying. "You think I should stay?"

Fabien shifted his weight and looked down, running a hand through the wilds of his hair. He shrugged. "Nothing better comes to mind."

"It's settled then!" Darius jumped on the end of Fabien's

words. "Let's start with something for the pain." He shoved the jar into her hands. The ache was climbing higher one rib at a time. But it didn't hurt bad enough yet to make her drink the off-color sludge. She glared skeptically into the container.

"I've kept you asleep most of the time to heal you faster. You don't even know how much you're going to need that." Darius gave the glass a flick. A bubble burst the surface.

"Tell me," Verenna blurted to distract herself from the vomitus prospect of downing the potion. "If you're so good at this, why do you live out here and keep it all a secret?"

"Here, I am with those who need my services the most. Also, burning people for sorcery wasn't that long ago. They'd still be doing it too, it's just that exceptional people learned to hide their talents. Canterford is not ready to see all of what I can do. They'd never understand it."

It was Verenna's turn to scoff. "Sounds like a pretty poor excuse."

Fabien chuckled, watching Darius adjust his collar in restrained frustration. "I have faith that the contents of that jar will prove my skill. But only if you drink it."

His insistence made her nervous. After all she had no idea what was in the cup. "I'd rather not, thanks."

Darius shot up, jaw tight and fists balled, towering above her. "You don't know how lucky you are. The fact that you can sit up and sass me is a testament to my triumph over death. I'm offering to show you the future of medicine first hand with no charge and you're being stupid about it."

Verenna wound up to slap him but Fabien caught her arm. She tried to fight her way out of his grip but pulling that hard sent a ripping pain through her middle. Her face gathered into a silent scream that made Fabien drop her arm and help her back onto her pillows, catching the jar before it slipped from her fingers. She clutched at her side and tried to slow the gasping breaths that threatened to tear her in half.

"Don't do that," the doctor mocked in a sing-song tone.

"Are you really going to laugh at this?" Fabien rose to his full height. He puffed out his chest and moved in on the doctor. Darius simply shrugged.

"Who's laughing? I'm very serious. She shouldn't be flinging her limbs at anyone, especially in this state."

Verenna caught her breath enough to interrupt.

"Fine," she blurted. "I'll stay the night. But you'd better convince me you're a miracle worker by the morning or I'm leaving. Give that here." She pointed to the jar. The bout of agony had made her eager for it. Fabien passed it to her, assuring it was secure in her pain-weak grasp.

"Consider that the first miracle," Darius gloated.

Before drinking, Verenna considered one last time what this could mean. If it worked, it would put her in their debt. If it didn't...it could be poison. Then again, if no one had harmed her in the week she'd been unconscious, they weren't likely to start now. They weren't telling her everything and she couldn't afford to believe their reasons were completely innocent. But whatever their aims, there seemed to be some vested interest in making her well.

"I want to make a deal," she demanded.

Darius rolled his eyes, though Fabien was far more open to it. "Go on," he prompted.

"I'll drink this. I'll stay and let you treat me. But I want answers. All of them. I'm serious, all the details on everything I ask. Yes?"

Clearly upset that his services were going at such a low price, Darius barked his agreement. "It will be arranged."

"Do I have your word?" She raised the glass to her lips, unable to ignore it's sour, sap-like stench.

"You do." He bowed his head once.

Verenna took a deep breath. She looked to Fabien for a last bit of confirmation. He nodded his encouragement and she downed the liquid.

The taste choked her immediately. Oily bitterness clung to her tongue and slid down her throat. The scent of it snuck into her nose making her recoil. "You're an ass," she sputtered. "You could have warned me."

"If I had would you have taken it?"

He had a point. If he could have found the words for how truly awful it tasted she never would have accepted it. "Well, I've done my part. When do I get to ask my questions?"

"This evening. There are a few people who would like to be present."

"Who?" Verenna demanded. "Your other patients?"

"Hardly. The other occupants of the abbey. They'd like to meet you."

"Why?"

"Having met you myself I haven't the slightest clue. Politeness, I suppose? You're a guest after all." He took the jar from her, setting it on his table and laying a tablecloth over his tools. "The medicine should be taking hold soon and you'll be in no state to move."

Verenna grabbed Fabien's hand. "You won't leave me here with *him,* will you? Not when I can't defend myself." As soon as the words were out of her mouth she questioned them. Fabien might be in on the whole thing. Just because she'd known him before didn't mean he wasn't up to something now. Their only real contact had been flirting in the flower shop. She'd have to take the chance.

"I'll stay if you like." A smile danced in his green eyes. It comforted her to an extent, though she couldn't shake the bone deep feeling that she'd made a mistake.

"You'll do no such thing," Darius chided. "I am a medical professional. You are a hoodlum. I will not have you anywhere near this room when the nurses come to change the bandages. It would be grossly inappropriate. I'm sure even your sense of decency extends at least that far."

Fabien's answer was calm, but his voice had an edge to it. "I will remove myself to the hall when they come and wait till they finish. If the lady does not wish me to go, I will not go. I'm sure even your sense of sympathy extends that far." Kneeling beside the bed he asked Verenna, "Shall I stay?"

Flustered by the sudden chivalry, she stuttered out "Y-yes."

"Very well. Stay I will." He set himself in the chair by the door, slouching and getting comfortable. "Besides, Darius, it seems like you need the protection. If I hadn't been here she'd have slapped half your face off by now."

Darius sent him a scorching glare that put an end to his kidding.

"Fine," Fabien muttered, leaning his head back and closing his eyes. "If anyone troubles you Miss, just call for me. I'll set 'em straight."

As the room went quiet Verenna felt her hands and feet start to tingle. A warm numbness glided up her limbs and coated her whole body from the inside. Even the worried knot between her brows released as the pain vanished like steam. She looked to Fabien. His legs outstretched, hands clasped over his stomach; he might already be asleep. She'd follow him soon.

These people needed her for something. She could only hope that, whatever it was, it wouldn't kill her.

Chapter 5

Again the smell of smoke shocked her awake. Verenna gagged as she searched her hazy view of the room for someone to blame. She found Darius standing over her with one of his smoldering sticks. He tamped out the ember on its end to halt the bitter gray trail.

"Wha-why?" Verenna managed around her spluttering.

"They work better than smelling salts, that's why. These will bring you out of almost anything."

"You could have just shaken me."

"Trust me, I've thought about it."

Her palm tingled with the rekindled urge to slap him, but the memory of nearly ripping her stitches with the last attempt made the option less attractive. Her hand ran across the new bandages to discover a long, sore line beneath. She looked around for Fabien. Her shoulders sunk. He had vanished while she slept.

"I take it you still have questions about the abbey?"

"Yes," she rushed, momentarily forgetting her discomfort.

"Good news. That's why I'm waking you. It's time to start on our end of the deal. One of the women here lent you a dress. It's there." He nodded to the chair by the door. Spread across it was a deep green dress with buttons gleaming up the bodice. It parted in the front to show mint green underskirts. The garment wasn't half the disaster she expected it would be. Simpler than her own things at home, where lace and or embroidery were inescapable, but not at all upsetting.

"Thanks, um, petticoats? And I'll need a corset."

"No one needs a corset. Especially not with your kind of injury."

"If you want me to look like a loose woman…"

"Dear, you'd hardly look like a loose girl."

"Pig!"

"Name calling does nothing to prove me wrong."

A knock at the door rippled through the room. Fabien's muffled voice reached them through the wood. "Everything alright in there?"

"Just fine," Darius called to him. "Yes, he's waiting in the hall. You can stop pouting now."

"I wasn't." She looked down and fiddled with the edge of the blankets.

The doctor shrugged at the lie and made for the door. Before closing it he instructed, "Dressed. Upstairs. Quickly. Fabien will show you the way. We'll be ready for you."

"Who's we again?" Verenna's words didn't make it out before he'd gone.

She swung her feet over the edge of the bed and carefully stood. Suspicious that her knees might betray her, she moved slowly across the room, bracing herself on the bed, then the table as she made her way to the chair. Leaning on the wall for support she held up the dress. The whole thing was much more form fitting than anything she'd been allowed to have at home. Seeing no other option, she sighed and fought her way into the skirts.

Verenna struggled to manage without the assistance of a maid or two. The buttons up the front had to be redone three times for poor alignment. Finished, she scanned the room for a mirror. No luck. Not so much as the shining face of a clock to see herself in. What time was it anyway?

Light no longer bubbled in through the cracks in the shade. The two lamps in the room had been left to do the job. Curious, and fairly certain it wouldn't be allowed, she tiptoed to the window to have a look. Glancing over her shoulder to reassure herself no one watched she undid the latch on the shutters. It's jangling made her flinch.

The smell of dust and the heat of a hot day gone swirled in through the newly open window. She glimpsed the purple sky of late evening, edged by the rough lace of trees already heavy with shadow. Only the high stone wall of the abbey grounds held their darkness at bay.

Movement caught her eye below. A figure crossed the lawns with a bundle in arms. Firewood, she thought, they're starting the fire. The figure vanished around the corner of the building. Verenna pulled the shutters wider and leaned out in an attempt to keep the figure in view. Who was the pyre for tonight?

A wrap on the door and she slammed the window shut again. Heart in her ears, she threw her back against it, calling out, "Yes? Who is it? What?"

"Just me, miss. You alright?" Fabien sounded perplexed, likely due to the sound of the window slamming and the sound of her quick, wobbling steps she took towards the door, knocking into every piece of furniture along the way.

Verenna took a moment to brush tidying fingers through her hair before yanking the door wide. A tug of pain complained in her side. Ignoring it she blurted "Fine. I'm ready. I just need...oh." Only now with the cold of the stone floor sinking into her feet did she realize she had no shoes.

"Thinking about these?" He held a pair out to her; delicate things with flowers on their sides.

"Thanks," she took them to the chair and slid them on.

"Don't thank me. They're certainly not mine. Calla's old things. They're yours, she says. The dress too if you like it."

"I don't know if I do. Haven't seen myself in it." She stood and immediately grasped onto Fabien's offered arm for support. Heels did nothing for her shaky balance, nor did the distracting pinch in her toes. "Nice of her though. Whoever she is."

"You'll meet her. That is if you don't break yourself walking in those things." His crooked smile eased the jab to her pride. "My advice though? Keep the dress. You look like a jewel, Miss."

She cleared her throat and looked away, unable to meet his sparkling gaze. "Thanks very much." He seemed to notice her awkward shifting and moved the conversation along.

"Shall we?"

Verenna took in a deep breath to quiet her buzzing nerves and stepped with him into the dim, stone hallway.

The sconces that lit the passage were few and far between, one light fading almost completely before meeting the glow of the next. She could imagine how easy it would be for someone to hide in the gap between. Sturdy doors dotted the way. Tapestries too, beautifully woven, wearing the musty smell of their years. Some had dragons, others family crests, a few had what appeared to be historical scenes though she did not recognize their stories. From what she could tell in the sparse lighting, some of them might be trimmed with gold or silver.

"Interesting aren't they."

Verenna startled at the sudden sound of his words. They seemed to echo endlessly down the corridor before them.

"Most of them are at least two hundred years old. They don't redecorate much around here."

"They're nice."

Fabien slowed his walk and brought her close to one of the hangings. "Have a closer look if you like. Here, this one."

It was in quite a state of disrepair. The once neat stitches had frayed, each color at a different stage of going brown. A man with wild, graying hair and a red streaked beard stood in the center.

Clad in deep blue and clutching a staff, his lips sewn in the shape of a soundless command.

Behind him on each side scenes from the tales of King Arthur played out in exquisite detail. Above, three women in ornate frames of gold thread. The one to the right looked down shyly with her arms open and hands upturned. A thin circlet of shine over her head suggested a halo. The one to the left had tangled black hair, her mouth open and screaming, fingers outstretched as if to claw at the failing stitches of the sky. In the middle, a calm face, sitting patiently with a sand timer in her lap, forever frozen halfway through its pouring. She gazed out into the world beyond the tapestry with an eerily knowing expression.

"I'm sure you know who that is." Fabien said pointing to the man in the middle.

"Merlin," she replied. "Who are they?"

"His daughters."

Verenna raised an eyebrow. "He had daughters?"

"Aye, he did. Most haven't heard their story. When Merlin was on his deathbed, he decreed that his three children were to equally inherit their father's power after he passed." He gestured to the clawing woman. "When the eldest found out she'd have to share with her sisters, she was outraged. As the first born to him she felt it should be gifted to her alone. She plotted to kill both younger girls." He hovered his finger above the other woman's subtle halo. "The second sister died trying to protect the youngest, who was only a child at the time. A martyr, really. Despite the sacrifice, the eldest sister killed the youngest too."

Verenna thought for a moment. "Then why doesn't she have a halo?"

"Because she survived."

Verenna squinted up at him. "How?"

Fabien leaned in close, his voice dropping to a coarse whisper.

"Because Death himself brought her back."

A chill ran down Verenna's spine. A week ago she would have laughed at him, but what she'd seen in the street that night had her in the mood to believe. Goosebumps rose on her neck as he continued.

"Death keeps careful records you know. Everything balanced on a never-ending ledger. Who is born, who will die, where, and exactly, to the moment, when. Seeing inaccuracies in his books he went to investigate the cause. And when he arrived he found the eldest sister, standing bloody above the dead bodies of her siblings. It was then he knew that if the woman before him were to inherit all of Merlin's power alone, a woman dripping with the unjustly spilled blood of a child, of her own family, it would ruin the balance between life and death. She would create such destruction, wreak such havoc upon the world, bring so much untimely death that he could not allow her to go on."

"What did he do?" Verenna murmured, spellbound.

"What he wanted. In those days, Death had free will and a fierce temper. In a rage he reached into the beyond to bring the sisters back to life. The second sister was too far beyond the veil, but the child hadn't long passed. He pulled her back to this realm, but something had to fill her place. The balance must be kept. In his fury, he banished the eldest sister to the afterworld in her stead, pressing her down and down, to the very deepest Hell. *I banish you to the bottom of the pit*, he said. *And if you are ever to walk this earth again, Hell, in all its ire, must rise before you.*"

Verenna blinked in wide-eyed awe. She could picture a seething ocean made of the same darkness that had chased her into the streets. "What happened to the little girl?" Her voice came breathless, as if the Death he spoke of might hear.

"She lived again. But that's when Death realized his mistake. He had bound the eldest forever to the world of the dead. And now, to keep order, he must bind the child forever to life. In doing so, he created what you would know as Vampires. They wander, tethered to life, unable to pass on. Unable to die, they are not alive. But oh how they crave it."

He leaned closer to her ear so that the wash of his breath caressed her neck. "That's why, on night's when the moon is dark, they go out to hunt. To taste the life they are bound to, but will never truly know again. They stalk the darkness to feed."

The prickling hairs on Verenna's neck implored her to look over her shoulder, to see if the wraith from the staircase had finally caught up to claim her. She thought she saw movement in the distant corridor. She went to gasp but her lungs were already full of held breath.

"Do...do you think...that could be true?" Verenna stuttered.

"Ha, no idea. It makes for an awfully good story though, doesn't it?" She turned to find a rascal grin painted across his face. He'd been teasing her.

"Shut up!" She punched him in the shoulder, pursing her lips to keep from smiling. The joke put her at ease, though it lasted only as long as it took the sobering draft of the hall to inch closer to her bones. "Don't ask me to forgive you," she mumbled as he led her around a corner to a flight of stairs. The steps spiraled gently upwards like the inside of a seashell, filled with a smell like cool earth. A tower.

"Wouldn't dream of it."

They started the climb. Fabien set a leisurely pace that Verenna was silently thankful for. Sconces were far more frequent here. She could feel the heat of each on her face as they passed. Her cheeks began to warm from the steady exertion. To distract herself from the unending plod, she tried to get a glimpse out of the arrow slit windows. A hint of the dying purple dusk beyond was the only reward.

Her legs burned. She didn't dare look up, afraid of how many stairs she'd see ahead of them. They had to be nearing the top. Verenna could hear her heart almost as well as the resounding click of her steps. In an abrupt mercy the stairs flattened into a landing. They faced a massive wooden door studded with metal bolts that shone like dozens of eyes in the torch light. It was cracked open just enough to hear the faint sounds of conversation from the room beyond. She recognized Darius's voice right away.

"We need to be careful of how honest we're being."

A woman's airy tones answered him in a slight stutter. "I d-don't see much harm in telling her the truth."

"You will if the town gets wind of it."

"What makes you think she'll tell them?" another man questioned. He had a plum-like roundness to his speech.

"She's been a challenge since the moment I woke her. We were hardly able to convince her to stay. I think she'll…"

The rest of his words were covered by Fabien's coughing.

"Excuse me a moment. Just...wait here?" He left her leaning against the wall for support and hurried behind the door. The room hushed instantly. A few hand-wringing seconds later, the entrance widened and Fabien gathered her inside.

They were greeted by twenty to thirty gawking faces. With such variety in class, dress, and cleanliness, it was hard to imagine how all of these people had ended up in the same room. Some, like the thin necked woman with the caked-on powder, smiled encouragingly. Others seemed awestruck and whispered to their neighbors. Though the majority of the room could be described somewhere between worried and terrified. These must be other patients.

"C-come. Sit." The powder faced woman patted a chair next to her.

Verenna followed the woman's instruction, leaving Fabien's

arm and taking a place atop the gold embroidered seat. The room held plenty of light, rich fabrics hanging between the multitude of windows, cushioned chairs and tables sporting intricate carvings. Such a lavish space came as a shock after the grim halls they'd walked to get there. How suspicious to be hiding all this in an abbey.

"Make yourself comfortable dear. We sent for tea. Sh-shouldn't be long." Verenna leaned back and nodded wordlessly. The lavender wafting from the powdered woman was strong enough to taste. She either had a bundle of it under her mound of graying hair, or she'd rubbed her entire gown with it.

"Allow me to welcome you to our home. I'm Lady Madeline Ren. And what is your name?"

"Verenna Dellins."

A din of murmuring went up, animated chatter, these strangers all with something to say about her name. Darius shoved the weighty door shut with a clap, quieting them all.

"How are you feeling?" he asked.

"Fine," Her palms were sticky with sweat, her mouth dry and her knees quivering, but it was easier not to mention it.

"We'd heard about what happened. Terrible shame that. Very glad you're looking so well. Lord Alric Ren, by the way," the man with the plum voice proclaimed. A rounded stomach protruded before him, making more than enough work for his strained belt. He had on some sort of uniform with seven gleaming metals dangling over his heart. Their polished sheen countered by the pair of mangy boots loosely strapped to his feet. Again, Verenna nodded without comment, looking down to her pinching shoes. What was there to say to these people? No one thing could possibly fit all of them. Perhaps they were all sick or dying. She wasn't sure, but she felt that it should somehow change the greeting.

"I'm glad to see you like the dress. It suits you well I think." A woman in the corner crooned with the slightest ghost of an accent. Her face a moon in the center of her dark, gathered locks. A narrow smile perched above her high, ruffled, red collar. "Forgive me. I'm Calla."

"Thanks." Verenna replied. The woman only winked.

"For the sake of my nerves can we skip the rest of the pleasantries?" Darius complained as he took a chair. "Everyone, meet Miss Dellins. Miss Dellins, this is everyone. The residents of the fabled 'Falseman Inn'. It may surprise you to see them looking so normal. We do work hard to make everyone think we're a leper colony."

"Darius! What kind of a joke is that?" Lady Ren scolded, fanning herself.

"The kind that keeps people from poking around where they shouldn't."

Verenna fixed her eyes on the rugs dressing the floor, anywhere but meeting the eyes of these strangers.

"You're scaring the girl."

"Am not. I'm telling her that's *not* true."

"I had heard a lot of things around town. Rumors, all of it. I mean, you all look so...ordinary. Though not in the boring sense. I mean, I…" Verenna clapped a hand to her mouth to stop it running. There was nearly thirty of these people, with who knows what wrong with them, and she'd insulted them in their own home. To her relief, Darius spoke up and spared her more stumbling.

"Not all rumors. I do run a practice here. And it is only for the most serious of cases. People society needs to be protected from as well as people who need protection from society. Neighbors are more fatal than the flu if you're not careful. Regardless, this place isn't the disease ridden pit the simpletons say it is. I'm sure you can see that. But the rumors do buy us a sort of peace and quiet that's hard to come by."

Verenna searched again through the strangers. She recognized a few from town, though they'd never spoken. The beggar she'd seen on her street sulked in the back of the gathering, eyes flicking with nerves. Two old women she always saw gossiping at the tea shop. A dapper man in all gray seemed familiar as well. And of course, there was Fabien.

"I'm sorry to seem rude, but, what does all this have to do with me? I don't know any of you really, and I'm not sick."

"Not anymore. Thanks to me." Darius snapped.

Calla attempted to calm him. "Darling, your temper."

"Don't." The warning muted the room.

"Then why keep me?"

Everyone present dangled on the edge of some unspoken secret that no one wanted to breathe to life. Eventually, Lady Ren cleared her throat, "Fabien, would you?"

The young man bowed his head and knelt beside Verenna. "Miss, you are not like anyone else. Not at all."

In any other situation she could think of she would have been overjoyed to hear those words from him on bended knee, but the timing told her this would not be romantic. "How do you mean?" Verenna asked, voice sharpened with worry.

"Everything that's happened to you in the last weeks has happened for a very important reason. What you saw the night you were chased? That's not something everyone sees."

"You know what chased me?"

"Yes. We've seen them too."

"Well, what was it?" Her ears started to burn with frustration. She could not know fast enough, yet all of them seemed content to exchange blank stares between every phrase.

A timid word from the back answered her. "Demons." The

beggar came forward.

"Oh, ha ha. And how would you know?"

"He of all people would know. He was watching your house." Darius leaned and steepled his fingers, content to watch her unravel on the vagrant.

"You!" she squeaked in a mixture of surprise and outrage. "How dare you!"

"I meant no harm by it, my lady. I was there to help keep you safe." The man looked wistfully to the ground, sinking into some somber depth within himself.

"How long?"

He paused, unwilling to say. Verenna's autumn eyes locked onto him, their hot copper demanding a reply.

"A week, going on two, before the accident."

Her ears turned flame red at his answer, fingers gripping the arms of her chair as if she'd re-carve them with her nails. "I was attacked! Chased and attacked! What do you mean accident?"

"I meant," the beggar started, only to have his words roared over by the girl's tirade. "Two weeks watching? Fat lot of good that did. Didn't see you when it counted."

"The blame's with me." The shabby man groaned like the timbers of an aging house. "I lost sight of what I was doing, why I was there. I wasn't myself. But that's never an excuse. My failings put you in danger. For that I am truly sorry. I can't begin...I can't begin..."

He was somewhere else when he spoke, mired in his own private horrors, so lost in memories that Verenna thought she might be able to see them reflected in his welling eyes. He held out empty hands as if he might find words in them. Something about it drained her of rage.

Darius interrupted the man's struggle. "We have more important things to discuss than your regret, Mortimer. I'm sure the lady is still wondering why she was being watched in the first place."

"I'm glad you're sitting down," Fabien breathed, allowing Darius to launch into the explanation.

"The reason you were being watched is because a certain chain of highly prophesied events are unfolding. You happen to be one of them."

She would have laughed if he'd given her any shred of evidence that he was joking. The rest in the room seemed to agree; not a single doubt uttered or indicated on their long, grave, expressions. Verenna scoffed. She had never been a part of so much as a sewing circle. A prophecy crossed the boundaries of belief.

"Hard to take in, I know. You seemed useless when I met you, but there's no way around it."

"There is no need for cruelty, my boy. Times are hard enough," Lord Ren scolded, taking a pipe from his pocket and pointing it at Darius like a wagging finger. The doctor shrugged and took a seat.

"Fine. Someone else care to take over?"

"Yes, please," Verenna grumbled, the heat of anger ascending her cheeks again. Lady Ren took the girls hand and looked again to Fabien.

"Did the two of you discuss the tapestry?"

"Sort of. The story anyway. But I'm not, um, really, I…" Fabien glanced around the room for support but no one offered to take up the subject for him. "That tapestry I showed you. I pointed it out for a reason. Do you remember what Death said to the eldest sister? *'If ever you are to walk the earth again, all Hell must rise before you.'* Yes?"

"No."

"We just talked about it."

"I remember, it's just that that's a story on a hanging rug. And I have a feeling you're about to try and convince me it actually happened."

"Do I have any reason to lie to you? Merlin's eldest daughter has finally found a way to tear a hole in Hell. Now it's open and things are rising out of it. Things like what came after you. Can you really say you don't believe me at all after what you've seen?" He said it as if he were begging.

"So you think he's right? You think it was a demon?" The chill of belief surged cold in her veins, threatening to overtake her.

Fabien nodded. "Of some kind. I don't know much about their types, but I can tell you for sure that's what you saw. And that was only one of them. There will be a lot more soon, if there aren't already. Eventually, all Hell will come bubbling up if we don't do something about it. From what we hear, the Four Horsemen are already riding...What?"

It began as a low chuckle that grew to an empty, humorless, laugh. Verenna tried to stop herself, honestly surprised that the sound came from her. "I just, I can't, not to be rude, but you're all sold on this?"

The quiet answered. Yes. The feeling of falling gripped her. Alone with no way home, surrounded by an ogling group of people she'd never met, accepting a story about the Four Horsemen as fact...a thousand potentials took root in her mind.

"And who am I in all this exactly?"

Darius chimed in again, rising to stroll the space between her and the door, like a professor in a lecture hall. "Merlin's only living descendant through his youngest daughter. The one that Death brought back. The only child of an only child for as long as anyone can remember. At least on your mother's side, if I'm not mistaken. *'A child to tempt Death at every turn but still he will refuse.'* Tell me, were you sick much when you were young? Reckless maybe? A lot of narrow escapes from horrible fates?"

"How do you know that?"

"Therein lies the beauty and danger of prophecy. You don't have to know anything. It's all written out for you."

"You're lying. My mother must have told you when you saw her. Why would my being an only child have anything to do with it?" Verenna felt the collar of her dress grow humid with sweat, her palms rewetted, the tremor back in her knees.

"Death has to make sure a power struggle like the one between the Merlin sisters never happens again. The world had too much to lose by it. So, only one surviving child to each generation. Death protects that child until they produce the next heir. Or until they're called upon by the prophecy."

By the time Fabien had finished speaking Verenna had gone a shade of bloodless white. Her lips trembled out her fear. All she could think of were the licking flames at the base of the smoke trail she'd watched. Without an heir, she had a feeling she knew what the prophecy called for. "You're going to sacrifice me."

"Good h-heavens, no!" Lady Ren put one bony hand up to her neck in shock, the other squeezing the girl's wrist.

"Not after all the work I put in saving you," Darius added.

"If Death were really protecting me, you wouldn't have had to work at all."

"Well, technically your mother is still young and just healthy enough that she could produce another heir if something were to happen to you. So perhaps you can die. Who knows? Why risk it?" Darius leaned against Lord Ren's armchair as if he were discussing nothing more than the weather.

"I have no powers," Verenna fought.

"Of course you don't. Without consistent practice in the family those qualities will go dormant. It does not detract from who you are or the bloodline you come from. I hate it almost as much as you do but you are the one meant to fix this whole demons and Horsemen business. Now back to the original point. It would do no good for anyone to sacrifice you."

Her life might be secure but there were still thousands of undesirable ways to live it. What if they kept her locked up here, starved her, tortured her? She could feel her chances of seeing home again dwindling by the minute.

She shot out of her seat and hurled herself towards the exit. The crowd rushed a few steps forwards only halting as Fabien caught her at the door. Verenna clawed at him but he got hold of her arms and pinned her against him.

"Listen, Verenna, please. There's more you need to hear. No one is here to hurt you. We all need the same thing. We can help each other." The words rushed out of him like water she would not allow herself to drink.

She quit her attempts to free herself and met his gaze, leaning in to whisper, "I'm going home." With that she raised a knee, hitting him squarely in the groin. Fabien crumbled. Verenna leapt over him, wrenching the massive door aside without a thought to the splitting pain in her side. Half falling, half running, she plummeted down the stairs, a cascade of voices echoing after her.

There was no knowing what they said, not over the thunderstorm of pursuing footsteps. The faster she fled the faster they came. She reached the bottom of the stairs and plunged into the dim hall, sprinting blindly until her eyes adjusted. The orange splashes of pulsing torch light on the walls made the corridor look like the innards of a snake. Each door became a rib, each rib aligned in hopeless sameness, on and on as she passed them praying for an exit. The throb in her side, the clench in her throat, the smothering sound of the crowd behind her drowning out all thoughts but escape.

Verenna rounded a corner at full speed and toppled. The sounds behind her swelled. There was no more running left in her legs, she knew. Rolling to the side of the hall she curled in a pool of shadows the torches did not reach. With sweating palms she slipped the clacking shoes off her feet. The following footsteps ceased. Voices rose and she listened.

"Come on! We can't have her getting out in this condition. She went this way." The words belonged to Darius, their echo dying out with no reply. "Why are we stopping? She's not far ahead."

"Because it's wrong how we're going about this." Verenna couldn't be sure who spoke, but it sounded like the beggar. "You think being chased by a mob will earn her trust? She's got to be scared out of her mind."

"We don't have time to argue," Darius growled. The mumbles of the crowd increased.

"Then don't. We need to split up. Search in smaller groups." The beggar commanded. Others joined in, offering their help.

"We can take the north corridor."

"We'll keep heading down the east."

"I'll head towards the library." Fabien added.

"Don't go quietly. Talk. Call to her. We aren't sneaking and we want her to know that." The beggar had hardly finished when Darius tore into him.

"You gutter wash, Mortimer. None of that will matter if she gets too much of a head start. And since when do you make the decisions here?"

"Since when do you? Go, everyone, start looking." Lord Ren interrupted and dismissed the search parties. Verenna half thought everyone had gone and dared a peek around the corner. They had not. Darius and Lord Ren stood alone. She ducked back and hid herself again as the graying man spoke.

"Mortimer was right. A mob was no solution."

"He's is a lowlife. He's..."

"I fail to see what his station has to do with anything. He may be a bit dirty, but so are my boots and there's nothing I trust more. You should listen to him more often."

"When he isn't drunk."

Lord Ren sighed. "Darius, you're like a son to us. That's why it's so disappointing to see you like this. You've gotten bitter. Mean, even. We have a hard lot here with this condition, perhaps you in particular. But if I hear you talking about girls and beggars like this again you'll find someone else's estate to practice on."

Departing footsteps; one set calm, the other stomping in her direction. She held her breath as they died out and peered into the light again. No one. She rose slowly, soundlessly against the wall. A toe reached forward to test the ground. Then something seized her, wrapping her from behind.

Verenna shrieked as the vice tightened. She dug her nails into the flesh of the creature that had crept up on her, digging them deeper and deeper until she recognized Fabien's cries.

"Agh! Verenna! Damn it would you stop it! Listen to...look at me!" He turned her to face him.

"It's me," he breathed to her as if it would be a comfort. Her spit landed squarely on his cheek. Her claws snagged where it had landed, leaving three blood dark paths. Hurried footsteps in other passages gathered speed. More were coming. Her screams of rage melded with wails of pain. She'd awoken her gashed side.

"Hold still. You'll hurt yourself. Verenna, please!" Fabien begged as he worked to keep hold of her writhing body. Phantom forms appeared at the end of the passage, rushing towards them. Fear filled her lungs until she could no longer feel air enter or exit her.

"Stay back!" Darius shouted to the rest of the specters. Babbling their worry, they obeyed. The doctor pulled a folded paper and one of the incense sticks from a pocket as he rushed forward, striking one against the other until it sparked and smoldered.

"No!" Verenna kicked at him and missed.

"Yes! I can almost guarantee you've torn your stitches. Do you want to bleed to death?"

Verenna kicked again, catching Darius's shin. He swore under his breath before closing the distance between them and waving the smoke beneath her nose. Instantly her limbs gave into exhaustion and she crumpled towards the floor. Fabien brought her back up before she hit the stone and draped her between his arms. Verenna tried to spit at him again but she could hardly hold her head up.

"I am sorry, Miss. It's for your own good. And mine." Fabien sounded regretful though she could hear relief in his voice. "I'll be damned if she'd not a fighter. Poor thing. This round wasn't fair."

"Wait till you see what she did to your face. Then decide what's fair," someone called from the group.

"I'll live."

A few cynical laughs. Darius was not among them. "Very funny. Follow me, Fabien. I need to check those stitches right away. Everyone, good night."

Cloudy faces drifted in and out of her vision as the throng disbursed. All except one. The familiar man in the gray suit lingered and watched them go. She couldn't tell what he meant by it, if he looked on with pity or worry or satisfaction. Her hand went up to reach for him in hopes that he'd help the girl he'd surely recognize from town. 'I want to go home,' she thought as hard as she could, hoping the right sounds would form on their own. But the gray man turned away and vanished like the rest.

"Well," the word hummed in Fabien's chest, pushing Verenna even closer to sleep. "That went as bad as it could."

Darius murmured in return, "Let's hope she fights half as hard to save us."

Chapter 6

Verenna came to in bed in the dark of her room. The faintest glow from the oil lamp near the door lit the chamber. It surprised her to find herself alone. No guard, no doctor, no strangers waiting for their eyeful of whoever they thought she was. She noticed the pain in her side had gone as a deep breath stretched her lungs. The cool of the air told her it must be deep night.

All she'd been told earlier that evening came trickling in to form a murky and wholly unbelievable picture of the situation. Logic said they had to be lying. But what she'd seen that night on the stairs, what else was there to call it but a demon. No animal moved like that. Certainly no human.

Fabien seemed convinced of all of it, though that meant less and less as she thought about it. He could be one of them. They seemed to know him far better than an occasional delivery would allow. Perhaps he was a prisoner too. They could be keeping him here just like they kept her. That seemed more likely. And if that turned out to be the case, escape together would be easier than alone. Of course, that depended on if he turned out on their side or hers.

Verenna rose, careful of her side, and went to the window to survey her options for an exit. She hadn't realized before, but the room was quite high up, at least four stories. There were no branches or trees anywhere close by, just a sheer facade dotted with shutters the same as her own. They'd probably put her there because of it. No way out but a straight drop down. Her bedsheets weren't half long enough, even tied together, to ensure she wouldn't break an ankle.

From the shape of the building it might be easier to walk out. Her hall was pin straight. At one end or the other there had to be stairs to the first floor, and somewhere there, a door to the outside world. The wall surrounding the abbey might be a problem, but she could sort that out when she got there.

Verenna crossed to the door and put her ear to the wood. Cracking it ever so slightly, she held the oil lamp to the gap. No one waited as far as she could tell. Now might be her only chance to explore.

She turned the key to brighten the lamp. One of the still smoldering sconces crackled. She jumped, expecting the worst and nearly dropped her light. Steadying it, she checked the dark around her for signs of life.

On the balls of her feet, she crept along the hall the opposite way Fabien had taken her. Around that corner she met with a friendlier passage. The high ceilings were held aloft by elegant arches. Between them, tall windows let in cascades of moonlight. She crawled onto one of the stone sills for a view of the landscape outside. Her heart thrilled with instant hope. She could see town. Canterford's little chimneys puffing against the faint yellow glow of the street lamps. It looked warm. It also didn't look all that far away.

She found her own reflection in the glass. Having not seen herself in days her rumpled hair came as no surprise. As she attempted to smooth it, she noticed her image was not alone in the glass. Something stood behind her. Verenna toppled from the sill. Hitting the ground knocked the air to scream right out of her.

"Miss! Are you alright? I didn't mean to startle you, I swear."

"You," she growled. The beggar had turned up.

"You can't be very happy to see me."

"I'm not," she informed him, back tight against the wall.

"Can't say that I blame you. Especially after tonight in the tower. That's why I brought a peace offering." He gestured with a silver tray he carried. It was covered with a white napkin, a large bump sticking up in the middle. Verenna tracked his every move as he knelt, set the tray on the ground, and uncovered it.

There sat a huge slice of cherry pie. It hadn't occurred to her until that moment that she was starving. A wave of nauseating hunger lurched in her stomach.

"Back up," she tested him.

He bowed his head, rose, and moved halfway across the hall. Taking her stillness as his cue, he took one more stride backwards before sitting.

Verenna took a critical look at the pie. Nothing seemed out of the ordinary. She picked up the fork, cut a piece and took a bite. It was ambrosia, the sweet tart of the fruit and butter smell of the crust; easily the best thing she'd ever tasted. She barely resisted the overwhelming urge to drop the utensil and eat with her hands. With a huge effort she set the fork on the tray with a dainty tap. She wouldn't let him see weakness.

Verenna looked up and caught him watching her just before he glanced away to toy with the ragged edge of his pant leg. A dirty leather coat flopped open and pooled at his sides. He scratched at a thick layer of stubble wrapping his chin and neck, framing an expression that managed to be both humble and desperate. Growing uncomfortable with the silence between them, Verenna asked, "Your name is Mortimer?"

"It is, Ma'am."

"And your last name?"

"Oh that's not so important anymore. I'd much prefer you call me Mortimer. If that's not too informal."

It struck her how well he spoke. People of his station usually went without schooling. Yet even his voice was pleasing; deep, calm, oaken.

"Mortimer," she repeated thoughtfully, pausing to allow herself another bite of pie. She swallowed around a knot in her throat. "Are you going to tell anyone you found me in the hall?"

"What's to tell? You weren't doing anything wrong."

"Thanks." It would have been the end of her escape plans. She could imagine the doctor putting a lock on her door if he found out she'd been snooping around at night.

"Why come find me so late? If you wanted to bring me something to eat, you'd have a better chance finding me awake in the morning."

He shrugged. "I thought it might be hard for you to sleep after hearing all you heard today. It might not feel like it right now but you are a guest here. Something to eat should be the least of our hospitality towards you."

Verenna took another bite as she studied him. A gentle half-smile creased the corner of his eye. He was the oddest combination of shabbiness and manners.

"May I speak freely, Ma'am?" he wrung his hands as he asked, so much like her father. She nodded cautious agreement. He took a deep breath and launched into what he had to say.

"The reason I came to you tonight was to apologize. I was the one sent to guard you and I failed. I know it will do nothing to repair what's happened to you. Now I can only hope you'll forgive me for it."

Verenna placed her fork down with a clank. She had nearly forgotten his role in putting her here. His failure was the reason she sat on a stone floor with cold seeping into her legs instead of her own bed at home.

"You could have warned us," she hissed.

"Would you have believed me? Look at me. If I showed up and

told your family demons were in their house, what do you think they'd say?" Mortimer shook his head, weary at the thought. "Even if they did listen to me, it would have only made things worse. Demons are drawn to panic and fear. They feed on it. When you panic, you become a beacon for them. Telling you would have endangered you all."

The hair on Verenna's neck prickled as a shiver trickled through her. "My parents? They're still there."

"I wouldn't worry about them. Those creatures were searching for you. In fact, there might even be less of them in the house now that you've gone. Your parents are likely safer than before you left."

Verenna sank against the wall again. "And how do I know I'm safe here?"

"It's hard to tell, isn't it? I've been around this place for a lifetime and sometimes I still don't know. For you, you mustn't feel safe here at all. Strangers telling you you're involved in some world shaping prophecy, saying demons exist and they're after you, claiming Merlin was real..." He trailed off into a breathy laugh. "It seems mad, but believe me dear, you're the safest person in this place. We need you far more than you could ever need us. Trust us or not, that should reassure you we'll keep you protected."

Verenna stared down the remnants of the pie slice, the pulp of its red center smeared across the plate. Helplessness, loneliness and confusion formed a lump in her throat that heralded tears. She held on fiercely to her composure, looking down into her empty, fidgeting hands. Luckily, Mortimer's voice distracted her before her eyes overflowed.

"I don't know if it will make any difference to you, but I promise I will not fail you again. You'll have my protection as long as I live. I swear it."

The solemnity of what he said made her look up at him. His very presence changed as he uttered the words, his hazel eyes open and clear as he spoke the oath. She had no idea if he had the ability to protect her. Regardless, there could be no doubt that he meant every word.

"Thank you," she shivered. The cold of the floor had taken hold of her. Mortimer noticed, immediately reverting to a servant's demeanor. "Why don't I walk you back to bed? It's awfully chilly in a place as big as this. Especially at night."

Verenna nodded and rose. He stopped to pick up the tray, taking up her oil lamp as well, moving steadily as not to frighten her. Even as they walked together he kept to the opposite side of the hall. When they reached her door he returned her lamp and set the plate of pie inside on the chair. "I suspect you'll want the rest of this."

She smiled for what felt like the first time in months. "Good night, Mortimer."

It seemed to please him to hear her say his name. "Goodnight, my lady."

"Verenna," she corrected him.

His smile broadened as he bobbed the slight bow. "Goodnight, Verenna."

The girl watched as he stalked off down the passageway. The dying sconces threw his faint shadow against the opposite wall, growing and shrinking it. At the end of the hall he turned back to her and nodded a last farewell before dipping off into the night.

Verenna nodded in return and closed the door. Perhaps it had been her weary mind, or a trick of the dim light, but at the very last second of his gaze, Verenna could have sworn she saw his eyes flash green.

Chapter 7

Another week came and went, each with less soreness in her side. If it weren't for the sneaking suspicion that everyone was hiding something, the time might have been enjoyable. Ten or so new faces had stopped in to introduce themselves, bring her tea, escort her on walks. They answered questions freely, and there hadn't yet been a single room they wouldn't show her. The visitors even explained the smoke. Apparently, it was in fact the huge amount of wood it took to heat the building. So they said.

There were still plenty of halls unwandered; ample space to keep whatever secret brought them here. The abbey held people from every station of life, faraway places, sick and well, with no obvious connection aside from their residence at the abbey, and every one of them with a convenient tale of their arrival.

On her almost daily trips to the library with Fabien, she'd wait until he fell asleep on one of the reading couches and hunt through the vast collections unattended. The starts and stops in his soft snoring dictated when it was safe to continue. She checked miles of titles for something about the true origin of the abbey, what it was really for, perhaps some kind of map if she were lucky. But the history section yielded nothing more than brief summaries of its building, minor battles for its possession, and after becoming the home of a man sharing Lord Ren's name, it's eventual abandonment. And none of it touched the most recent three hundred years.

Regardless of her failures in the library, Verenna had had considerable success remembering the layout of the corridors

Fabien lead her along. It was as if he were showing her the same route again and again, hoping she'd catch on, teaching her the way out one walk at a time. They'd never gone all the way to the ground floor though. Verenna assumed there would be guards to prevent them if they tried.

The trouble would be telling Fabien she was ready to escape without tipping him off to her plans if he didn't feel the same. She had sat up most of the night working out what to say and how, finding phrases only desperate ears would understand. Finally, half way through their walk back from the library, she got up the nerve to try. After a healthy pause in their conversation she threw out the first question.

"Do you like it here?" It came out with such abruptness she startled herself.

Fabien's eyebrows rose in surprise. "I mean...This place isn't for everyone." He pursed his lips and screwed them to one side in thought. "It serves its purpose though. Lord and Lady Ren are more than generous with everyone. They've taken in so many people Canterford has shunned. Fallen women, the sick, beggars and the like. Darius makes them well, then they can stay and work here if they like. Canterford isn't a great town if you're anything other than normal. But all things considered, I suppose it's alright." He paused and checked they were alone before continuing. "Between you and me, if things were a little different, I'd be somewhere else. Closer to the town pub, if I'm honest."

"You do live out here, then? You're not just by when there's flowers to deliver?"

Fabien flustered at the question. "Think less of me?"

"Not at all. I guess I still can't believe someone like you... You seem perfectly fine to me." He went silent as they strolled on, offering no more information on what brought him to this strange stronghold. Verenna calculated wildly in the next pause to find some way to draw more detail out of him. "So what else do you do? I know you work some days at the florists, but what's your role here?" Fabien was muscled in a way that simply lifting crates of flowers could not provide. There had to be more than that to him.

"I dig the occasional grave. Hunt, too. I'm pretty good at it," he told her with a shrug. "I practice with a sword now and again. My grandfather's. When weather permits, you could say."

His last words caught her attention. Trying not to seem to interested, Verenna spoke on a laugh. "How do you leave this place, anyway? I haven't seen a single way out." She clutched her own hands, hoping she'd walked close enough to the line between joking and seriousness that he knew what she meant.

"Some days I'm not sure there is one. But I manage. It'll be good to get out again soon, I'll tell you," he laughed in return.

Her heart fluttered. He'd admitted it. This place had some kind of hold on him. It had to be powerful. But with two of them, they'd make it for sure. They'd need a place to hide once they were out, just for the night.

"I'm sure you have friends in town. Why don't you go stay with them? If you don't like it here, I'm sure they'd understand."

"Perhaps they would for a while, but I'd wear out my welcome right quick I'm afraid."

"Come on, there's got to be someone," Verenna pressed him. A man as charming as Fabien would have friends on every street.

"A few. Now and again I can pull in a favor. They're still pretty far from town. About half way."

Verenna felt like dancing but fought back her bubbling joy. A listening ear could be pressed to any one of the doors they passed. She let the conversation lag for a bit.

"When do you hunt? I see you every day. When could you possibly have time?"

"Night. I prefer night," he said with distance in his voice. "There are lots of advantages. The cover of darkness is useful no matter what's being hunted."

They'd leave at night and head for this friend of his. "You said you were going soon?" She stopped walking, anxious for his answer.

"I was thinking of going tonight actually. You know, I didn't think you'd have an interest in something as risky as that." A corner of his mouth drew up into a smile that admired her bravery.

"Why wouldn't I be? It's exciting. And if it means leaving this place..."

"You are full of surprises, Verenna. You really are. I can't exactly march you out the front door though. Somehow I don't think the doctor would approve."

"Of course not," she agreed. Darius would go off like an alarm if he knew what they were plotting. She'd have to find a way to follow Fabien without running into anyone to stop her.

"I'll wave to you from the gate tonight. Watch for me out the window just before midnight. But you have to promise you'll wave back, now." He winked.

"Naturally."

♋

The wait for the doctor the day of her party paled in comparison to watching the night for Fabien's signal. Verenna had been uncharacteristically cooperative during Darius's last visit of the night. Anything to get him out of the room so she could go to work.

She fashioned a decent rope out of her bed sheets. It wouldn't take her all the way to the ground. But if she snuck to the floor below her it would get her close enough to make jumping reasonable. She hoped.

Confident in her knots and fully dressed, Fabien's wave was all she needed.

Finally, a pair of bobbing lights appeared on the lawn. Two lanterns, and in the yellow halo of their light the glint of the young man's golden hair. She watched as he found a thin inlet in the wall next to an overgrown vine that threatened to seal it. He raised a hand. Frantically, she returned the gesture.

He hung one lantern, and vanished through the door in the battlements. Hands trembling she threw her makeshift rope over her shoulder and took up her lamp, deciding to carry her shoes for the sake of stealth. With as much caution as she could muster against her urge to rush, she crept into the hall.

Most of the torches were out. Even when she reached the windows the meager slice of moon did nothing to light the passageway. The stairs were even darker. She clutched the lamp tighter and hugged the wall as she hurried down, the rasp of her frightened breath amplified by the soundless stairwell. Her feet fell faster and faster as a prickle on the back of her neck filled her with sureness that the dark itself followed her.

Skittering onto the third floor corridor she rushed to the first window, checking over each shoulder that no one watched. The lantern still hung, an amber beacon near the gate. She set her lamp and shoes on the sill and worried the rusted latch on the windows until with a scrape, it fell open. Clambering onto the ledge, she swung one window open and tied her sheet rope firmly to the handle of the other. Verenna tugged it tight with her full weight to be sure it held. After shoving her shoes into the pockets of her dress, she gripped the rope and dared a glance down.

A swooning dizziness took over as she realized the height. Forcing herself to look away, she gripped her climbing line, and let herself lean back into the open air behind her. The night breeze caressed the soles of her feet with each step, adding to her light headedness. The nauseating pull of gravity threatened to overcome her shaking arms with each painstaking step towards the ground.

Reaching the second floor windows she dared a glance over her shoulder. She couldn't find Fabien's lantern. Panic seized her. Had it gone out? Perhaps it had been taken. Someone could be watching. She turned further, hoping she'd just lost sight of it. In doing so her foot slipped and she plummeted the rest of the way to the ground. The fall winded her but as soon as she had her breath she was rushing for the spot she'd last seen light. Her stumbling turned into a flat run. Verenna reached the wall and followed the unruly mass of the vine to the inlet. The shushing breeze brought her the slightest scent of smoke from the extinguished lantern, still hung and clicking on its hook.

Verenna ventured a hand into the pitch, blindly seeking the door. She jumped as her hand met the wood. Shoving it as hard as she could, she burst into the world beyond. The excitement of her new freedom surged through her. She pushed her shoes onto her feet, suddenly aware of how soft the abbey grass had been compared to the rocks and weeds at the edge of the woods.

In the vague moonlight, she could see the road and on it the flicker of flame. Fabien! Electrified she almost called out to him. But the imposing shadow of the abbey walls silenced her. Moving fast she set out to follow him.

Grasses brushed at her ankles, knees, then sides, becoming brambles, then trees, beneath which lay an almost complete darkness. She swam through leaves and twigs. Only a few, dappled patches of sickly moon reached the ground from the fragments of sky that peeked through the canopy. They cast odd shadows that shifted in the breeze, growing and shrinking, begging her to take her eyes off the distant lantern.

The woods broke into a clearing that swayed with susurrating wheat. It might have been water for all she could see. The moon had been overtaken by a gauze of clouds that made the lamp ahead seem even brighter. She gained on it ever so slightly, jogging a few steps at a time to close the distance. Two more lights sprung up, still far off but dim and steady. As they drew closer, the faint smell of wood smoke rose to greet her. Then a sweet sight. A small, neatly kept farmhouse, it's two stories dwarfed by a massive oak tree at its side. The two distant lights had been the glow of a dying fire in its upper windows.

She reached the edge of the field and stopped, crouching in the grasses as Fabien approached the house. Best let him make the introductions alone in case his friends were off put by strangers.

Verenna watched him weave his way to the front door. Instead of knocking, he knelt and peaked in the front window, then rose and turned the corner onto the farthest side of the house. Peculiar, but perhaps they had some sort of system for situations like this. In a few minutes, he made his way back to her side of the building. He paused and scanned his surroundings with keen attention, then set down the lantern, took hold of a low bough of the oak tree, and began to climb.

Fabien reached a thick limb that ran right next to an upstairs window and shimmied onto it. Again he ducked below the level of the sill and rose just enough to look inside. He must have seen some signal between the parted curtains. He rose, took something from his pocket. He slid it along the seam between the two panes to undo the latch and climbed inside.

Confusion set in. If Fabien knew the people who lived in the house she couldn't imagine a reason for this type of entry. Verenna let her curiosity lead her to the base of the tree. Attempting to follow his example she struggled upwards. Climbing created an uncomfortable pull in her bandages that threatened to bring back the hurt in her side. Ignoring it, she pressed on until she sat before the window. Ducking low as he had done, she peeped through the fluttering drapes.

A pitcher of water and a basin on a table, a set of drawers, a small hearth with the last glow of embers emanating from it; a simple room without many possessions. There was also a bed with two sleeping people in it. And on the edge of it, sat Fabien.

He leaned down over one of the sleeping forms in a strange hunched posture, almost as if he were listening for a heartbeat, or perhaps whispering something.

Verenna could not place what she was seeing. Possibilities flitted through her head, but none matched. The breeze swirled through the leaves and chilled the back of her neck, sending a shiver down her. The oak issued a long, plaintiff creak, bemoaning the two unconscious forms.

Fabien's head whipped around at the disturbance. There was something red smeared at the corners of his mouth, darkening his open lips. Blood? Her vision swam. Something had gone wrong in his face. He'd become a wild-eyed, sneering version of himself she could not recognize. He charged towards her.

A scream rose out of her as she lost her hold on the branch, scraping her palms as she tried to grip the bark. Verenna landed in a heap on the ground. Her ankle twisted with the landing and took her breath. Disregarding the twinge running up her leg, she scrambled up and staggered towards the woods. A horrified glance behind her revealed a dark shape slithering down the tree after her. He'd catch her in an instant running. But hiding might save her.

Verenna threw herself into the wheat fields and ducked, hoping the shushing of the grass would hide her gasping. At first she mistook the sound of her own heartbeat as footsteps. Eventually the quiet of night overwhelmed her pulse. Hands pressed against the cooling earth, each nerve twitching the urge to run, she listened as hard as she could.

He swooped out of the silence. Wrapping an arm around her waist, he hoisted her over a shoulder and took off for the trees. Verenna kicked and flayed his back with her nails.

"Help! Monster! Let go!"

"Who's there?" A shout from the window. The farmer had heard.

"I'm here! He-"

Fabien put her down just long enough to switch his grip, putting her back to his chest and covering her mouth before continuing towards the woods.

"Get the neighbors!" the man in the window shouted back inside.

Verenna dug her heels into the ground wherever she could find purchase. She could feel him jolt in pain every time she hit his shin. He'd growl and swear but nothing slowed him.

"Stop it, damn you. They'll kill us. Stop," Fabien panted.

She clawed into his wrists, feeling her nails sink into the muscle.

"Gah!" he roared as she broke skin.

They reached the trees just as a chorus of alarmed voices rose behind them. Fabien bounded through the woods, dragging Verenna along as she fought. He stopped just long enough to throw her over his shoulder again before starting up a tree. As they ascended Verenna's struggles turned into desperate clinging. Higher and higher they spiraled into the branches until she could hardly see the forest floor through the leaves. Once in the canopy, Fabien halted and set her in the crook of a massive limb with her back against the trunk.

"Verenna," he began, extending a hand.

The girl recoiled. "Don't touch me."

Fabien slid closer. "This all makes sense if…"

"Don't get any closer or I'll bash your nose. You're a freak. What were you doing to that man?"

"Nothing."

"Then what's on your face?"

Fabien took his sleeve across his mouth and looked away. "I'm sorry you saw."

"What did I see?" she demanded.

"Why we're all at the abbey." He paused, the faint light through the leaves casting shifting patterns across his face. "We're what you probably know as Vampires. It's a dated term, but-"

Every sense told her to disbelieve. But with all she had seen, how could she? Twin urges rose in her throat; to shriek and be sick all at once. "Stay away," she gagged. Turning back the way they'd come she screamed to the forming mob, "Here! I'm here!"

The young man coiled and sprang, silencing her again with a thick hand over her mouth. His voice hushed and urgent, he explained.

"They will kill me if they find us. Please, Verenna, you know me. I've been this way the whole time. I've never hurt you and I won't now. Just please, don't help them find me."

The angry voices drew closer to their hideout, calling out to each other, calling out for her. Half way across the field, she guessed. If she screamed loud enough the sound might make it to them. Then, there was Fabien's pleading face. He looked completely himself, just as she'd met him in the flower shop. Handsome, sweet even. How quickly that could change. The beast she'd seen through the window couldn't be buried that far below the surface. Yelling for help might resurrect it.

"Please will y-ouch!" Fabien forgot his words and pulled back his hand as Verenna bit his finger.

"How's it feel, you bastard?" she hissed. "I didn't know you left without me because you were going to run ahead and eat someone first," Verenna spat.

"Left without you?" He paused rubbing his hand.

"We made a plan in the hall today. You said you didn't like it at the abbey, neither did I, and we decided to escape when you went out 'hunting'. If that's what you call this. You said you had friends. They might take us in. You even waved to me to give me the all-clear!"

"Is that what you got out of it? You thought I was trying to escape and take you with me? The abbey is the escape, Verenna. There are demons out looking for you and now a mob out looking for me. It's not safe anywhere else. For either of us."

Verenna felt herself cored like an apple as she realized the misunderstanding. "I thought that..." She didn't bother continuing. Of course he didn't like it there. Who would? An old musty abbey, part hospital, part asylum, and who knew what else. But if what he told her was truth, there was nowhere else for him. "But didn't you-"

"Shh!" Fabien held up a hand for silence.

"What?"

He pressed a finger to his lips, tapping another against his ear, and pointing farther into the woods. The calls of the farmers had just barely reached the trees. Yet from the other direction a new set of voices emanated from the dark, accompanied by the baying of hounds. Fabien lay flat on the branch, motioning her to press herself to the shape of the tree.

In hardly a whisper she began, "Who-"

"Hunters," he mouthed.

"What? More like you?"

He shook his head slowly.

"Do they hunt you?" Verenna didn't need an answer. The way he'd formed himself to the branch told her they did. He'd managed to make the whole of his considerable bulk nearly invisible amongst the gnarls of the oak. He motioned again for quiet.

"Promise to take me home," she murmured, purposefully testing him with the volume of her voice.

"Don't do this," Fabien begged.

"Home."

"I can't."

"That or…"

The din from the woods drew closer, overwhelming the shouts of the pursuing farmers. The smell of smoke reached them before the lanterns and torches appeared. Darts of light pierced the foliage as a cluster of forms, five or six, spoke below them.

"This must be what the dogs were on about."

"That?" another grunted.

"Girl's shoe."

Verenna broke into a sweat that made the breeze feel like ice. The toes of her bare foot gripped at the bark. The shoe had fallen off in the climb.

"So? No girl."

"We don't get paid for no shoe."

"Turn up something good for a change, why don't you?" A nasal voice complained.

Questions whirred through Verenna's mind. The band had been sent to look for her. A search party? The dogs would have to get her scent somehow, most likely from her parents hiring people to find her. Fabien took her hand and squeezed, one of his deep green eyes revealed in the light through a gap in the leaves. She'd never seen them so round.

"Gentlemen," a cooler voice calmed the group below. "We are not alone."

He squeezed harder and put his head down on the branch. In seconds they'd be discovered, she was sure. She'd be taken home.

Maybe. A forewarning dread told her not to climb down to these men; their strange voices and snarling dogs, their smell, sweat and burning. She clutched Fabien's hand in return as the calm voice called again.

"Hello! Who comes?"

"Search party!" someone called back out of the rustling brush. Verenna released her grip on Fabien's hand and let the building knot in her shoulders slide away. The mob had caught up just in time to distract the hunters. Their torches multiplied the shoots of light puncturing the canopy.

"There's a madman out tonight," a man panted.

"You don't say."

"Aye, we do say," a gruff woman joined them. "Woke up to some brute hanging over my husband with blood all over his face."

The cool voice did not rise to their excitement. It stayed steady and asked, "Are you hurt, Sir?"

"No. Bit of blood on me. But not mine as I can tell. Might be from that beast when I woke up and fought him off. Got in a few good knocks, I did. Almost had him. Then he fled right out the window."

Slow, heavy footfalls tamped the forest floor in the pause. Again the cool voice addressed his troop. "Well, we seem to be on the right track."

"Track of what?" the woman asked.

"Unusual things, Madam."

"Well, why ain't you caught him yet? He's huge. You couldn't miss him." Another one of the farmers piped. "I tell you, these pretty, rich fellows with all the time in the world. Hunting and never catching."

"I wouldn't say never. Our dogs caught a trail. We found this." Verenna peered down through the branches to see a man's hand holding up her shoe. "The thing that came for you is close by. I'd turn in for the night."

"And why should you lot handle it? It was in my home," the first man protested.

"Because, Sir, when you come to the woods looking for a monster, you will find one."

The farmer's wife screamed. One of the men dropped his torch, knocking out it's flame. Verenna tried to glimpse what went on, but saw no more than the farmer's horrified faces and the wide, brown brim of a hat that blocked her view of the man with the cold voice. The little war party set off running hard for home, leaving the hunters chuckling.

The one in the wide hat held the shoe out to the dogs.

Without hesitating, Verenna stripped the other shoe from her foot, wrenched back her arm and threw it as hard as she could. It went sailing. So far she hardly heard it come down. The dogs yipped and whined, straining against their leads.

"What was that?"

"Did you hear it?"

"Go. Circle around."

The band vanished, urged on by the pull of eager hounds. The sudden absence of their lanterns left Verenna's eyes unseeing and blinking wide in want of light. For the moment there was only the smell of earth and night. Fabien's words drifted through.

"You didn't turn me in. Why?"

"Does it matter? Let's go."

They clambered down the tree moving only when the wind did. Once feet hit earth they ducked and ran. Without shoes Verenna could feel each individual rock in detail as her feet pelted the ground. She pressed herself to keep going with the image of the mortified faces of the farmers. Especially the woman's. Her mouth had pulled so far down at its corners, her hand flew trembling to her mouth to cover her shriek, as if to keep from breathing the same air as the horror she had seen. What it had been Verenna did not know, but the urge to escape it pushed her feet passed bruising.

Fabien noticed her lagging and took her on his back. Verenna wound her arms about his neck and held tight as they dove through the brush. Carrying her didn't seem to slow him at all. The fear that drove him forward must have been infinitely greater than what had propelled her. He understood the things behind them, she could only imagine.

Chapter 8

After at least a mile Fabien slowed and set Verenna down. They kept a hurried pace, constantly checking the trees behind them for pursuers. Soon the woods returned to their usual night songs; crickets and the churning of windblown boughs. Only then did they dare to speak.

"Nice throw."

"Thanks."

"How'd you get it to go that far?"

"Practice." With her long history of tantrums, the statement was true enough.

"Well, that was a good bit of quick thinking."

They walked in silence for a while. The tendons in her ankle started throbbing from her fall. She tried to hide the slight limp to keep pace at his side.

"You didn't answer the question though."

"What?"

"Why you didn't help them catch me."

"I meant to. I forgot."

Fabien let out a scoffing laugh. "You did not. You decided to keep me."

"To spare myself. Those men didn't look any more likely to take me home than you did. I didn't do it for you, to be clear." Grateful for the dark, Verenna let the apples of her cheeks go red without a fight.

The young man smiled to himself. "You trust me more than them? Even knowing what I am?"

"Better the Devil you know."

"You're right about that. Then you're not afraid of me?"

"If you were going to try something you already would have. You made a good point." Another quiet lingered between them.

"I'm glad you think like that. We don't want to harm anyone. Most of us at the abbey are there because we're afraid of being harmed ourselves. That's why everyone thinking it's a hospital is so nice. They leave us alone."

"Most of us? You mean, there are others at the abbey? Are all of you…?"

"Not all. Some are mortal. Others are, well, other things," Fabien grumbled.

"So, Lord and Lady Ren? The doctor?" Verenna whispered, her world spinning with the realization.

Fabien nodded. "Pretty much everyone you've met is like me. Yet not a bit of harm came to you. I'd say you've done more damage kicking and scratching me."

"Yeah, um, sorry."

"Understandable," he shrugged.

Branches creaked and both froze. Only when the breeze moved them again, confirming the inanimate source of the sound, did they continue. Both had fresh injuries that might attract wolves; the blood on Fabien's sleeve and back where she'd scratched him, her palms and arms freshly scraped from her attempts to grip the tree as she fell at the farmhouse. Caution made the slower pace worthwhile.

"So that man. Is he like you now? Will he come to the abbey?"

"Thank goodness, no. The place would be overrun if it worked like that. It takes two bites, not one, for someone to be like us. And we can always tell when someone's already been bitten. There are traces of our immortality left. The first bite is kind of a trade. We take what we need, but we give a bit of our eternity in return.

That way they heal quickly. Probably also have the best night's sleep they've ever gotten. Some even look younger in the morning," he chuckled.

Verenna hardly heard him. She was lost with the word *immortal*. It hadn't struck her yet that that was part of it, part of him. She tried to keep herself from showing the awe that was settling over her, reminding herself that it could not possibly be true. They traipsed a long way saying nothing.

"I don't know if it's rude to ask but, how did you get to be the way you are?"

He stumbled a bit and cleared his throat. "Another time. We'll have a pint and a chat, you and I."

Verenna could not imagine herself with a pint in hand, and assumed that he meant never. Normally she would have pressed him but there was more on her mind. "What did that man do that scared those people?"

"You're full of the tough one's today. He's, um, the not-so-nightmarish way to put it is he's a Houndsman."

"What's wrong with that?"

"He keeps Hell Hounds. He sold his soul for the ability to have and control them."

"Those dogs?"

"Yes. Well, sort of. You don't see them how they really are until they have orders. Until they're turned loose to collect someone. Then they get...different. Their master's name is Lord Gawshire. He hunts us as a hobby. The thugs are new. It's usually just him and other Lords. He must have some nasty work he's about tonight."

"Oh," was all she had to offer. She had no energy left for shock. Never in her young life had truth required so much blind belief.

The woods gave way to grass once more. The distant black bulk of the abbey stood out against the royal blue of the coming morning. Bitter as she was that her escape had fallen through, a certain relief swept through her seeing it again. Thankful for the softer ground Verenna took a few steps out of the tree line, feeling the soft blades dance against her ankles.

Fabien caught her arm. She spun around, instinct assuming something was wrong.

"Thank you. Tonight could have gone badly. Very badly. For us both. You gave up a chance to go home to save me."

The girl stared down at her feet, into the shadows behind them, to the smoke trails from the town's distant chimneys, anywhere but at the man before her.

"I don't know why you did it. But I guess I don't have to. Just, thanks."

"If you can't die, why does it matter?"

"There are worse things," he whispered. That, she could believe.

"So...you won't tell Darius about all this, will you?"

Fabien shook his head and smiled with one side of his mouth. Verenna nodded her thanks, allowing him to carry her as they struck out for the abbey. The easy glow of dawn crept up above the trees, draping the battlements in the rosy glow of sunrise. They had almost reached the side gate when Verenna noticed movement on the road.

"Someone's there." She pointed over Fabien's shoulder. He turned for a glimpse and dropped below the level of the grass.

"They've caught up. Crawl for the gate." They wound their way to the iron and wood that had allowed their flight and slipped into its alcove, the ivy overgrowing it keeping them from view. Fabien fit the door handle into his palm to keep it from rattling and delicately lifted the lever.

Verenna watched the approaching group through the vines. The man with the cold voice lead them, his face still obscured by the wide brim of his hat. The group headed for the main gate only thirty feet or so from where they hid. She gestured for Fabien to hurry. He tried the door again, pressing into it with his shoulder. Leaning in, he breathed the word, "Locked."

Chapter 9

"What?!" Verenna rasped. "They're right there!"

"Just..." He went to work again, pressing, peering through the crack between the wood and the stone, tugging at the hinges. Verenna wrung her hands. The footsteps slowed. The violent rattling of the main gates made them both jump and freeze.

"Open up! We're here to speak with the doctor," one of the thugs shouted over the wracking clang of the iron bars. Verenna watched them through the ivy as they waited, grumbling. The dogs had their noses in the air investigating, black and brown like their bodies and chipped with the pink of countless scars. Luckily the breeze put the creatures upwind.

Eventually, one of the men with a meaty red complexion called out, "There he is!" The dogs took up his cry, whining and yelping at the coming stranger.

"Why's he walking so slow?" a man with a pock marked face complained.

"He's an old man. He walks slow."

"That's not him," the man in the hat corrected. He stepped in close to the bars and shouted, "Good morning, Sir. Is the doctor in today?"

"Give me a moment, I can't hear you," Lord Ren's voice answered him. "What's that now?"

"We are looking for the doctor who resides here. Is he in?"

"Docks? No, Sir. No docks. Dry land. All of it," Ren bristled. At any other time Verenna would have laughed to hear the sharp old man playing the idiot. Whatever plan he had in mind she prayed it worked.

"Amusing." The man in the hat gritted his teeth and gripped one of the bars as if he were wringing a neck. "We need to see the doctor. We know a particularly good one lives here."

"Doctor? Someone sick? You all look the picture of health to me. Young and spry."

Verenna suppressed a scoff. Except for their leader, each and every one of them was middle aged and some combination of scars, layers of dirt, missing teeth, and an odor that might be mistaken for decay. Verenna might have thought they were corpses if they hadn't been standing.

"I guarantee that we are in dire need. Now you will either let us in, or fetch him for us." The leader cracked a snarling smile.

"No. No, I'm in charge of intake. Hospital's quite full. Only the most serious cases allowed in."

"Hm." The man in the hat shrugged and looked back at his troop. Then in one smooth arch he drew a blade from his belt, whirled on the man closest behind him and slipped the knife across the man's guts. He fell, gasping. The rest of the group took a wide-eyed step back, but out of fear or confusion said nothing. Verenna looked away, feeling vomit rise in her throat as the sight of the red seepage boiling out of the twitching figure on the ground.

"Serious enough?" the leader continued, toying with the still dripping blade.

"Quite. Name please?"

"A man is dying, sir. Are you telling me that this is not what your doctor is sworn to prevent? I would say our need is quite dire. Introductions can wait."

"Name?" Ren insisted.

In a sudden, hardly audible outburst the man in the hat reached through the bars, taking hold of Ren's collared uniform and hauling him up against the iron between them. "Skip it, old man. A farmer was attacked last night. Seemed like Vampire activity. Which means one of the bloodsuckers the doctor keeps was out in the woods. It just so happens that it took something of mine."

Verenna looked again just in time to see the man holster his knife and wrestle her shoe from his pocket. A cold dart ran down the sides of her neck.

"That's yours?" Ren asked unflustered.

The man in the hat curled his fingers into a fist around the shoe as if he might knock Ren in the jaw. "This belongs to what we're looking for. The dogs took us right to it. The only problem is that it's got blood on it and no girl in it. And with a blood drinker on the loose, we put two and two together. Either you've got her in there or you know where she is. Tell me, is it familiar?"

"Wolves?" Ren suggested. "If you're looking for a girl, I'd try the pub."

The man in the hat gave Ren a shove. Verenna heard the old man hit the ground. The leader turned with open arms to his mob and laughed. "Did you hear that, gents? The pub. Funny old thing, isn't he?"

The group glanced at each other and nervously followed suit, chuckling and trying not to acknowledge the man still gurgling on the ground, though the dogs sniffed and prodded at him.

"Why, he's probably old enough to remember the burnings." The laughter stopped. "Every freak hideout in town, raided, wiping the land clean of undesirables. Now, they say they got them all. But if they didn't, I would bet they'd live in there." He nodded up to the heights of the abbey. "Call me nostalgic, but I do love to bring back old traditions. All it would take is someone with a little power saying the word..."

He hung on the gate, relaxed in his victory. "Of course, any unpleasantness could be avoided if you open these gates and let us have a look around. Perhaps we could have that chat with the doctor after all. As you can see here," he nudged the dying man with a foot. "Time is running out."

"Reasonable." Ren had recovered and come back to his feet. The grating, squealing sound of underused metal screeched in Verenna's ears as Ren unlocked and threw open the gates. "Have a look. Leprosy first floor, consumption the second. The third is plague and whatever that new one from Bronwell is. And I wouldn't ask about the fourth floor. You'll find out when you get there. That's where the doctor is."

The mob shifted in their places, none dared take the first step, not even the man in the hat.

"Come on. You'd better hurry if you want to help that friend of yours."

The dogs paced, soundless paws on bloodsoft ground. The plaintiff scrape of rusted hinges overtook the last wheeze of the man spilling into the dirt. The clanging lock tolled the close of the gates.

"Don't say I didn't offer," Ren shrugged to the troop he'd sealed outside.

In a burst of fury the leader shot a hand through the gate to grab for the old man's throat. He missed by a fraction.

"Tell your doctor, Gawshire sends his best," he spat and threw the shoe through the bars. "And I *will* be sending my best." He turned and hovered over the corpse before kicking it. "Keep this," he said over his shoulder. "Perhaps you have pigs." With a wave of his hand the group woke from their frozen terror and marched off towards the sanctuary of the shadowed trees.

Verenna and Fabien let out their breath as they watched the figures go, putting their backs against the door, eyes closed and sighing. "You alright?" Fabien took her hand.

"Yeah, I think." The words sounded ingenuine even to her. Her stomach threatened revolt every time the image of spurting red crossed her mind. A morbid part of her wanted to see the man who fell, to see the path his gore traced on the earth, to know what she might have looked like that night in the street. Before she could blink the thought from her head she felt herself falling backwards.

Someone had thrown open the door letting the both of them hit the dirt.

"Good God! What is wrong with the two of you? Get inside!"

They crawled in. Darius slammed the door behind them and turned to them fuming. "Do you have any idea, what danger you've put us all in. I can't..." He turned away, winding back and forth like a caged animal. "They almost had you! And you," he hovered over Fabien. Grasping at his own dark hair he roared, "You took her out of our walls?!"

Hearing Darius's rage, Lord Ren hurried over. Others who'd doubtless been watching from the windows came hustling to join them. Lady Ren bustled across the grass in the lead, fistfuls of her silken skirts held high. "What on earth? We saw those men at the gate. What's going on!"

On the edge of manic laughter, the doctor replied. "I'll tell you. Those two! They decided to take a little jaunt last night and were *this close* to being caught by hunters! They arrived so close together they might as well have been holding hands!"

"Darius," Ren interjected. "They'll be back. I suggest we put aside the upset and decide what to do about it. I think by now we all know what 'sending their best' means."

"Demons," a woman in her nightcap shuddered.

"What's that matter to us? We've been burning sage nearly every night. That seems to keep them at bay," another offered.

"Because they haven't been targeting us. Until now. Thanks."

Darius glared down at Fabien who scrambled to his feet to confront him.

"Listen here. I went out to hunt and she followed me. I didn't take her anywhere. I'm not an idiot."

"Well, you act like it!" Darius shouted, inches from his face. Fabien raised a fist, but before he could strike Mortimer broke from the crowd to separate the two.

"Stop it!" Lady Ren demanded. She extended a bony hand to help Verenna up. "My dear, a-are you hurt?"

"No. A few scrapes." She held out her stinging palms. "So that's what you've been burning? Sage?"

"Yes. Contrary to your burning bodies theory. I'm sorry to disappoint," Darius snapped.

"If not sage, then what? They'll be back at nightfall, latest," Marietta chimed in, wrapping herself tighter in her trailing red robe.

"And they'll be watching us till then," someone called from the midst of the forming crowd.

"We have to move." Mortimer chimed in. "If they think she's here they won't stop. They'll come at us until they get in. For the sake of the mortals living here we have to go. Now."

A murmur rolled through the group. Lord Ren nodded. "So be it."

"Wait…" Verenna tried to intrude but the bark of orders overcame her.

Lord Ren turned to his wife. "Darling, go with Marietta and pack the girl what she'll need. Will you dear?"

"Of course." She rushed towards the abbey. Marietta followed, but not before giving Verenna a narrow eyed once over.

"You there," Darius pointed to a young man in a dirty gray shirt. "Get the carriage ready. Hurry! The rest of you, make sure everyone knows what we're up against. Tell them to get ready.

Candles, fires, everywhere. Everyone inside! The sun will be up sooner than you think!"

The crowd split in all directions. Verenna tried to catch their sleeves for an explanation but no one stopped. With no luck she took hold of Fabien's arm before he could go. "What do they mean go? You said it was safe here."

"Not anymore."

"I want to go home. I'm not letting you take me farther from it."

"There's no choice. We have to leave."

"No. No! You said I could go home!" Verenna shrieked, hooking her nails into Fabien's shirt as if the fabric itself held the promise.

"You can. One day. Just not yet. It's not safe."

"And where is?!" Verenna wailed at the top of her lungs, her voice cracking with anguish and lack of sleep. "Where could you possibly take me? Why should I trust any of you?" Verenna threw Fabien away. She started as a placating hand found her shoulder. She slapped it off, finding Mortimer beside her.

"Verenna…"

"Get off me!"

"Good God, enough with the hysterics," Darius commanded as he marched to join them. "We've got no time for it. We have to move now. We leave or we die."

"I'll take my chances," Verenna stormed past him and up the front steps, the three men close in her wake. The vast main hall echoed with activity all the way to its vaulted rafters. It was clear that services hadn't been held there for years; not a pew in sight. The tables and chairs that now populated the space made the room look like one, huge parlor. But any homey feel the room had was disassembled as many hands upended the furniture to stack it as a barricade against the windows.

The throng piled firewood, lit candles, gathered supplies, a few men bore a stretcher out to collect the gutted man at the gate.

"Stop! I'm not going!" Verenna screamed, swiping several parcels from a table onto the floor. The hubbub subsided as all eyes focused on her newly flushing face.

"You ungrateful little sot," Darius spat as he caught up to her.

"Don't call me that!"

"Then don't be one!"

"She's got a right to be upset. None of us want this." Mortimer's kindness went unnoticed as Verenna flung another package, this time at Darius.

"I will not be spoken to this way by the likes of you!"

The doctor dodged the package. "The likes of me saved your life once already. And I'm about to do it again if you'll stop throwing things and cooperate." Fabien moved forward to restrain her but the girl circled to the other side of a table.

"I know what you are. What you all are!"

"What am I then? Go on. I'm sure we'd all love to hear," Darius prodded, arms thrown wide.

"Freaks! All of you! Monsters! Vampires!" she howled at the room, looking into the shocked faces of the silent onlookers. All familiarity had gone. Each seemed a hollow creature, entirely new and entirely empty.

"What?" Darius paled. A whisper ran around the room.

"You drink blood. Like animals!"

In the time it took her to turn to him, Darius had come around the table, seizing her and pinning her arms to her body, coming close enough that his eyes took up nearly the whole scope of her vision, the spray of his words misting her cheek.

"Listen to me," he rasped. "You listen because I won't say it again. You know what we are. That can't be helped. But I'll be damned if I'll hear you call us animals. These freaks that you spit at have done nothing but good for you. We shared our home when yours became too dangerous, we clothed you, we fed you, we found you bleeding in the street and sewed you back up. So don't you ever, ever, accuse anyone here of being a monster. Because if these are what you call monsters, wait until you see the rest of this world."

He released her and she staggered back, knees weak with surprise, and grabbed onto the table for support. Tears of outrage clouded her eyes. "You…" she tried for words. Darius waited, the whole room waited, until Verenna glanced away in defeat. Her fury boiled over into weeping.

The doctor straightened his vest, seeming to notice for the first time that they were being watched. In a hurry to be done with the situation, he raised his chin at three maids huddled in the corner. "You three, take her to my study and get her ready to travel. Don't let her out of your sight." Darius spun on a heel and left before any protests could be made. The three tidy women approached with considerable hesitation, looking from Verenna, to the parcels on the ground, to each other and back again, skittish like deer.

"This way, Miss," the tallest instructed. The other two linked arms with her on either side and the party took to the stairs. The tumult of preparation resumed as the women lead her away.

Verenna barely noticed the cheerful day beyond the rows of windows they passed. She followed the maids without a fight, hardly looking up from her feet. Something Mortimer said came ringing back to her. If her parents were indeed safer without her it might be wiser to go. The thought preoccupied her until they came to a humble wooden door at the end of a long, rug lined hall.

After knocking and listening the ladies took her inside. The door hid a lavish room, richly furnished with bold reds and purples, the furniture deep polished cherrywood, and bookcases climbing to the ceiling against almost every wall. Three hooded windows allowed in just enough indirect glow from the day to illuminate the room.

The two ladies on each side of her encouraged her to sit on a long, heavily padded couch. The three girls skittered about her. One brought a bowl of water and cleaned the scrapes on her hands and washed the grime of the woods from her feet. Another rushed in with a roll of bandages and began wrapping Verenna's ankle. In the chaos of their return she had forgotten it's soreness. A slight limp must have given her away. The third girl darted in and out of the room, first bringing tea, then a traveling case with a few clothes in it, then a new pair of shoes.

No one spoke in the process. Her earlier outburst had made them timid, though there was no longer any need. Defeat had stamped out Verenna's temper. She sat like a doll and cooperated as they tidied her clothes and brushed her hair. It was only as the trunk was clipped shut and one of the ladies poured the amber tea that Verenna finally found words.

"Thanks. For everything."

"It's no trouble, Miss. Is there anything else?"

"No. Actually, yes. Do you have paper? And a pen?"

One of the girls fetched the items from a desk across the room. "Do any of you go to town?"

Two nodded.

"Do you know where Pen Row is?"

Only one bobbed her head.

"Good. I'm going to write something. If I'm not back in a month, take it to this address." Verenna scribbled the numbers for her parents' house on the back of the parchment before turning the page to write.

Mum, Dad, I'm alive.

The words choked her and made her pause until she could be sure her tears wouldn't fall and ruin the ink. She could picture the roses, the green front door, how light glowed through the drapes of her room in the morning, how rain dripped in lulling cadence from the eaves.

It's the end of June now. I've been at the abbey in the woods, but I won't be for long. I don't know where they're taking me, but I believe it is safer for all of us if I go with them. They've been kind. I'm not hurt. I will be back.

The study door opened with a light bang against the wall that made her smudge her last word. Darius marched in followed by two men that Verenna recognized as the librarians. She scratched the last line in a hurry.

I love you both,
Verenna

Folding the paper, she placed it in the waiting hand of the maid. "Hide it. In your apron."

The girl shoved the paper into her pocket.

"Promise me you'll deliver it. Keep it a secret. Don't show it to anyone. Promise?"

"Yes," the girl whispered, locking her blue eyes with Verenna's copper.

Before she had time to thank the girl Darius interrupted.

"Progress?" He scanned each of them as if rooting out some lie. Verenna thought for a moment that he might have seen the note change hands. Surely if the doctor found it he'd confiscate it.

The tallest girl answered "Yes, sir. We've finished."

"Good. You're dismissed. But wait outside the door. We may need your help again." He narrowed his eyes at Verenna as he spoke. A warning against having another go at escape.

The three maids bobbed curtsies and slipped into the hall.

"Do you think you can manage to stay out of trouble a moment while we get organized?" He indicated the two men unrolling scrolls across the stout, dark-wood table near the windows. "I can always bring in someone as a guard if you feel you'll have trouble controlling yourself."

"I'll be fine," Verenna grumbled over the rim of her tea cup. The warm liquid helped distract from Darius's sarcasm and release the knot forming at the back of her neck. She could feel him staring down at her, but refused to cater to him by meeting his gaze. She looked fixedly into the distance until the Doctor relented and went to join the two librarians hovering over the spread of maps and papers.

She sighed and put down her cup. Exhaustion had arrived, but she had too much to think about to allow for sleep. She rose. Her ankle felt considerably better the way the maid had wrapped it. No pain at all, in fact.

She checked the group at the table. The three figures hunched over their papers and paid her no attention. Keeping them in the corner of her eye she explored the shelves that lined the room. Volumes of every size and sort, some layered thick with dust, others with spines cracking from use. Half were medical works. The other half were myth, lore, even fairy tales. Dotting the shelves, often as book ends, were jars containing plants. Some still grew, some preserved. One in particular that caught her eye held a sizeable beetle, it's iridescent wings splayed out, mid-flight in its liquid.

Following the shelves in ever increasing wonder she came across a book no taller than her hand, a noticeable dip between two encyclopedias. It's midnight blue spine could not be read, so she tugged it out to find its title. In thin, silver letters it read, 'The Practical Handbook for Identifying the Demonic'. She flipped through its pages, worn soft from ages of touch and use, which in itself was rather frightening. On an impulse, she slipped it into the pocket of her dress. If these people told the truth, it couldn't hurt to know what she was up against.

A rectangular structure stood in the gap between the next two shelves. About two foot or so taller than she and covered in a royal purple drape, it loomed high above a mahogany desk dotted with untidy piles of notes.

Unsure of what she'd find beneath she took a delicate hold on the edge of the cloth lifted ever so slightly. The light of the room flooded under the cloaking purple fabric. Glass, a case, with something smooth inside.

"Don't." A voice sounded behind her. She jumped and dropped the curtain. Mortimer appeared from behind her and hurried to shut the gap Verenna made in the drapes.

Recovering from the surprise she snapped, "Why not?"

"It's, um, not ready yet. It's a painting."

"An unfinished painting already in a glass case?" She cocked an eyebrow.

"Yes." The lie was clear, but the way Mortimer planted himself between her and the covered display dismissed all argument. Clearing his throat to break his own intensity, he changed the conversation. "I'm glad you're back safe. Those woods are full of wolves and men just like 'em. You have no idea the kind of danger you were in."

"Fabien was there. He did a fair job of protecting me." Verenna replied tartly.

"We can all be thankful for that." He straightened the drape to make sure it closed completely. "What's done is done. Just please don't take a risk like that again. It makes it awfully hard to keep my promise to you if you run off and I don't know where you've gone."

As he spoke she caught a glimpse of the sorrow that had brought him to his current state of ware. To avoid an uncomfortable silence Verenna looked down at her shoes and cleared her throat. "How long have you been in here anyway? I didn't see you."

"Just a few minutes. Sorry I keep startling you. I just came to make sure you were alright..." So began the pause Verenna feared. She watched gloom like gathering clouds veil the man's subtle gray eyes as he grew silent and distant. To stop his falling face Verenna blurted the first question she could think of.

"What's all that?" She nodded at the table awash with papers and pointing fingers.

Darius overheard and answered without looking up. "Sometimes people use maps when they travel. Revolutionary, I know."

Verenna stuck out her tongue. She intended to keep her cross-armed pout but curiosity took hold. Weaving around Mortimer she joined the men at the table, alternately standing on her toes and ducking down to get a good view of their work.

"We've compiled the three into one. Here," one of them took up a rolled hide in his stout fingers and rolled it out across the table. Verenna shouldered her way in for a look.

The contours of a familiar countryside lay before her. Surrounding towns, cities, even the meandering shape of the coast were all pictured in exquisite detail. X's dotted the landscape, most black, a few red, while long trailing lines of blue ink wavered across like veins. Though they were not the rivers. Each had what appeared to be a name. The first line zig zagged with the roads, stopping altogether, then cropping up again in the next town. The label read 'Souris'. The other drifted about in a graceful, sweeping arches and had been named 'Malagrir'.

A black spill of ink in the upper left of the map drew her in next. It appeared to be a mistake that darkened a whole corner. Yet beside it there was a name. 'Marhasim'. Perhaps it was a place, though she'd certainly never heard of it. She would have asked if one of the librarians hadn't launched into an explanation.

"These circles here are all of the suspected sightings of The Horsemen. These ones, the lines, the way they've come. And the x's are confirmed cases of Cold Fever. Black for deadly, red for survived."

Verenna's brows furrowed. Spindly x's decorated city names like lace. So many afflicted.

"Each x is ten of course."

The girl's jaw dropped. Death by the hundreds. Right where Bronwell should be. She searched and found the name almost completely obscured by black marks.

"Right," Darius's nodded his grim approval. "We'll take the back roads and hope for the best. That avoids most areas with over ten fatal cases. There aren't many people out that way, no major cities or sources of news. They should be calm, and from the looks of it, relatively unaffected so far."

"Where are we headed?"

The men went quiet, unsure if they should elaborate.

"Why, Bronwell of course." Darius answered with an uncanny smile.

All the color washed from the girl's face as she gestured to the spot on the map where the city lay. So many x's, overlapping, layered in heaps like the near countless bodies they represented, one on top of the other.

"But all those marks-"

"You're underestimating Bronwell's population. It should still be a fully functioning city. A few hundred dead, yes, but thousands still alive. And we're going to help keep it that way. What? You were so interested in Bronwell before. It's your chance to see it for yourself. " Darius rolled up the map and slipped it into a canister with a carrying strap. He slung it over his shoulder before addressing Mortimer who hung back near the desk.

"That damned horse still alive?"

"Somehow, yes. I came to say the carriage is ready."

"In that case, I bid you farewell gentlemen. Thank you for your work." He patted the canister. The two men wished the best of luck and departed.

"We're off." Darius said heading to the hall in a way that suggested she follow. Mortimer took up the bag the maids had packed for Verenna and lagged behind with her as Darius forged ahead down the corridor. Verenna felt her throat tightening the farther they descended. She worried the edge of a sleeve with a shaking hand.

When they returned to the main hall they were greeted by a hundred wordless stares. A mass of people awaited them, residents and workers alike, some she'd met, other's she'd never seen. The crowd parted for them with many best wishes, handshakes and words of advice.

Verenna gave a tense nod to those she knew from the tower and from visits in the week. The sheer number of people watching them made her back and shoulders stiff. All of them seemed to know what to expect of the journey but her. And to turn out in these numbers to say goodbye, the stakes must be dire. It felt like she was walking in her own funeral procession. She peered around for the comfort of Fabien's face but saw him nowhere. He of all people would have turned up to see her off. If anything had happened to him on her account for last night she'd never forgive herself.

At the end of the gauntlet the man in gray she remembered from the hall gave her a lavish bow. She looked down and curtsied, nearly colliding with Marietta as she rushed forward with a traveling cloak.

"Here you are, dear." She held the item out to Darius, giving Verenna a once over as she did.

He paused before taking it, his mouth a flat, exasperated line. "Many thanks."

"And you took the draught? You have some with you?"

"Yes. Plenty. I'll be fine." He pushed past her and pulled open one of the immense front doors with a heave. "We're short on time. Come on." Darius threw the cloak about his shoulders and plunged into the daylight beyond the door, the hem swirling like ebbing tidewater behind him. At Mortimer's urging, Verenna took a deep breath and followed him into the blinding bright. The others did not follow, but loitered just inside the shadows of the building.

She shielded her eyes and took in the sizable carriage waiting at the bottom of the steps. The box could hold four easily, and other than being well used it looked quite comfortable. The problem was with the horse. The poor thing was ragged. It had a steely gray coat, blotched from either dust or ill health, and there was no ruling out a combination of the two. The animal's mane and tail hung like dead grass at both ends of its countable ribs.

"Can it run?" Verenna whispered to Mortimer. He chuckled to himself.

"He looks his age, doesn't he? He's been with us for decades. A strangely long time in fact. There are younger but no better. You'll find that out soon enough I imagine." Mortimer fixed her bag into the luggage rack on the back of the cart. He helped Verenna inside before reaching for the ladder to the coachman's seat.

"What do you think you're doing old man?"

Verenna leaned out the window to find Darius blocking his ascent.

"I'm going along."

"And who decided that?"

"I made a promise to the lady that I'd keep her safe. Can't very well do that from home."

"We must travel light. Be as small a group as possible for speed. You'll be dead weight."

"I am sure you'll find use for me."

"We leave now. We have no time for you to prepare."

"I have nothing. What's there to prepare?"

The tendons in Darius's neck stood out like columns, his lips thin, his breath coming in huffs. He jabbed a pointed finger into Mortimer's chest for emphasis. "Fine. Get on. But the moment you lag behind, you're left behind."

"Nothing new," Mortimer shrugged. The old man sidled up the ladder and took the reins without a second glance at the fuming doctor.

"Missing something?" Called a voice from the steps. Fabien rushed out of the building, a scabbarded sword and a bag bouncing across his back. For the first time that day, Verenna smiled.

"Only valuable daylight. We leave now." Darius scolded.

"Then I'm in perfect time." Fabien jogged up to the carriage, gave a wink to Verenna, and with an effortless swing, set himself atop the luggage rack on the back of the cart. The horse stirred at a combination of the jostling and Darius's shouts.

"Good God, is everyone coming?" He marched over to Fabien

to berate him. "Also, how are you out in the sun?"

"Borrowed one of those vials in your desk. I thought it was rum, but when it turned out it to be Sun Draught I thought, why not come along and be helpful? Those give you three days each, right?"

"You went through my study? My study?" Darius shook the cases Fabien sat on to try and dislodge him. He held firm, his chuckling spinning Darius into a barely containable rage.

"May I suggest we get started?" Mortimer interrupted from the top of the carriage. "This contraption can carry six and we've only got four. Let the boy come. He's bored."

"Thank you." Fabien called over the cart.

"He went through my things!"

"And it was rotten of him. But you said it yourself, we've got to get moving." The old man reminded.

"I only brought enough sun draught for one." Darius barked.

"What do you think these are?" Fabien held his bag high.

"Thief!"

"Get in, Darius," Mortimer groaned.

"You'll pay me for those." Darius clambered inside the cabin, snarling.

"Let's go!" Fabien patted the back of the wagon as Mortimer spurred them into motion.

The carriage lurched forward and turned toward the main gate. Verenna's palms went slick. She didn't want to go, but the wheels had already turned. Even if she jumped out now there was no better option. She'd be put back in the cart and packed off anyway. Her stomach knotted. There was nowhere to go but out.

The lolling motion paused before the gate and Darius leaned out the window to give instructions. "They'll be watching from the woods. We'll have to take off at a run, and keep it that way until we lose them. They have hounds, you hear me? Don't slow.

For anything."

Verenna leaned out the opposite side of the cart. Two people, cloaked against the sun, stood at either side of the towering iron gate ready to heave it aside.

"Close it as soon as we're out. Clear? Brace yourselves. On my signal."

Verenna held her breath. The smell of heat and dust, the sound of birds, the breeze, everything melted from her mind except a rush of panic as Darius gave a single sharp whistle.

The gates parted, Mortimer snapped the reins, and the horse burst onto the road. The sudden speed knocked Verenna back into the carriage. She hit the back wall, rolling off the seat and onto the floor. Darius hauled her up just in time for a rut in the road to send them both toppling.

The cart plummeted towards the tree line followed by the bellowing of men and the frenzied baying of hounds. Their cries weren't as distant as she'd hoped.

"Stay down," Darius commanded. Verenna hugged the floor and shut her eyes against the carriages violent rocking. The barking drew even nearer. She could see tree branches whizz by in a blur of green through the wildly flapping drapes.

"We're going to crash! They'll catch us!"

"Just wait. Wait." Darius breathed.

Chapter 10

Verenna kept curled, head covered on the floor of the wagon, listening until the sounds of pursuit faded into the brush and crack of branches against the cart slowed to gentle clatter. Fabien let out a wild laugh from his seat on the luggage rack.

"We beat 'em!"

"I'm going to be sick," Verenna moaned.

"Not in this cabin you're not. The window's there," Darius threw a thumb in that direction.

She hauled herself up and clutched the edge of the window. Thankfully the splash of the breeze distracted her from the sour in her mouth and she sank back onto the seat without event. Even with her eyes closed she could feel Darius watching her from the opposite bench.

"What?"

"What do you mean what? We've got a lot to talk about. We're heading for Bronwell and you are grossly unprepared."

"Now?"

"Yes now. When else?"

"I'm tired. I'm going to sleep." Verenna fluffed the slim seat cushions beneath her and lay herself down with a huff.

"Should have thought of that before you ran away last night."

She crossed her arms, determined to hear none of it. To her great surprise, Darius relented.

"Fine. Sleep. But when you wake up, no excuses. I'd rather talk to a well-rested brat than a tired one."

Exhaustion let her ignore him as she gazed at the world

through the open curtain of the opposite window. Her lids grew heavy watching the world drift by, reciting its poem of gold and green, field and forest, again and again and again. The carriage slowed further to a swaying trot, rocked by the shallow grooves in the ground carved out by previous travelers. Soon the smell of dust and the steady fall of hooves grew distant and sleep overtook her.

℘

By the time her eyes fluttered open the window held the colors of sunset. She glanced over to Darius. He appeared to be asleep; his chin on his chest and arms crossed. She let out a sigh, enjoying the hazy peace of a freshly awoken mind before it remembers the day.

Verenna readjusted to ease the crick in her neck and felt something with corners prodding her from the pocket of her dress. A searching hand produced the book she'd taken from Darius's study.

"Hey," she said aloud to test if the doctor was truly asleep. No answer.

She examined the book's sapphire cover, feeling the embossed silver lettering. It was old, well used but well kept. She ran her thumb across the edge of the velveteen pages, making them flutter like hummingbird wings before turning to the first. Holding it close to the window for what dim light evening provided, she began to read.

A dedication adorned it in fine calligraphy. It read, 'For Sir Martin, when the need may find you.' On the next page was a disclaimer.

'The advice herein has been derived from extensive study and personal

experience. No action prescribed by this book is meant to be carried out by the untrained individual. May the reader be warned that any dealings with otherworldly entities are ill advised. Best wishes for continued health.'

Verenna's fingers tingled with both apprehension and some trace of excitement as she started chapter one, entitled, 'A Brief Overview of Demons and Their Varieties'. The first type explained was a low demon. A Crawler, as the book called it. They traveled close to the ground and were fairly small in size, often mistaken for large black cats or dogs. The hair of her arms stood up with a chill of morbid fascination as she pressed on.

'Crawlers are relatively delicate, having to consume mortal substance, the soul, regularly and often to keep themselves on this plane. They can pass easily into this world; however, they are also quick to fall back to their rightful realm if they do not feed. If they do not consume a soul within one to three days, even the strongest of them would be forced to return to Hell. They are also fairly mindless and easily tricked.'

In her excitement Verenna rushed ahead to the next section, entitled 'Runners'. These ranged anywhere from the size of a large dog, to that of a man.

'They can last weeks on earth without feeding, the longest known record being three months. They are fast, somewhat clever and often travel in groups. Hell Hounds fall into this category. Others in this classification often appear as a liquid-like substance suspended in the air, comparable to ink dropped into water. When they sense prey, they shrink low to the ground, becoming a dense blackness and swaying side to side in preparation for attack.'

Verenna's slapped the book shut as if reading any further might summon the creature from the stairs out of the pages. Something stirred across from her. Verenna let out a squeak of fright, clapping a hand over her mouth and recoiling.

"What's the matter with you now? What bloody time is it?" It was only Darius. She'd been so enthralled by the book she'd forgotten he slept.

He glared out at the sky and swore. He reached and gave the ceiling three hard knocks with the bottom of his fist. Mortimer guided the horse to the side of the road and they came to a stop.

The throat clenching feeling of being hunted returned the moment the cart stopped rolling. "Why have we stopped?" Verenna demanded. "What if they're still after us? We have to keep going."

"Oh they're still after us. You can bet your life. We've got some distance on them though." The nonchalant tone he'd taken frightened her even more. She shoved the book back into her pocket and tried to draw reasonably sized breaths as Darius leaned out the window to call to Mortimer.

"Please tell me you didn't pass Sansbury."

"It's a mile ahead, maybe. Maybe less." Mortimer shouted back.

"Shouldn't we be quiet? They'll hear us," Verenna blurted, though no one seemed to match her concern for noise. Darius completely ignored and continued his instructions. "We'll stop there for the night. That monastery has been hospitable in the past."

"We're staying at a church?" Fabien joined. "Are you joking? There's all sorts of inns and pubs and you're going to have us stay in a monastery."

"They'll look for us everywhere else. You'll live. Let's go."

"Yeah, but I won't be happy about it!" Fabien declared before his protests were lost to the grating of wheel over rock and dirt. Mortimer hurried the carriage as much as he dared in the failing light as they charged towards the edge of the woods.

In the dark, Darius's shape became unnerving. Though she knew it was him, her mind could not help but replace his form with the creatures she'd read about. His stillness and silence made her restless and set her fingers twitching. Finally her nerves bubbled over into speech.

"Do you really need to sleep? I mean, doesn't it become unnecessary when you're...like you are?" The answer wasn't important as long as he kept talking. His voice was the only reassurance she had that he was not one of the ink blot shadows from the book.

"Yes. Not near as much as you. We won't die without. But insanity sets in eventually which is not ideal."

The threat of a pause spurred her on. "What about the sun? It hurts you, doesn't it?"

"Sun Draught takes care of that. Not well mind you. It's uncomfortable, but bearable."

"Why is the sun so bad for you in the first place?"

"Because when a mortal is changed into one of us, the soul crystallizes. The sun hits you, the crystal focuses the light, it burns you from the inside out."

Verenna shuddered, remembering the feeling of burning her finger in the kitchen as a child and trying not to imagine the same sensation turning her torso into a furnace.

"Why the sudden interest?"

"Curious."

"And are you at all curious about why we're going to Bronwell?"

"Does it matter? Thought you were taking me there whether I like it or not." As her fear faded, bitterness took its place.

"True. But it will matter to you soon enough. From what we've gathered, Bronwell is where this whole mess started. There's a plague brewing in the city, a bad one. People dying in scores. Hysteria follows. Those kinds of conditions are perfect for demons to gain a foothold on earth. Plenty of death to fuel the fear that makes mortal souls such easy targets. Like furious little fires begging to be put out. People flee. And where prey goes, so go the hunters. Demons are pouring out of the city like an angry nest of ants. That's the only source we can be sure of anyway. It's the biggest at least. Which means Souris will likely be there."

"I saw that name on the map," Verenna's breathless voice recalled.

"You did. Souris is a far more ancient name for what you know as The White Horse, Pestilence. A creature which in essence is the god of disease."

"Why the Hell are we going there? You were supposed to keep me safe. That's the whole reason we left!"

"We will keep you as safe as possible. But it's made clear in the prophecy-"

"That I haven't seen." Verenna crossed her arms and stared out the darkened window. "How can I believe you if I've never read it for myself?"

Darius sighed. "Would it make you believe me any more if you saw it written down? My guess is you'd accuse me of writing it to trick you. Shall I go on?"

The girl gave no answer and allowed him to resume.

"The prophecy tells us that you are important to Souris's fall. It says you are to 'wash clean the city'."

"And what does that mean?"

"We don't know yet."

Verenna slammed her palms on the seat beside her in a flash of outrage. "You don't know? You dragged me out of my house, out of my town, and you can't even tell me what it is I'm supposed to do?"

"We didn't drag you anywhere. You came. Which was the best and only choice if the goal is your survival and the safety of your family. We know Bronwell holds the first key to unraveling this thing. We are as sure as we can be that Souris is there and that you are the one to do something to slow or stop him. That's why we're going."

"I can't believe you. You've been alive for who knows how long, known about the prophecy and THIS is how prepared you are," she said gesturing around at the carriage. "Great use of time."

The cart jolted as the ground went from dirt to cobblestone. It stopped the argument and had both clutching the walls to stay in their seats. Verenna checked the window and instead of darkness found the dim glow of street lamps.

Quaint thatched roofs lined the narrow street, flower-draped window boxes, and above it all a clear night full of stars. The streets broadened as they wound through rows of shops and houses until they finally opened into a wide town square at the foot of a huge edifice. It reared skyward, opulent in comparison with the town around it, with buttresses and spires like sewing needles piercing the indigo sky.

The carriage ambled up to the cascading front steps. Fabien jumped down from the luggage rack and hurried to open the door for Verenna.

"Apparently, this is our stop," Fabien offered his hand. She took it and clambered down, joined shortly by the other two.

"So, shall we knock?" Fabien took a few jogging steps towards the doors.

"Tsh! Get back here!" Darius hissed. "There's an etiquette to this. We wait. They approach. And Good God man, hide your sword."

"They might not even see us out here!"

"Oh they've seen us. In times like this they'll have a lookout over every entrance. Especially at night." Mortimer reassured the young man.

Fabien sauntered back down the steps, took off his sword and shut it in the cabin of the cart, making sure to swing the door hard enough for a good snap. "I guess we wait for them to get off their fat, robed asses then."

"Exactly. And when they do, I'll speak to them. You lot go along with what I say and we'll be safe for the night." Darius instructed.

Just as he said it one of the cathedral doors opened a crack. A man in white robes stepped out, followed closely by a monk in brown. The monk held a lantern suspended from a rod high over the other man's head. They started the journey down the steps at a stately pace. Their painfully slow descent made Verenna restless, shifting her impatience from one foot to the other.

The two reached the top of the last series of steps and came to a halt. The one in white held up his hands as if calling for a silence that had already set in. His clean-shaven face was smug and jowled. Wisps of gray hair streaked backwards to cover his coming baldness. Darius stepped forward and bowed, staying low until the man in white spoke.

"Good evening, my children. What brings you to our doors so late?"

"Father, good evening. My name is Doctor Matthew Carter."

Verenna forced herself to hide her surprise at hearing the name. Matthew Carter had been her family's doctor since she was a child. He was well known and liked and thus an odd choice to impersonate, even in the next town over. She listened carefully as Darius improvised.

"We're seeking sanctuary. We were robbed on our way from

Canterford. Until I complete my appointments I have no way to pay for a room at an inn. Might there be a room you could spare us?"

The man in white considered what he'd heard with a skeptical brow. "Perhaps. And who travels with you Dr. Carter?"

"My servants," Darius answered with ease. Mortimer did not react, but from the corner of her eye Verenna saw Fabien's head snap in his direction.

"This is Christopher," Darius indicated Mortimer. "And this is Samuel." Fabien looked straight ahead, though Verenna could feel the rage of being re-named and called a servant rolling off him like smoke.

"And the girl?" asked the holy man, clearly suspicious of a young woman traveling unattended with three men.

"My wife. Lilith," Darius answered. Verenna suddenly understood how Fabien felt.

"I see no ring," the old man pressed. She clasped her hands to cover the flaw and moved closer to her supposed husband. Darius issued another lie without flinching.

"The bandits took that too. A group of men came out of the trees, ambushed the cart and we barely escaped with our lives. They took almost everything in our trunks. We have nothing until I'm paid for my work."

The priest looked them all up and down, taking in each stitch of their clothing. Finally his brow unknotted and a benevolent smile parted his jowls. He raised his arms again, this time in welcome. Two more monks hurried down the steps summoned by his gesture.

"Thank the Lord your travels brought you here, my children. We have plenty of room. A place for you and your wife, as well as your men. Brothers, please see to the horse. The poor creature looks exhausted. Put him in the rose garden for the night." The monks bobbed bows like newly rung bells. The horse snorted and stomped as they took hold of its tack, untrusting of its new handlers. Only with Mortimer's encouragement did it allowed itself to be lead away.

"Your generosity is astounding. We cannot thank you enough, Father," Darius flattered.

"Father Ignatius, my child. And it's nothing. We should be ready at all times to give in the name of the Lord. Please, follow me." The Father and his assistant turned to lead them up the steps.

Darius offered Verenna an arm. "Who do you think you are?" she whispered.

"It's for appearances. Just-" he jutted his elbow out for her to take hold. She did, looking up at him with a saccharine smile as she sunk her nails into his arm.

"Whatever you say, dear."

He grimaced and locked eyes with her before giving her a yank to start her up the stairs.

The group followed the Father and the monk into a cavernous hall. At least fifty pews lined each side. Stained glass interrupted the heavy stones with their color, dimly glimmering like dark jewels in weak light. As they approached the high altar the room got brighter. The glow issued from one of the transepts. A statue of a saint spread its graceful arms above a swath of countless candles with three hooded figures lighting them.

"We pray for the safety of our flock every night these days. Bronwell is spilling its sickness out into the rest of the countryside. It's not just disease coming from that cursed place, it's desperate people. Dangerous people. We must all be vigilant."

"Truer words there never were," Darius agreed.

They were lead away from the statue into the dark transept on the opposite side of the church. To their surprise it hid a spacious flight of stairs. After that the building changed, halls resembling long, straight tunnels, a warren dotted with tiny doors.

The Father held up a hand and the party stopped. Two rooms stood open, each with two, thin beds, covered by harsh wool blankets. Identical narrow windows separated the beds, along with a table holding a single, tallow candle. The monk hurried in and lit them with his lantern.

"These rooms are yours. Rest well." Ignatius nodded his goodnight.

"Thank you. We will." Darius returned.

With that the Father and the monk faded down the hall, drifting through the dark in their pool of lamplight.

Once it was clear they were alone Verenna spun and slapped Darius on the arm. "Your wife? I am not sleeping in the same room with you."

"And I don't much like that servant bit either," Fabien glowered.

"Not the most believable," Mortimer agreed, crossing his arms and leaning on the doorframe.

"Shh! All of you. It echoes in here. And what, can you think of something better?" Darius whispered, rubbing the sting out of his arm.

"Doesn't matter. I'm not staying with you." Verenna gathered her skirts and bustled to the room farthest from him.

"Then who with? I'm supposed to be your husband. If they find you in a different room it'll open up all sorts of questions we can't afford to answer."

"You told the story. Tell another one," she retorted.

"It's non-negotiable." Darius gripped her wrist as if he'd haul her to the other chamber. Fabien flew to her side to defend her but Mortimer wedged himself between them before a fight could begin.

"This ends. Now," he snapped. "Verenna, you have to stay with Darius. Myself and Fabien will share the other room. It's the only way to keep up appearances. It's one night. I think we can all be adults about this."

"If he can," Fabien breathed.

"Stop. It's over. Good night."

Darius and Fabien locked eyes, clearly with more to say. "Good night, then." Fabien growled.

"Good night," Darius repeated, smirking at Fabien's ire.

Verenna whipped her hand out of Darius's grip and stormed into the room behind him, falling onto the bed closest to the door to pout. The fall jarred her, the bed being far less giving than she'd expected. Crossing her arms she stared at the ceiling, following the arched stone with her eyes and straining to hear the muted words exchanged in the hall.

Darius slid into the room shortly and shut the door. He tossed a small parcel onto the bed beside her.

"Here. Mortimer brought it up from the carriage."

"What is it?"

"Food. Eat."

The stress of the journey had distracted her from her ravenous hunger. She grabbed the package and perched on the edge of the bed to open it. Tearing away the brown paper and string she found a plump pasty. Its crimped edges left buttery dark spots on its wrapping. The crisp sound of the first bit released the smell of potatoes and rosemary that overpowered even the strong must of the old room. Verenna took another bite, closed her eyes, and lay back on the lumpy pillow.

"Now, those bandages. We need to change them."

Darius took a roll of gauze from his pocket, pulled up a brittle, angular chair from the corner of the room and began to unwind the roll.

"Tomorrow," Verenna groaned around another mouthful of pasty.

"Tonight."

"I'm eating."

"I'm aware," Darius's nose flared with mild disgust. In answer, Verenna met his eyes and crammed her mouth with a massive bite.

"That is grotesque."

"Then don't watch."

"I'd love to stop, but I can't until I change your bandages."

"Touch me and I'll scream," Verenna said it as if mentioning the weather.

It gave the doctor pause. His gaze flicked almost imperceptibly towards the door. Likely they were picturing the same thing; Verenna's shriek, the boom of Fabien's boot kicking open the door, and Mortimer's failed attempts to keep him from taking Darius to the ground.

"I don't have time to fight with you. In the morning. First thing." Darius broke their staring contest and shoved the chair back to the corner, tossing his jacket, vest and shoes onto it before settling huffily into bed. "First," he added, holding up a single threatening finger.

"Whatever you say," Verenna agreed, only half hearing him over the rapturous crunch of crust. She kicked off her shoes and let them clatter to the floor.

Darius cleared his throat. He'd tied his cravat around his eyes to block out the light of the candle on the table between them. "I hope that wasn't the sound of you chewing."

"I'm not that disgusting."

"Well..." He turned on his side to face away from her without finishing. Verenna pulled a face and consumed the last of the pasty. She debated whether or not to throw the crumpled brown parchment at him, but decided against it to prevent more arguing. Verenna stared at the masonry of the ceiling again trying to let the memories of the past day and a half slip from her head so sleep could take hold. She looked to Darius.

"Hey."

"Good God, what could you possibly want now," he grumbled without budging.

"How old are you? You, Fabien and Mortimer?"

"Well, that's rude."

"Oh come on. If you'd just found out immortals existed wouldn't that be your first question?"

Darius rolled over, lifting the band of silk away from his eyes, revealing a weary squint. "Will the answer make you sleep?"

"Yes," she lied, an unexplainable excitement boiling in the pit of her stomach.

"At the time of our respective incidents, Mortimer was forty-six, Fabien nineteen, and I was twenty-four."

"I meant how old are you now." Verenna lay back and folded her arms, her head finding a cradle between two lumps in the pillow. The following silence went on so long she thought he might have fallen asleep. But to her surprise an answer came. It rang around the sparse chamber and filled the air with a tremor Verenna both loved and hated.

"You meant how long have we existed. I'll be two hundred seventy-two in a few months, Fabien is around seven hundred, maybe a bit more, and Mortimer, he doesn't talk about it much. But from what he's said while drunk, we estimate he's been here over a thousand years."

"Why wouldn't you talk about it? That's incredible."

"Spoken like a mortal. Living a long life is one of the most desired things in the world, but too long and you outlive the blessing of it. Everything good is shorter lived than it should be and the rest never seems to die. It becomes a cycle. Repeated loss. Everything grows, blooms and dies, and it's beautiful but..." his words faded and he stared unseeingly down at the floor. "You have your answer. I believe sleep was your part of the deal."

"Fine. It won't be easy though." Verenna set the pasty wrapping on the bedside table and tucked herself below the blankets. "It sounded like you were just getting to the good part."

Darius replaced the band of cloth across his eyes and scoffed. "There is no good part. The best part is what you've got right now."

"Huh, very funny." No answer came. Either he'd already fallen asleep or had mastered pretending. In a few minutes the measured rise and fall of his chest told her he was unconscious. Without taking her eyes off him, she slid up to sitting in her bed.

"Pst! Hello!" With no response to her call Verenna took the book from her pocket. She ran a finger across the silver letters and peered at the seams of the door to make sure it was closed, that nothing seeped in at the hinges to search for her. She took one page at a time between her fingers to make sure they did not rattle and wake the doctor. Skipping over the rest of the Runner section with a shiver, she turned the page to the next. 'The Old Guard'.

'They are usually quite massive, ranging from the size of a man to the size of a bear or larger. They are fast, and more importantly, intelligent. They are able to plan, wait, trick and deceive, and sometimes speak human language. Some may even take on a human form, either by generating the appearance of who they were in life, or by living inside the host they feed on, controlling the husk of their body.

The Old Guard are seated deep in Hell. It takes enormous energy and effort for them to rise, usually with the help of someone on earth who, in exchange for freeing the creature, controls it for as long as it remains on this plane.

    These beings are particularly dangerous because those who keep them owe a debt to the ruler of the realm from whence their charge came. Not only do these beasts have their own appetites, requiring countless souls as prey, they are at the whim of the evil that raised them.'

Verenna checked the room again to make sure nothing from the book watched her from the corners and flipped forward until she found a page emblazoned with the words 'Detection and Defense'.

    'Signs of demonic presence are not as obvious as one might at first think. For instance, the most common indication is the uneven burning of candles. Fire reacts to demonic presence and passing. This can be useful for detection, as well as creating distractions and defending one's self, which will be discussed later in the chapter.

    Because the nature of flame is similar to that of the human soul, demons often mistake fire for prey. In the case of candles, the flame is pulled towards the creature as it drinks in the energy. This melts one side of the candle much faster than the other, leaving wax pooled on the side closest to the location of the specter.'

She tossed the book to the end of the bed and pulled herself as far away from it as possible. The candle in the study on the night she'd been chased out...The flame had raged on the wick, sending a stream of wax down one side and shocking her hand just before the creature appeared on the stairs. It had been a warning she had not known how to heed.

Verenna checked the candle beside her, smooth and steady, a single tear of wax on its side. It was enough comfort to take up the book and hide it once more in her pocket. Verenna pulled the scratchy wool blanket till it covered her head and curled up as tight as she could. A single opening allowed her to keep an eye on both the candle and the door. With luck, the flame might last until daylight.

Chapter 11

The lantern swung and rattled as Mateo jogged to keep up with Father Ignatius. As soon as the four strangers were out of sight, the priest made for his study with a haste the monk had never seen from him. They barged into the Father's chamber with Ignatius demanding the door be shut and barred even before they were through it.

"Close it. Hurry."

The monk rushed to do so. Once it was secure, he turned back to find the priest rummaging through his desk, his usual stately motions reduced to floundering. The monk went to the old man's side and tentatively opened a drawer to indicate that he'd like to help.

"No," said the priest, shoeing him away.

He stood back and watched, wondering what the man's frantic search would yield. Never had his vow of silence felt like such an inconvenience. Finally, the search produced results. Out of the desk came a leather bag. Holding it as if it were his own life Ignatius hurried to the fire.

He opened the draw string and poured a fine gray powder into the palm of his hand. The old man tossed it into the blaze. It flared up brighter, taking on a glaring white. Mateo shielded his eyes until the light calmed.

Utterly baffled he looked to Ignatius. The tension had gone from the old man's shoulders and he'd stopped shaking. He looked oddly at peace. He turned to his assistant and spoke, his voice placid.

"Now we wait, my boy. They're on their way, I suspect."

The monk shook his head violently, waving his hands as if he could refuse what the old man talked about. A few weeks prior, a group of men had stopped by to see the Father. They were rough men, unclean and uncouth. A band of hunters, except for one; their well-spoken leader in the wide brimmed hat. He'd demanded to see the priest alone in his quarters. But once Mateo had led them there, the Father had banished him to the hall. Unusual, as he was the man's near constant attendant.

From what he'd gathered listening at the door they were on no ordinary hunt. The leader of the group asked if the Father would notify him if a certain red headed girl came to them, possibly in the company of a doctor. If they attempted to take refuge in the cathedral, the priest was to send for him at once.

Mateo had been offended that Ignatius had even considered a proposition that included turning over those who came to the church for sanctuary. He'd pressed himself against the door to learn more but the voices inside had dropped too low. The men looked displeased when they left. He had assumed that Ignatius had turned down whatever they'd offered and sent them away. That must not have been the case.

The priest ignored Mateo's gesturing and ordered, "Open that window will you, my boy?"

The reluctant monk did as instructed. He pulled aside the drapes, undid the latch, and was bowled over by the shutters as they flew open with a whipping gust of wind. He turned over to find something materializing out of the fire.

Ink-like darkness bloomed into the air, swirling like petals dropped onto water, accompanied by the most unholy sound of breathing. It began as a feeble wheezing noise that grew by the second. Soon the rasping became powerful like the sound of pumping bellows. The darkness expanded in size with the sound, tugging at the fire, drinking it into a gasping absence of a mouth. Mateo watched in horror from the floor as the ink rose into the shape of a man made of gathered smoke. It was the man from before, he was sure of it, though the shadow's only features were two eyes like glimmering coals, and the long dark line of his hat.

Ignatius had taken shelter behind his armchair, clutching his cross and muttering psalms. A deep grating chuckle rang around the room followed but the familiar, well-spoken voice.

"Come out, Ignatius. I can see you there."

Pale as his robes the priest slid out from behind the chair. "Lord Gawshire, I...I summoned you as soon as I could. They arrived not even an hour ago to stay the night. They're here now. The girl with red hair and the doctor. I, I did the best I..." the priest trailed off with a bowed head. His hands shook violently around his crucifix.

"You've done well. There is no need for fear," the form comforted.

Mateo shook his head to try and rid himself of what had to be a hallucination. The scene did not fade.

"Then, am I safe? The reward," Ignatius ventured.

"Oh, I remember what I promised you; safety in the coming times, immunity from the ride of the horsemen, kingship in the new world that's upon us." The form took in a deep breath. The fire reached towards him from the hearth as he did, dying back as he let out a sigh. "Feed the fire," he demanded. "It's getting cold, don't you think?"

Ignatius crept with trembling bones to the corner of his desk where he'd left the powder and poured another handful into his palm and threw it into the flames. The fire went white once more and clamored higher.

"More," the apparition ordered.

Ignatius threw in another palm full.

"More."

At the shadow's command Ignatius shuffled closer and emptied the entire bag above the blaze. The fire swelled until an explosion of light forced the priest to stumble back and shield his eyes.

The flames roared up the flue as if pulled by an unseen force. A growl issued from the chimney, followed by the scraping of claw against brick. Something large stirred in the hidden space. It moved closer until it's grunting breaths splashed ashes and embers off of the burning wood and onto the rug.

A nightmare emerged from the fire, taking on a solid form as it clambered forth. The smoke knitted together to create it. As it condensed Mateo could see the creature's teeth, long talon-like strikes of bone. It seemed to be baring them but soon he realized that it had no lips to cover them at all.

With another rumble of exertion the beast reached forward two appendages and took hold of the rug near the hearth. The fabric crumpled in its grip as the beast dragged its massive body into the room.

Mateo could see through most of its fog gray bulk, easily seven feet long and five feet at its shoulder. No feet could be seen touching the ground, yet heavy footsteps like the fall of gigantic paws could be heard every time the creature drifted forward. It circled the room, its bending sides shining silver as it turned, coming to the fire to open its maw and drink. The flames poured into its throat feeding the smoke of its body until it took shape. Naked sinew wrapped it like wire, its form resembling a gargantuan, skinless lion. Its muscular ribs expanded and contracted both building and devouring the fire with its thunderous breathes as it drank.

"Fumus," the dark figure of a man called out. The beast responded instantly. Its head snapped away from the fire as it rushed towards him. It stopped just inches away. He instructed it in Latin. "Habeo mandatum tibi." As soon as he uttered the words the creature sank and lay at his feet.

Mateo wished he didn't understand, but after years of copying texts he knew exactly what the man said.

"Find the girl in this house, The Bright One. Find her and take her light, and the light of any who get in the way. Do it quickly before there is the chance to escape. Understand?"

The beast writhed with perverse excitement, undulating like a snake, and to Mateo's eternal shock, it spoke. Struggling, it croaked a single mortifying word.

"Man..du...corrrr,"

"Yes, Fumus. Manducor," Gawshire repeated the word lovingly, as if to a child. The creature let out an exhilarated shriek like the cry of ten men in the throes of agony. Mateo covered his ears and curled into a ball, contracting from the sheer ruthlessness of the sound, sickness rising in his throat to think what was about to happen to the people who'd come to stay. The word *manducor* meant eat.

The shadow man held up his hand. The beast froze and watched him intently as he went to Father Ignatius. The old man could barely stand. His grip on the armchair was the only thing keeping him from the ground.

"Now, as to your reward," Gawshire began.

"Yes," Ignatius whispered, breathless with relief. "Yes, my liege."

"You've done well. Especially for a holy man with no experience dealing with demons," the man chuckled darkly and drew close to the priest's face. "However, there is one thing you should have assumed about us. We like to lie."

He seized the old man by the throat, his fingers gathering the man's paper skin, and threw him to the ground. The beast leaped upon him, inciting a myriad of screams, prayers, shrieks, gurgles and eventual silence. Mateo lay trembling on the floor. The smoke of the beast's body had shielded his eyes from the attack itself, but when it rose, glutted, the shriveled form of the Father lay motionless. His eyes and mouth, open in shock and pain, were dripping black, tar-like liquid. It oozed down his face and pooled around his head like a dark halo. His white robes rumpled around him like well tread snow.

Rooted to the spot in terror, Mateo prayed that he'd been forgotten. Shutting his eyes, he lay absolutely still in hopes the man would think him already dead.

The ghostly footsteps echoed through the chamber drawing closer to the monk's huddled form. They ceased. He could feel the man's presence hovering over him and stopped his breathing.

A hand wrapped around his neck and dragged him to his feet. Mateo choked for air. He pried at the grip that held him but it would not release. Biting cold hooked into his throat as the hand around it constricted. The smoke man lifted him so he could hardly touch the floor. The monk could feel his weight leave his feet. He dangled helplessly in the demonic grip, toes straining for the ground.

"Brother, perhaps you'd be kind enough to tell us where your guests are sleeping. In light of what you've seen, I don't think I need to explain the alternative." The man indicated with a graceful wave the place where the priest lay bleeding. The beast lingered beside the body. Mateo could not tell if it had eyes, but he could feel its hungry gaze. The vice around his neck loosened ever so slightly. It was just enough for a gasp of air. Formulating a lie, the monk pointed skywards.

"Up? How far?"

The monk held up five fingers.

"Five? That must be the bell tower. They're sleeping there?"

Mateo nodded furiously against his captor's hand.

"Such a hiding place. I wouldn't have guessed. Good work, Brother. I believe a reward is in order."

The monk tried to struggle free, fearing he'd share the same fate as the Father. Gawshire laughed at his panic.

"No, no, not like that. I will grant you safety." Then the man leaned in and breathed, "Pity the only safe ones are dead."

Gawshire let the monk fall and the beast rushed into him. Mist rolled inside his eyes. It was as if his entire body had been filled with freezing water, simultaneously icing his veins and suffocating him. He flailed to free himself of the feeling he was sure would be his end. Then the pain set in. Somewhere inside his chest the creature took a bite. His guts seized and he let out a ragged scream. He writhed onto his side. The same tar-like substance that dripped across Ignatius's deceased face spattered the ground before him. The world closed in. Darkness bled towards the center of Mateo's vision and was about to overcome him when the attack ended. He lay exhausted and barely breathing.

The shadow man made his way to the door, lifting the bar that locked it and tossing it aside. He pointed out into the hall repeating his order to the beast.

"Manducor."

The creature sprinted out into the darkness, it's heavy breaths growing faint as it headed for the bell tower. Gawshire chuckled and went to the open window. He dissolved, vanishing like ink on black cloth into the background of the night.

As soon as the room stood empty the monk propped himself up one arm, then two, then pulled himself to his feet with the edge of a table. Wiping the back of his hand across his mouth he found a trail of clotted maroon from fingertips to wrist. He was as good as dead, but that did not mean the travelers had to be. Stumbling out into the hall he started for their rooms as fast as his weakening legs would carry him.

Chapter 12

Verenna awoke to Darius's nudging and shushing her.

"What's going-"

"You're snoring."

"I do not snore."

"Hush. Listen." He crept to the door and put his ear to the crack.

She took the blanket over her head and groaned. Listening expired with the sun.

"Quiet. There's something out there. Stumbling. I can hear the steps." As he whispered the old wood scent of the room drifted back to her. The mustiness, the scratch of the blanket against her cheek, the lump of the book in her pocket against her leg, summoned the memory of where she had fallen asleep. Tearing the blankets off she threw her legs over the edge of the bed and stood ready to run regardless of the lack of exits.

Fumbling, awkward steps, approaching fast, then stopping, then starting again out of the silence.

"Stay back," Darius mouthed, and gripped the door handle, to hold it shut or throw it open, she couldn't be sure.

Something thudded against the timbers outside. The door shuddered with its weight. The mass slid down, sinking to the floor. Verenna pressed herself against the back wall. The stone chilled the nervous perspiration on her hands and back.

A cough sounded from the hall. A sick, gurgling, complaint. Darius wrinkled his brow at her as if to ask if she'd heard the same. He was going to open the door. Verenna couldn't find the air to say no. She shook her head until she was dizzy but the click of the latch came regardless. As soon as it opened a hooded figure fell through at the doctor's feet. Verenna clapped a hand over her own mouth to stop her shriek.

"Please. Please," a weak voice rasped. Darius knelt and turned the form on its back, revealing the pale, bloodied face of the monk that had accompanied Father Ignatius. Even in the dim Verenna could see a collar of fresh red bruises forming at his neck and dark spatterings at the corners of his mouth. She let the wall guide her to the ground as her knees protested the iron smell of blood that came when the monk coughed.

"What happened? What's going on?" Darius urged him.

"Ignatius," the monk wheezed, voice feeble from disuse. "He sent for the hunters. They're here. They brought a creature. Fumus. It killed him. Ate him. That's all it said. All it said was eat." He curled weeping into Darius's chest. The doctor lifted the monk to the bed as running stripes of tears streaked down his face.

"I told them you were in the tower. They'll know I lied when they reach it. Go."

Darius barked an order as he began to tend to the man. "Wake Fabien and Mortimer. Tell them to get out and get the carriage."

The urgency in his tone made her snatch her shoes into her pockets and scurry for the door on all fours, fighting to her feet against the wishes of her queasy stomach and tilting vision. She burst into the next room, half falling on top of Fabien and shaking him. "Wake up. Wake up. Please wake up."

A groggy smile stretched across his face. "Well, isn't this a nice surprise." His arms went to encircle her but a quick slap shattered his dreaming.

"Listen to me. We've been found."

"What is it?" Mortimer struggled out of his blankets.

"The hunters are here. Looking for us. They brought some

creature with them to eat us."

"Fumus," Fabien's voice quavered as he said the name.

"Gawshire's here. We've got to get the carriage," Mortimer blurted.

Fabien sprang from the bed, nearly throwing Verenna to the floor as he did. The two men rushed their shoes onto their feet, Mortimer taking up his coat and Fabien thrashing back into his shirt. The group poured into the next room as Darius spouted more orders. "You two. Run ahead and get to the carriage. And if you see that thing wandering the halls, distract it. Verenna and I will follow you."

"We need to get her out of here now," Fabien's insisted.

"I know that! Don't you think I know?!" Darius snapped back.

Mortimer held up his hands. "There's no time for this. We'll go ahead. We can't risk charging into a trap with the girl. If we run into anything we'll take care of it."

"Sure was a good idea leaving my sword in the carriage, wouldn't you say?" Fabien bit.

"It's no use against these kinds of enemies, boy. Start running." Mortimer shoved the young man towards the door but Fabien caught himself on the frame. "We'll be waiting for you," he nodded to Verenna before glaring at the doctor. "And you. Get her out alright. No matter what. Hear me?"

"Just go!" With one last shove Mortimer managed to launch Fabien into the hall. Verenna leaned out only to find they'd already vanished into the depths of the corridor.

"Come," she heard Darius say, turning to find him trying to lift the monk from the bed.

"No. I'm through. Breaking the vow will be worth it if you survive. Please, go. I'm happy here. Right here."

Verenna felt him go, like the moment the sun leaves the skin and dips over the edge of the world. An absence hung around them, a hole torn in a spider web. She wanted to sew it closed. Her fingers wrung the pattern as a few dry sobs trembled through her. Darius crossed the man's arms over his chest, reaching feather light fingers to close his eyes.

He jerked his hand away, stumbling from the bed to shield Verenna as black fluid bubbled forth from the man's lips, from his eyes, overwhelming them and dripping into his hair. A white lace of frost enveloped his hands and throat as the slow rolling fountain leaked from his jaws.

"Get out!" Darius screamed, seizing her hand and fleeing.

The pounding of her bare feet on stone ached up her legs. Her lungs burned, her breathing went ragged. No amount of air was enough.

They reached the last, short hall. In the center of it, the stairs. Darius extended an arm to hold her back as he checked around the last corner. Verenna put her hands on her knees, her ribs stretching to their limit for her desperate lungs. The dull throb in her side begged for attention against her best efforts to ignore it.

"Hurry," he dropped his arm and ushered her forward only to tackle her into the shadows again. "It's there."

"What?"

Darius put a finger across his lips. He checked the passage ahead once more. He mouthed a silent swear. Pressing her into the darkest recess of the wall he came so close their foreheads nearly touched and whispered a command. "Stay until I say run. Then get out. Don't stop."

She nodded. Then to her surprise he darted around the corner. Verenna crouched down and peaked after him. He slunk along the wall, skirting something she could not see. She leaned farther.

A dark mass loitered between her and the stairs. At first she thought it might be smoke. Then it moved. Resounding footfall and a huffing breath, a creature somewhere between the size of a bear and a horse, it's bulk made entirely of deep gray mist that shone silver as it moved. Its head, or what could be its head, bobbed and swooped as if it could sense Darius but not see him.

The creature grunted like a foraging pig then paused. A deep grating growl issued from it and it pivoted towards her hiding place. Verenna ducked back. The beast stocked closer. It's heavy steps stopping so close by that she could feel the gusts of its breath spilling around the corner.

Instants before the creature discovered her Darius's shouts rang down the hall.

"Over here, you damned animal! Here!" The beast whirled to the sound and charged. Darius dove to one side to dodge its headlong pounce. "Run!" he screamed and rolled aside as the shadow reared and came down to crush him. Awestruck by what she saw it took a moment for the word to travel from her mind to her limbs.

"Go, you idiot! Run!" he shrieked again. It shocked her legs into action. She made a break for the stairs under the cover of Darius's calls to the creature.

She'd taken less than a quarter of the steps when an unearthly noise rose behind her. A chorus of anguish and hate woven together into a roar. Verenna looked back. The darkness of the creature's body tumbled after her like the waters of a flood. She pushed her failing legs to move faster but her speed was already at its peak. She'd never make the door. It would catch her before the end of the stairs. The beast had fixed her in its sights and would extinguish her.

Inspiration struck. She didn't need to get to the door, just to the transept. If what the book said was true, she would blend into the hundreds of candles and vanish from the monster's sight. Verenna jumped over the last bit of banister to skip the remaining steps. She could hear the clatter and fall of the creature's feet as it made a failed grab for her. Sprinting past the altar she wove her way between the forest of candlesticks and candelabras to the foot of the statue and crouched amongst the flickering lights.

The beast rushed to the edge of the candles. It grunted and growled, darting to one side, then the other, swaying in frustrated confusion. It stormed out into the main hall to search. Thrashing and screeching it overturned pews, it's claws leaving finger width streaks down the boards as it threw them about the room like sticks.

Having vented some of its rage it returned to the field of candles. Verenna held her breath as the beast paced before her, seeming to calculate its next move. The flames burned sideways, following the creature's movements, pointing to it like a thousand glowing compass needles.

Then the beast opened its mouth. It's teeth a jagged edge of silver on both sides of a yawning expanse of darkness. It inhaled and gathered the candle flames towards the infinity inside its jaws. Verenna felt the pull as well, not just in the fluttering of her skirts, but inside her chest; the feeling that something in her center would be ripped from her body.

The mouth closed and the wind stopped. A few wicks at the front smoldered and died, others were left small and struggling. The beast yawned again, sucking in more light, drinking and drinking until over half the candles were gone. The thin trails of smoke rose to build the opacity of the beast's form.

Verenna's hands clutched at the stone behind her as if she might tear open an escape. But there was no outlet. She'd backed herself into a corner of stone and stained glass with no way out. Through the smoke of the creature's body she could see Darius creeping down the stairs. He slunk through the main hall, low and quiet. In the time it took, all but the candles within arm's reach of her had gone out. The hall darkened incrementally with the death of each tiny light.

Her short gasping breaths burned from the smoke of the failed candles. The beast stepped forward and drank again. She turned her head, refusing to look into the nothingness of its maw before it took her. The last candle went out.

She felt warmth. Darius had slunk in and wedged himself between the monster's open mouth and Verenna's huddled form. The beast shut its jaws with a snap. It circled the statue hunting for where it's prey had gone, as if Darius had somehow rendered her invisible to it.

Enraged once more the beast barreled off into the nebulous dark of the main hall to bellow its fury. Before she had time to overcome the shock of it all Darius slung one of the candelabras through the stained glass behind them and heaved her up. They plummeted through the opening together. Darius shifted himself beneath Verenna as they fell through the bushes, hitting the glass littered ground in her stead. He groaned and swore. The girl scrambled to her feet, grabbing Darius's arm to haul him onto his.

Across the lawn they could see the carriage, and next to it a festering brawl. Mortimer and Fabien had been beset by the waiting hunters. The fight was two to one.

Fabien's broadsword flashed, a deadly silver arch, catching the moonlight as it traced through the air. He hollered out insults and laughed in his element. Mortimer strained to keep up. He had an arm locked around one man's neck, choking and dragging him around as a shield against the knife of the woman with the crow's nest hair.

The horse reared and kicked, eyes wild in its tossing head, trying to fight off a man attempting to unhook it from the cart. Darius made a grab to hold Verenna back from the fray but his hand closed on empty air. She'd already taken off running.

Verenna dashed towards the man near the horse. At full tilt she landed a foot on the man's lower back, sending him to the ground with a lurch. But all sense of victory died as he rose for revenge. The girl inched away as he came to tower over her at his full height. The lanterns hung on the carriage lit one side of his face, round and red, with black gaps in his vicious smile. He lunged. Verenna jumped back but he'd caught the hem of her skirts bringing them both to the ground. The man took fistful after fistful of her dress, climbing towards her along the dirt. She aimed kicks at his chin but couldn't land a single one. A creaking laugh rose out of him, each higher grasp on her dress giving rise to a new bought of cackling.

Verenna made a desperate slash at his eyes. Her nails missed but dug deep into the side of his face. Roaring, he rose out of her reach to tower over her, made of clawing hands and hot breath and the hungry emptiness of his missing teeth.

A thick, thudding sound, and her attacker collapsed beside her, limp and lifeless. The rearing horse caught him with a hoof to the back of his skull.

Her stomach and throat burned with bile and disgust as she struggled upwards. Shaking, Verenna dodged behind the cart, hoping the other hunters hadn't noticed her. She'd never win a fight against any of them one on one. And they'd have to end things fast if they were to make an escape. That thing, Fumus, would find its way out to them any moment. It had better be over by then.

Then again, that might be the solution. In a surge of panic and ingenuity she climbed up onto the carriage and took one of the lanterns. Scrambling down she snuck along the edge of the fray to the bushes against the building, hiding the lamp from view with her skirts.

Once below the broken window she dashed the lantern to the ground. The tiny flames leapt onto the oil spattered leaves. A quick glance behind told her she hadn't been noticed. She ripped out handfuls of grass and weeds to feed the blaze. It had to be higher. She flapped her skirts to fan the fire. A check over her shoulder assured her she hadn't caught the attention of the brawling mob.

The spiked edges of the broken glass glimmered like wet teeth as the flames reached the sill. A wailing cry burst through the opening closely followed by the boiling blackness of the beast's body. Verenna dove and rolled under what few bushes had not yet caught fire.

The beast tore at the flames as if they were flesh, clawing and snapping to bring more and more of the light into its voracious mouth. Verenna could not see the creature's talons. She could only hear them scrape against the stone of the building, seeking prey. It howled, empty handed. Enraged by the trick, it turned to the men fighting on the lawn, barreling towards them to vent its fury.

Hunters scattered in all directions as her three companions hurled themselves out of the way. With Fumus and the attackers distracted Mortimer scrambled to the top of the carriage and took the reins. Fabien gave some chase to the fleeing men, sword brandished, roaring at the top of his lungs for the cowards to come back and finish what they'd started. Darius screamed her name over the mayhem as he struggled off the ground near the cart. Rolling out of her hiding place she stumbled into a run for the cover of the coach. The distant shrieks of one of the men echoed pitifully in her ears against the cacophonous screeching of the creature consuming him.

Darius flung open the carriage door and Verenna barreled inside. He'd hardly clambered in himself when Mortimer spurred the horse into motion.

"Fabien, you bastard, get on the cart!" Mortimer called as they lurched forward.

Verenna hung out the window. She searched the darkness for him but there was no sign. They were gaining speed. Something heavy landed on the back of the carriage setting it rocking. Panic flooded her at the thought of Fumus clinging to the luggage rack.

Thankfully, Fabien's voice called from out of sight, "I'm on! Go, go, go!"

Mortimer snapped the reins and the horse took off at full tilt. Verenna felt herself yanked into the carriage, landing hard on the ill padded seats.

"Good God! Get away from that window! There's either nothing to see or things you wouldn't want to," Darius ordered.

The girl hugged her knees and squeezed her eyes shut. The bouncing of the cabin combined with the flashes of street lamps sickened her. Both she and the doctor recovered their breath in silence.

"Good thinking." Verenna opened her eyes, the bursts of light through the window revealing that for once Darius wasn't mocking her. "Using the lantern fire to call Fumus. How did you know to do that?"

"Well, when we were in the hall it seemed like it couldn't see you. I just thought if it couldn't see you, but it could see me, it must be because you're not mortal. So it would chase the hunters off and leave all of you alone."

"Huh...And hiding in the candles? Where did that inspiration come from?"

"I just sort of did it. I mean, if Fumus sees me as fire, I should hide where there's fire."

"Mmhmm. And where did you learn all of this? Because I know we haven't told you."

"I heard it somewhere once."

"Where?"

"I don't know. Around."

Even in the dark Verenna could read the disbelief in his squinted eyes and crooked mouth. "I may have taken something from your study. A book."

"Which?"

Verenna grumbled and removed the shoes she'd stashed in her pocket, finding the little handbook beneath them. She tossed it onto the seat beside him and leaned back to sulk.

"Ah," Darius took up the book. "The Practical Handbook. Definitely one of the most straightforward. You chose well." He extended the book as if she should take it. Her hand rose but didn't reach.

"So," Verenna eased. "You're letting me have it?"

"Might as well. It saves me explaining things and it seems you've already put it to good use. I'm not pleased with the stealing, mind you, but at least you have decent taste. Take it. Go on."

Unconvinced that the offer was genuine, she set the book at her side instead of her pocket. "Thanks," she muttered in confusion at his sudden generosity. Darius simply nodded and leaned back to gaze at the darkness beyond the drapes.

Quiet fell between them, disturbed only but the sound of rocks and earth passing under the spinning wheels. Time meant nothing as they flew down the road. There was nothing to puncture the pitch of the night, or mark the difference of a minute from an hour. Eventually Fabien's voice rang out from the back of the carriage.

"Woah now!"

Mortimer echoed the call from his position up top. The horse slowed and turned off the road. The eerie scrape of leaves and branches along the sides of the cab had Verenna imagining the claws of a monster dragging them into the trees.

The carriage came to a stop and ended the noise. She heard Fabien and Mortimer hop down from their perches. Fabien swooped the drapes aside and peered in, his face fretful and tawny in the orange of the single remaining lantern.

"Stay in here till we have a fire. It'll just be a tick, Miss."

Darius slid out of the cab leaving the door open as he went to rummage about in the luggage. Mortimer saw to gathering the wood Fabien felled as he made a clearing with his sword. The shifting muscle beneath the young man's shirt, the effortlessness of each swing, had the girl mesmerized. She could never have imagined a blade over half her height wielded so gracefully, such a precise instrument in his hands even in his obvious ill temper. Each staccato clip through a branch marked his frustration.

Having felt her watching, he turned over his shoulder. She hardly looked away in time. Out of the corner of her eye she saw him half smile and carry on about his chore with considerably more flourishes.

The green smell of night and trees whisked past her cheeks on a soft, humid breeze. It rattled the leaves and guided her gaze to the murky gaps in the undergrowth. But Mortimer started the fire before she could sink to far into wondering about them.

He motioned her towards the cheerful blaze by patting the ground beside him. She slid on her shoes and joined him.

The others gathered too, though no one spoke. Fabien plopped down against a tree and produced a cloth from his pocket to clean his blade. Darius returned from the cart with his medical bag and began fiddling with its contents.

"Who's hurt?" Verenna inquired. Other than scrapes and possibly a few bruised ribs from the fight everyone seemed remarkably intact.

"Me if you must know," Darius grumbled, bringing forth a tarnished hand mirror, a polished silver case, and a pair of tweezers. He took a seat on an old stump at the edge of their clearing and eased off his jacket. He grimaced, letting out a low growl as he peeled himself out of it.

"What is it?" Verenna asked.

The doctor tossed the garment towards her in answer. "Remember?"

She held it up. Thin slices in the fabric dotted the back, outlined in deep red.

"The glass!" In the chaos she'd forgotten about their tumble out the window.

"My favorite coat, I might add."

"What happened there?" Fabien pointed.

Darius answered him as he balanced the mirror in the twigs behind the stump. "Had a bit of a run in with a stained glass window." He removed his shirt and angled the silver case so he could see his own back in the mirror.

"Fumus cornered her, we broke the window to escape, and I landed first."

"Sorry..." Verenna grumbled.

"I'm glad to hear you say that because I definitely blame you." Darius made an attempt to free one of the shards in his shoulder with the tweezers. It slipped from the forceps with a clink, making him hiss the pain through his teeth. Fabien shook his head and scoffed.

"Ah, quit cryin'."

"Who's crying?" Darius smarted back.

"Haven't we had enough of a fight tonight?" Mortimer interrupted. The two younger men went quiet and the night resumed its calm. "Need some help with that?" he offered.

"Not from you. You have table legs for fingers."

"Let me at it, then," Fabien argued. "If you're not scared it'll hurt too much."

"It's not that I'm scared, it's that I'm not stupid. Your whole profession revolved around hacking things to bits. I'll manage myself."

Another attempt and another failure made Darius grit his teeth. Verenna winced with him. "Let me," she blurted, unable to stomach his trial and error.

The doctor gave her a wry look. "And your qualifications are?"

"Needle point. It's delicate work. I did quite a lot of it at home."

"Somehow I can't imagine that."

"Neither can I at the moment," she shrugged. "I sort of owe you after all."

Darius narrowed his eyes, his lips going thin, and scanned her up and down. "Fine," he uttered under his breath and handed her the tweezers.

Verenna took them and made her way to the other side of the stump to take in the damage. The colored shards glistened like gems protruding from his skin. Dried traces of running blood splotched the pale of his back. She had to look away to keep the vomitus feeling from rising too high in her throat. With a deep breath she went to work, taking hold of a large emerald fragment and tugging. Flesh slid away from it as she drew it out. His shoulder twitched but he made no sound. It was safe to continue.

Sliver by sliver the glittering fractions of window came forth and were tossed in the fire until the last sickle of glass slid from Darius's shoulder. Other than the few muttered profanities he hadn't made a peep. Proud she hadn't given in to nausea she sat back to admire her work.

Half of the cuts had vanished. She watched in awe as one of the smallest closed itself, becoming no more than a thread-like line. "How- how are you doing that?" Another injury slid shut. Her eyes ached from how wide they stretched in shock at this miracle.

Darius stood and retrieved his shirt from where it hung in the bushes. "One of the few benefits of being what we are. We heal quickly. The downside, the pain's no different."

"You can get as hurt as you want. But you'll always live. And that's not always as great as it sounds." Mortimer added staring into the fire.

"Either way you get better so there's no use whining, is there?" Fabien sheathed his blade with a snap.

"Speaking of which, may I ask what's bothering you?" Darius questioned as he finished the last buttons of his shirt.

"Bugger off."

"What? Still not a fair enough fight for you, two on one?" the doctor persisted.

"That's not what it's about and you know it," Fabien looked down, his hair falling to cover a face taut with rage. The darting line of his jaw grew harsher as he held back his temper.

"Poor thing. Must be a waking nightmare winning every fight you enter."

Fabien could no longer resist. He rose to his full height, hand on hilt. "What would you know about it? A warrior's worth…"

"*A warrior's worth is in the risk of losing.* This might actually be the hundred thousandth time you've said it."

"I should-"

"You should sit down the both of you," Mortimer said, putting himself between them. "There's no sense in tearing each other apart. Just, sit."

Neither of the young men so much as blinked. The blade peaked out of Fabien's sheath, winking silver in the firelight. Darius smirked and shrugged. "I've got better things to do anyway."

With a final taunting glance at Fabien, the doctor stepped off to rummage through the trunks once more. Fabien sank back to his place on the ground, picking a leaf and shredding it one slow pinch at a time.

It didn't take Darius long to retrieve the map. He lay it out across the stump he'd been seated on and studied it intently in the glow of the fire. He pursed his lips and grabbed his chin to think.

"Don't tell me we're lost," Verenna begged.

"Not at all. Just recording the death toll of the fever. I'd guess twenty or thirty in the monastery. I believe that's the number of monks there.

"How do you know they're dead? We didn't really have time to stop and count."

"It's an estimation. But given how fast Cold Fever can spread, and with people living in such close contact, there will be next to no one alive in that church by morning. Especially with Fumus running around.

"So things like Fumus are the cause of the fever?

"By all indications, yes. I believe the disease occurs when a demon infiltrates the mortal soul and consumes it. You saw an example in that monk tonight. Such a rapid progression is unusual, of course. It usually takes a few days to reach the final stages. My guess, it was the work of Fumus himself. A demon that strong might be able to consume someone in seconds."

"And Fumus is a Hellhound?" Verenna tried hard to keep her words from quavering with the tremor in her spine.

"Yes and no," Darius's answer came with a note of hesitation. "It's far more powerful than Hellhounds. A creature like that would even be able to drag an immortal to Hell for a time. Something average hounds would need a whole pack to accomplish. But it's usually brought out of Hell and controlled by a Houndsman in the same way. To create a door for something like that to rise…" Darius paused and shook his head. "Someone must have sold their soul, not to mention the souls of countless sacrifices. They'll have to keep those souls coming too if they want to pay off their debt to the underworld. A beast as big as Fumus has to be fed scores of mortals to stay on this plane."

"How? That's so many?" Verenna whispered.

"A Houndsman's whole profession depends on trading the lives of other creatures in exchange for dark powers and the right to control Hellhounds. If they aren't efficient at what they do, they risk being dragged to hell themselves. They will do whatever it takes to keep their charges fed."

"That's Gawshire, isn't it?" Verenna breathed, clutching her knees to her chest.

Mortimer let out a slight chuckle that cocked one side of his mouth higher than the other. "You don't miss much do you? It's Gawshire, alright. But I wouldn't worry about him tonight, Miss. He'll keep the beast at the church to wait for the congregation in the morning."

"To eat them? We have to warn them!" Verenna stood as if she meant to march back to the church on foot.

"We did. As best we could. The town will have heard the row we kicked up. And they'll see the signs of a fight in the morning. Hopefully they'll stay clear." Fabien grumbled, shredding the remainder of the leaf he held.

"That's not good enough! That won't save them," Verenna shrilled.

Darius halted her outburst. "Neither will going back to suffer the same fate. I'd get some rest."

"Ha. How?" Every time she blinked she was afraid she'd be faced with the dying monk, or the image of Fumus flooding down the stairs after her, or the creatures gaping jaws as it drank the light from around her.

"Try. The carriage is yours for the night."

"We'll be up standing guard, Miss. Don't you worry,"

Mortimer offered, though even he seemed unconvinced that it would be any comfort.

"Fine. Be heartless," she rose in a huff. "These shoes hurt anyhow."

Verenna made herself as comfortable as the cab would allow. The firelight from the window filled her eyes with a weary burn, but she could not bring herself to close the drapes. The woods seemed to come alive as she waited for sleep. Every tick of falling leaf became the snap of a twig underfoot, every rustle of the breeze the breath of the beast. Each crack of sap bursting in the fire sent a cold gasp rushing into her lungs.

"It's a bad time for this." Mortimer's voice rose soft above the sounds of night. She almost mistook it for the groan of a bough in the wind. "We're heading right into the dark moon."

"I tried to take care of it beforehand. I knew things weren't going to stay easy," Fabien joined. "I can't speak for this one over here though."

Verenna held her breath to listen, her own heartbeat almost enough to cover their whisperings.

"I'll be fine." Darius' temper sizzled in his words.

"Will you? Self-control can only keep madness away so long. You'll have to hunt," Mortimer was cut short by another hiss.

"And you're one to give advice? Just because we allow you into the abbey does not mean you understand us. I will be fine."

"Say it all you want, but I saw you the last time you let a few dark moons go by without hunting. Near went on a killing spree when someone got a nosebleed," Fabien challenged.

Verenna eased herself up to the window and hid just behind the curtain. Their voices came through clearer. She dared the slightest peek beyond the drape. Darius still hunched over the map. Fabien stood on the opposite side of the fire making slow, arching practice swings with his sword.

From his cross-legged position on the ground, Mortimer held the strained peace between them. "You'll need to feed too, Fabien. You can't pretend the most recent time was enough," he soothed.

"Yeah, but I'll go hunt if I have to. He'd rather sit and starve himself crazy because *'he's not an animal'*."

"I'm not," Darius spat as he shot to standing.

"We all are," Fabien growled. "The sooner you recognize that, the safer Verenna will be. I need blood. You need blood. And the closest is hers. We can't afford to go hungry if we mean to protect her."

Darius looked ready to lunge. Fabien braced for impact, but Mortimer held up his hands. "Shh! I'd rather the lady be asleep for this conversation, wouldn't you?"

"I'll hunt when I have to. Not now. Not yet," Darius grumbled and settled back to the map.

"Yeah. Just make sure you're not too late."

Their aggression died out against the sounds of the breeze stoking the fire. The night drew in close, lapping like tidewater at the edges of the light. All three men had turned stone sullen, each mulling their own thoughts.

It had been easy to forget in their days together that they were anything other than human. Verenna lay back down and crossed her arms over her face, the coursing of her pulse so loud she wondered if they could hear it. A parade of awful possibilities marched through her mind, one scenario after another. If something were to happen to her out here, if they turned on her, there would be nothing she could do. No one would ever know except the three men and whatever pairs of unholy eyes might be watching them from the trees.

Her parents would receive the note the maid promised to deliver. Might receive the note. But even if she had a pen and paper before her then, she had no way to describe her situation in a way that they could fathom. And tomorrow? If she lasted the night, how much stranger would things become before she saw home? If she ever did.

Before sleep conquered her, a familiar sound echoed through the cacophony of her thoughts. A sing song warning in her mother's voice.

"Be careful, dear. Be careful."

Chapter 13

The night was empty of rest. The death of the monk, the idea of pursuing hunters, and thought of her traveling companion's growing hunger kept her up most of the dark hours. Each time she dared to closed her eyes the pitch would become Fumus' yawning maw open to consume her. She'd startle and sit up ready to fight until the pale orange of the campfire gave her the courage to lay back down. Eventually it went out.

Darkness wrapped her, snug against the shape of her so she dare not move to wake it. She breathed softly to keep from taking it in. The night clung tighter, laboring her breath. She forced the rise and fall of her chest against the pitch, unsure if her eyes were open or shut in the ink of night, unsure if she slept.

Something pressed down on her. A weight atop her ribs. Verenna struggled for air beneath it but found herself locked in place by its bulk, her body unresponsive. Not even her rising panic could force her lungs to expand.

"I see you, you know," a mocking voice spoke mere inches from her ear as two hazy white orbs opened before her. The darkness atop her cracked a wire thin smile like a frozen strike of lighting.

Verenna's mind screamed for her arms to move, to push the hovering face away, but they would not obey her. The entity spoke again.

"Your flame draws closer every day. Closer to my new city. Come. You are welcome."

By the slight glow of its eyes Verenna could see it raise a hand, a spindle like a dead tree branch. She watched, helpless, as its jutting fingers grew into perverse mutations, weaving themselves into her hair.

"Silly little mouse to come to my stronghold. All the same, I would love to meet the one who thinks they will wash Bronwell clean of me." The being chuckled. "We are many, little mouse. And you are one."

The creature's mouth cracked wider to allow its frenzied laughter. "By all means, come see for yourself. I look forward to the reward of dragging you under myself."

Verenna's vision flickered as she struggled to stay conscious against the constriction. The creature's fingers bound her neck like vines, squeezing until she was sure her throat would be crushed in their stranglehold. "Come and fight. Come and lose," the creature hissed. Something like a snake's tongue flickered against her neck.

Just as she thought she'd pass out in the being's clutches, it unknotted its grip. The weight vanished from her chest. A gasp of air filled her as the pulse rushed again in her neck. She sat up choking on her new-found breath. Her freshly opened eyes met the gray light of morning. It had all been a dream.

The muffled sounds of the others picking up camp declared the start of a new day. Verenna threw wide the carriage door in a cold sweat, eager for daylight. It slammed open and startled the three outside.

Mortimer said a confused good morning and passed her a scone the maids had packed.

"Anything the matter?"

"No. Dreams. Just bad dreams."

She sat on the sideboard to eat, pushing her bare toes through the leaflitter without looking up. She didn't want to meet anyone's eyes for fear she'd have to try and explain what she'd seen. Talking about it would only make it more real.

They were moving down the road again within the hour. Mortimer drove the horse, Fabien kept guard from his seat atop the luggage in the back, leaving Darius sitting across from Verenna deeply scouring the map. After the conversation, she'd heard last night his thin face suddenly looked starved. He licked his lips in concentration as he traced their route. She couldn't help but wonder how much of it was focus and how much hunger.

Verenna pulled herself to the opposite side of the cabin and tried to forget; the dream, what she'd heard, what these men really were. She crossed her arms on the window of the cab, laying her head on them to watch the countryside roll by. The lullaby of the rocking cart and the reassuring warmth of the sun on her face was almost enough to allow her doze off, until Darius interrupted.

"Awfully quiet today. The quietest I've ever seen you."

"That a complaint?" she grumbled.

He let out a breathy laugh and might have replied if the cart had not started to wobble. Fabien had clambered from his perch on the back, to hang off the side of the carriage and speak into the window.

"What are you doing? I'm trying to read," Darius scolded, but Fabien ignored him.

"There's a group up ahead on the road. Do you think-"

"Can't be. They should be behind us by well over an hour." Darius pushed Verenna aside and leaned out to see for himself. She slapped his hand off her shoulder and shoved him over a few inches to have her own look ahead. Sure enough, scattered figures dotted the path in the distance as if waiting to receive them.

"I can't tell if it's them," he slid back into the cabin. "But whoever it is they've seen us. Their blocking the road. It'll look suspicious to turn around now."

A few wraps sounded from the top of the carriage from where Mortimer sat. "I hope you're thinking up a plan. I can only drive so slow without stopping."

"I'm trying," Darius called, thumping a frustrated fist against the roof.

"Who do you think it is?" Verenna whispered as the potential gravity of the situation took hold.

"You know they can't hear us yet, yes? And we don't know. Pay attention." Darius dismissed. He knocked again on the top of the roof to call Mortimer's attention.

"Keep the pace. We don't want to look like we've got anything to hide. Our story is this. I am headed to Brightly Township for a medical call. That's a day North of Bronwell and gives us reason to be passing near the city. Mortimer, you're my driver. Now, you," he rounded on Fabien. "Have they seen you?"

He shook his messy, blond head, "Nah. They can't at this angle."

"Good. Make sure they don't. If it's the same bunch we ran into last night they'll remember that damned knife of yours."

"Sword," Fabien corrected, leaning into the cabin like he might climb in for a fight.

"We've got bigger worries, boys," Mortimer warned, his dismay evident even above the clatter of the moving carriage.

Scowling, Fabien let the issue go. "I'll follow along in the trees. I'll step in if things go poorly."

"And what are we doing? Are we just going to roll up to them and hope for the best? That's stupid!" Verenna grabbed indignant bunches of her dress.

Fabien winked an emerald eye at her. A slight scar at the corner of his mouth tucked into a dimple. "I'll take you along with me. Can't risk anyone recognizing you."

For the first time his smile did not entice her towards him. The idea of being alone together held no glamor after overhearing the men's chat overnight. His grin had the same number of teeth, the same red cravings, the same appetite as the doctor's. Before she could stammer out her answer Darius snarled his own.

"Like hell you will."

"Well what, then? If it's them they're sure to recognize her. We'll sneak around and meet you up ahead," Fabien insisted.

"You can shake that dream right out of your skull. Here," Darius shed his jacket, bundled it and tossed it into her lap. "You're pregnant."

"WHAT?"

"That. Put it under your skirts. Until we're through this you are Mrs. Collins, my wife. That jacket is our child. Hurry up."

Verenna leaned out the window for another look.

"Good God! Get back in here!" Darius pulled her arm but she jerked it free. Four figures swayed in the heatwaves ahead. Even from some ways off they bore little resemblance to the rough, misshapen brutes they'd run across the previous night. On closer inspection, they all appeared to be a wearing the same deep blue. Police?

Her parent's faces immediately leapt to mind. They must have sent out search parties after all. This could be one of them. A road block. Searching for her.

"No," Verenna threw the coat to the floorboards. Her copper eyes challenged the two men to convince her. Each tried silently to prompt the other to answer.

At a stalemate, Darius finally turned to Fabien. "Go. I'll handle this."

"Call out if you need me. I'll be ready," Fabien answered with a worried wrinkle in his brow. With that, he released his hold on the carriage and slid deftly into the trees.

She looked down at the coat on the floor between her and the doctor, then raised an eyebrow at him.

"You'll handle this, will you? Those look like police to me."

"You don't understand."

"Tell me what it is I'm misunderstanding then," she demanded, clenching the fabric of her dress tighter. Her knuckles formed white crowns across the tops of her hands.

"There's a roadblock up ahead. There shouldn't be. The first legitimate stop to check for Cold Fever is ten or more miles north of here towards Bronwell. We're headed the right direction, but it's far too soon."

Verenna made no move for the rumpled jacket. "So who set this one up if not the police?"

"Anyone but."

She took another peek up the road. Sun punctuating the silver buttons down their blue-clad chests. "Anyone but? Hm." Her voice dripped with disbelief. "Funny. They look like police to me."

"Listen to me," he hushed. "Why would four men, probably the majority of the closest towns police force, be all the way out here? We're miles from anywhere." He glanced out the window again, his words spilling even more rapidly and dropping in volume. "Now get that under your dress. We're getting closer."

"No. Those men have come to get me. My parents sent them. And I'm going with them. Before you get hungry enough to kill me."

Darius could not cover his shock. "What do you - what you heard ..."

Verenna did not allow him to finish. "I know exactly what I heard. You're going to need to hunt. I'm the closest prey. When you finally eat, it will likely be me. I'm not waiting around for that."

"Never. You don't know the first thing. Never in my life..."

She'd never seen him stumble for words before but it satisfied something in her to see him struggle. But soon anger replaced his fluster and he took her by the shoulders, hissing a hand's breadth from her face.

"None of that matters now. You're damn right they came for you. But they are not the saviors you think they are. Now get that jacket in place. And here." Darius rushed the cravat off his neck and ushered the long, white silk into her hands. "Cover your hair too. They'll remember you with that red mop."

"I won't," Verenna held the fabric as if it were a snake. "My parents. I know they'll have told the police I was missing. They'll take me home." She looked up from the winding white clutched in her fingers.

"It's not what you think."

"Oh, I think it's exactly what I think," she retorted. There would be no wordy escape for him his time. "Those men are there to take me back. And I'm going to let them."

"You don't get it. This is serious..."

"So am I," she threw the tie to the floor as well, her confidence growing as she watched the doctor wring his hands. "You. Kidnapped me. You. Are a criminal. And if I stay with you much longer, who knows what will happen to me. I'm going home. I'm finished. With all of this."

She spat on the pile of clothing at her feet and sat back to watch him squirm. Her chest filled with ecstatic hope and the relief of knowing it was all about to be over, that she would escape a dark moon in the woods with these monsters.

Darius leaned forward, his hands out to her. "You can't do this. You have to believe me. They're looking for you, but they are not police."

"Uniforms?" Verenna questioned with the snide tone of victory.

"Fake. More likely stolen." He checked the road again and pulled the drapes closed on each side.

Verenna scoffed in disbelief. All the frantic trappings of an unraveling lie were playing out in front of her. Still he tried to sway her.

"With all you've seen in the last few days, do you really think going home will be this simple? That you can just walk away from all of it? Good God! If you have any sense of self-preservation do what I've told you. We're coming up on them now."

"I'll do no such thing," she said with a laugh, amused at how the once proud doctor peered through the curtains like a timid child. Verenna was all but giggling with delight at the power she held. They'd underestimated her. All of them. Smug, she asked him, "What sort of idiot did you take me for when you stuffed me in here?"

"I hope you wanted the answer to that question." Darius let go of the curtains edge. The cabin grew darker, whether from the covered window or the new timber of his voice she could not be sure. All of her humor vanished as he spoke.

"You decided to take a jaunt in the woods at night. Despite the wolves, despite the type of people you know roam in those trees in the dark, you thought you were going to walk home. So yes, I thought you were a massive idiot. I still do. Because you didn't take a long enough look out that window to recognize the people ahead of us. Which is fine. They'll recognize you. That's the same group that ambushed us at the abbey. The grabby one quite liked you, I remember. He'll probably want to thank you for the trenches you dug across his face. Verenna, if you set a foot outside this carriage, that is the last anyone will ever see of you."

Verenna seared him with a glare, an attempt to hide the fact that her entire body had been consumed by a cold wash of dread. "The same..." She searched him for any signs of the lie she'd assumed he'd been telling. He didn't blink or move, only waited for the truth to settle with the dust motes.

"Whoa there," a stranger's voice called a little ways in front of them. Mortimer echoed the command gently to the horse and the cradling motion of the carriage drew to a halt.

She grabbed the curtain. The syrup yellow daylight dripped through the tiny crack as she peered outside. Two of the men took a stance in the middle of the road to block their leaving. Another with thick shoulders came towards them. He squinted in the sun causing a glint of grease on his wide, pink nose. The memory of the man's hands tearing at her skirt sent a shock through her entire body. Sweat settled on her skin, a shroud of panic. They'd been fighting face to face. He would surely know her on sight.

Verenna flung herself onto her knees to gather the jacket. She smashed it into a ball, stuffing it between her dress and layers of petticoat. Fumbling to hold the bundle in place, she struggled to restrain all of her wild hair under the white streamer of necktie. Every attempt slipped through her swiftly numbing fingers. Darius pulled her up from her scrabbling on the floor and planted her firmly on the bench. He took the ends of the cloth and knotted them snugly under her chin. "Don't talk. We will get out of this. Understand? And open those other drapes. If you're backlit it'll be harder to see you." She rushed to do as he said.

Thunderous pounding shook the door. "Police! Routine check, open up."

With one last warning glance and a finger across his lips, Darius pulled aside the curtain.

"Can we help you, my good man?" Darius said, deftly leaving all worry out of his voice and exchanging it for a false geniality that made Verenna cringe.

Daylight added even more sickening detail to the man's meatish visage. The pockmarks and crater-like scars were interrupted by three bright scratches streaking down from under his eye where Verenna had clawed him. He spoke with a surprisingly high timber for his size.

"Yes, sir. This is a checkpoint. We're stopping every carriage that comes through."

"What are you blokes looking for? Can't be that disease can it? This far south? Tell me it's not this far out of Bronwell already." Darius rattled off questions so quickly the man at the window had to regroup.

"Never mind that. We're not looking for sick people. We're looking for three criminals. They've got a kidnapped girl. Who's in there with you? That a lady?" The man peered into the cabin, shading his view with a thick hand for a better look at her. Verenna gathered the white cloth tighter around her face and shifted to look out the other window.

The woman with the matted hair stood some yards from the cart loitering by the trees that lined the thoroughfare. The dogs lay at her feet, tethered to saplings. She casually checked their leads. Her long-nailed hand tugged sharp on the leather straps to loosen them, as if leisurely preparing to set them free. The dogs made no move. All six of them were thoroughly involved in chewing on the scraps of some poor, dead creature in the grass. Though all seemed to have eyes on the carriage.

"It most certainly is a lady," Darius boasted. His sudden gusto distracting the man. "That is my wife. She's pregnant, however, and I'd ask you not to have her out of the cabin. She isn't feeling well."

The man grunted, obviously unconvinced. "Where are you and the misses headed then?"

"I'm on business towards Brightly Township. I'm a doctor."

"And you brought your wife?"

"I certainly can't have some other chap delivering my baby if I'm out of town, now can I?"

"Well, ain't that nice." A sneer grew across the stranger's face, drawing up the curtain on his missing teeth. "Step out, please."

Darius turned to her quickly mouthed, *stay calm*, before undoing the latch with a quiet click and sliding from the cabin. The dull thud of his boots on the dusty ground made up a for few of her missing heartbeats. With the door open, there was nothing between her and the stranger in blue.

"Alright. What now?" Darius asked. He looked slim, almost adolescent, in comparison to the bulk of the man in the police uniform.

"What did you say your name was?"

"Dr. Phineas Collins. My wife Mrs. Collins," he said with a sweeping gesture to the open cabin. "And our driver, Mort. And yours?"

The pink-faced stranger didn't reply. He was busy squinting up at the driver's seat. "You," he barked. "Down 'ere."

The boards above Verenna creaked as Mortimer clambered down the side of the carriage. The horse let out a discontented huff and stomped a few times in place. His hop to the ground sent a tinkling shiver through the horse's tack and a wave through the carriage as he let go of the ladder. Across the road, the dogs stirred and looked up from their meal.

"Your name?" Darius repeated, working hard to keep a tone of camaraderie.

Verenna used the cover of their conversation to slide across the seat. She held her breath and reached to close the door. The stranger turned towards her making her jerk back inside.

"Read the badge," the man dismissed. He took a few heavy steps towards the carriage. His shoes ground like teeth against the grit of the road. Resting a thick forearm against the doorframe he leaned in and screwed up his face in an attempt to make out Verenna's features.

A long tear on his sleeve opened and closed like an eye.

Verenna held her breath and looked down at the floor. The man sniffed as if smelling for some trace she might leave on the breeze. She froze, hoping her stillness would erase it.

"I can't see your badge," Darius called. "Not while you're looking at my wife, anyhow." The upset in his voice was convincing enough to turn the man away from her. Verenna shuddered with momentary relief, happy to be out from under his gaze. It was Mortimer and Darius's turn for scrutiny.

"Fine," the stranger shrugged. He aimed the shiny silver badge upwards and grimaced at it. "Conover. See?" He tapped a dirty nail against the gleam. "Now that we got the formalities out of the way, why don't you tell me where you came from? And why don't you both just answer at the same time." He pointed back and forth between Darius and Mortimer, smiling at the genius of his trap.

"No looking at each other, now," the man added. "I'll count from three and we'll see if we're all on the same page. Three," he held up three stocky, callused fingers.

Verenna cringed. They'd have to tell the same lie in perfect unison.

"Two…" he dropped one, sneering. The men blocking the road exchanged amused looks. Verenna wrung her hands. The hounds, perhaps sensing the tension, stirred and whined, eager to investigate.

"One."

"Alma," two voices chorused together miraculously. A murmur of surprise rippled around. Even Darius seemed shocked.

"That so? Alma's a long way off. Funny talking town, that."

"Port cities often are. You'll spend a great night there though, if you know what I mean. And I'm sure you gents do." Darius attempted to joke through the rigid quiet but no one responded.

"Stop anywhere in between? Anywhere we might need to know

about?"

"Just for the night," Darius answered.

"Shut up you. I wanna hear it from him. Old man, where'd you stop the carriage?"

"Martin's Moor, Aston," Mortimer droned, but the man cut the list short, clenching his gapped teeth.

"You know the place I'm getting at. Sansbury. The criminals were stopped there last night. Caused some trouble for us. Put up a real fight. You didn't happen to spend a night there, did you? Because I gotta say, fighting the police is a jailing offense, and you two look a titch familiar." The nervous hum of summer insects rose to fill the pause that followed. Darius opened his mouth, but nothing came out. He kept his face calm, though his right thumb worried the writing callus on his middle finger.

"What do you mean by that? Are you calling me a criminal?" Darius said the last word so crisply that spit flew onto the man's cheek, though it was so covered in sweat and oil the man didn't notice.

"If I am?" The stranger's glossy, pink face drew close, challenging Darius to look away.

Clenching his fists to hold onto his composure, the doctor stared unblinkingly back. "We have nothing to hide."

"Are you sure?" the man rasped in his ear as he circled them.

Verenna took a breath in and quelled her violently fluttering pulse. She wanted to call for Fabien. The way the man passed around them she could see the situation headed towards another brawl. Just before she called for help, Mortimer spoke again.

"If I may be so bold, I recall you said you were looking for a group of four traveling this way. Three and a girl?"

"Aye…" The man in blue crossed his arms, the tear in the uniform sleeve gaping near of the elbow.

"There's only three of us in total."

Darius caught on. He planted himself and squared his shoulders. "My driver is right. Unless you're counting the baby as the fourth criminal we only have three with us. Also, if we'd just been in a fight, I think we'd be a bit more busted up. Look," he turned in a circle. "Not a scratch."

"What are those holes? In the back of your shirt."

The world stopped once more. One of the hounds strained at its lead. Ears pricked and attentive. Darius stalled, having completely forgotten how the glass had shredded his shirt.

"Moths," Mortimer blurted. "Can't seem to keep them out of the trunks."

The stranger set his jaw. "A moment." The man lumbered over to join the two others blocking the road. Muffled grunts of alternating agreement and dissent reached Verenna through the window as the men discussed the fate of their group.

A dog snapped, catching Verenna's attention. One of them, with a dirty black coat, had taken over the meal. The nape of its neck bristled, legs wide over the carcass, a low warning growl spilling around the end of a bone clenched in its teeth.

The other animals hung back at the farthest reaches of their tethers as their leader drug the grisly prize closer to the base of the tree. In the shorter grass the size of the bone became clearer. It was nearly half the length of the hound with bits of ragged flesh still clinging to it.

The animal seemed to watch her as it gnawed. Its keeper watched too, her arms crossed, back against the sapling, unfazed by the gore at her feet. Sunlight springing off the woman's badge stabbed at Verenna's eyes. The girl squinted against it, noting that the blue crispness of the woman's uniform was ruined by a stain that ran from her ribs to her right hip. The burgundy color streaked vertically with the direction of the material, as if someone had tried and failed to scrub it out.

Verenna knew exactly where the uniform had come from.

The tatter in the first man's sleeve and the mark on the woman's shirt had come from the same event that had earned the dogs their current feast.

She felt sick rising in her throat. She threw open the door and wretched into the dust. The imposters in blue jumped and took a rushing start towards the carriage. The dogs abandoned their spoils to bark and snarl at the sudden hubbub.

"She's escaping!" One of them shouted. "Don't either of you move!" Another screamed at Darius and Mortimer. It didn't take long to realize that the sudden movement hadn't been an escape attempt. The sight of Verenna hanging on the open door, weak and green in the face, seemed enough to sooth them. Peering through into the cart Darius called, "Feeling better darling?"

The saccharin sound of false worry almost made her heave again. He had a way of making even concern sound like I told you so.

"Yes, dear. It's just the baby." She spat out a sour welling of spit, purposefully aiming towards the feet of the dog handler. The woman noticed the insult. She met the girls glare with a shrug and a grimace that drew down her thick eyebrows. Verenna snapped the carriage door shut. Once sealed inside she hung her head and clutched her knees, shuddering under the weight of the knowledge that the tangle of red and white in the grass, had once been human.

"As I said, sir, we are in no fighting condition," Darius reiterated.

"You're too familiar," grumbled the stranger.

"I'm sure I can't tell you why. Unless you make a habit of fighting pregnant women."

The man lifted his fingers to the red stripes of scabbing skin, three trenches beneath his cheek bone. He ground a heel into the earth and turned again towards the carriage. Marching up to the door he looked Verenna over one last time. She straightened up from her hold on her knees so that the bump the jacket created would show.

Scowling, the man traced her silhouette with his eyes hesitating over the lump in her dress. Verenna followed suit, looking herself over, hoping to catch anything out of place before the man had a chance to notice. After what seemed like half an hour, he stormed towards Mortimer and Darius.

Verenna's hand flew to her mouth to stifle the thin moan of fear escaping it. It would be last night all over again with worse circumstances. There were no darkened woods to escape to and miles until help. Darius's words rang in her ears; *the last anyone will ever see of you.*

She recoiled into the corner and shut her eyes but no fight ensued. "Get gone. You're holding up the road." The troop backed lazily out of the path.

Both men moved cautiously. Darius took slow steps towards the open carriage door while Mortimer moved sideways for the ladder to his perch.

"Get gone I said! Before I haul you off anyway."

The carriage rocked as Mortimer scrambled up the side. Darius tried to keep his pace stately though he nearly tripped over himself stepping inside. The door snapped shut behind him and the reins flicked the horse forward. They slid away into the afternoon.

Verenna watched out the window until she could no longer see the flash of the sun off the men's buttons. Until every bit of their stolen blue vanished behind the plume of dust struck up by the wheels. The second they disappeared she flung the drapes closed, threw Darius's crumpled coat to the floor and pulled the scarf from her hair. Her unbrushed, ruby locks tumbled free, pressed and misshapen by the binding. The corners of her mouth downturned, she tightened her face against the coming onslaught of tears. It did nothing to quell the flow. She swiped the salt water from her cheeks with her sleeve. The fabric had once been the color of cream, but the edges had gone dingy with wear and sweat, and begun to smell like the dust of roads that might never lead to home.

☙

They drove on in bitter silence well into the afternoon. Words held hostage by grievance.

"River up ahead!" Mortimer called. "The horse needs water. We can wait for Fabien there."

Verenna watched their approach from between the drapes. A grass covered bank melted into a shallow ford. The water jumped over stones and chattered at the edges of boulders. Easily the most pleasant place they'd stopped so far.

"Stay inside. We won't stop long." Darius slid from the carriage.

Paying no mind, the girl kicked her shoes off and set out for the riverbank. The plush feeling of the grass beneath her feet eased the tension of the hours they'd spent cooped up in the dim cart, shut inside with their shaken nerves and worry, brooding in their own uncertainties.

The dogs hadn't left Verenna's mind the whole distance. The sound of teeth scraping bone had been etched into her memory. Mercifully the wind had taken the stench in the other direction.

"Where do you think you're going?" Darius demanded. "We're leaving as soon as Fabien's here."

Verenna heard but did not answer. She rolled up her sleeves, hiked her skirts high and pressed on toward the water, determined to ignore him.

The grasses rose to her waist and turned into reeds as she came to the top of the bank. She gripped the slender branch of a dead, gnarled tree that hung out over the incline, using it for balance. Verenna reached to part the cattails. Something wrapped around her ankle.

She shrieked and kicked to stomp out whatever creature had taken hold of her. Her nails dug into the branch she clung to but she could not keep her hold. Her hand slipped, raking her forearm against the jagged bark of the tree. Crashing into the reeds she struck out in all directions in the hopes that one of the blows would connect. Her fist found a target behind the green and whaled at it until a familiar voice begged mercy.

"Verenna! Miss! For crying...ough! It's me!"

"Bastard!"

Fabien parted the grasses. "Gah! Every time with the claws and the hitting! It was a joke!"

"This is your idea of funny?" No amount of charm could have spared him the resounding slap across the face. She had almost gotten her hands around his throat by the time Mortimer reached them and pulled her away. He looked like he might join in the fray. But in an instant, he realized it was only Fabien and turned the girl loose.

"Stupid," he muttered, shaking his head in utter disappointment.

Darius arrived a moment later. "What is it?"

"Nothing. Boy played a prank. I've got to see to the horse." Mortimer lumbered off, shoulders tight and head low, clearly fuming over the false alarm.

"It meant it as fun." Fabien stood and rubbed the handshape print across his cheek.

"Well, some fun," Verenna bristled.

"No one's in the mood, Fabien. We'll be moving on as soon as we've watered the horse. Do not wander. And no more jokes."

Fabien dusted bits of shredded grass from his shirt. "What's gotten into you all? It was a roadblock, not a funeral. Everything looked like it was going alright."

"They almost recognized us. They..." There was nothing she could say that would make him understand. The sickening sheen of the man's oily skin, the dead stare of the dogs as they consumed what was surely human remains. Those things were hers alone now. She changed the subject.

"How did you get here so fast anyway?"

"A quick jog and a shortcut and I was back on the cart again. I kept quiet though. Wanted to make it look like I beat you on foot. It was going to be part of the joke. Turns out I'm not that funny."

"You're certainly not," Verenna pouted. She began to tidy herself, pushing her hair out of her face. A tart pain raced up her right arm.

She looked down and noticed red springing up from a long scrape on her forearm. Gasping she covered it with a hand. A warm drop paused at her elbow before splatting onto the dirt with a weighty thud. She looked away and swallowed hard, blinking to clear the image.

"What's happened?" Fabien asked.

What if he could smell the blood? If he saw it, would he charge her? The moon was only a pale sliver in the afternoon sky. In a day it would be gone. What if his instincts took over?

"I'm fine."

"You're a liar. Let me see."

Verenna tucked the injury behind her. "Don't come any closer."

"If you're hurt, it's my fault. The least I can do is help you fix it up as an apology."

"No, it'll make you...stop. I don't want your help!"

Fabien prowled towards her with a grin that seemed too thin and wide for his face. "At least let me see, would you?"

"I said stop it!" Verenna tripped as she backed away. The reeds softened the landing but made a quick retreat impossible. The thick grass served as a spider's web, holding her as wiggling prey before a predator. "Don't!" she squealed.

"You're bleeding."

"Stay back. Don't think I don't know what you want. Get closer you'll lose an eye."

The young man plopped down in the grass beside her with his eyes on his own feet. "So how did you figure it out?"

"I heard you three talking. The dark moon means you'll be hungry. And I'm the closest thing," her words trailed away as she watched them shift his expression. His brow fell and his shoulders sank.

"I never want you to be afraid of me. I can't help what I am but once you've been around as long as I have, you do get control of it. And I promise you, it is under control." He took her hand, lacing his fingers with hers. The honest green of his eyes made it hard to doubt him. She found a comforting weakness in his smile. "Here. Let's wash that out before it gets infected."

He hopped up and took a few sloshing steps into the water.

"What are you doing?"

"Cleanest water is mid-stream. Don't want any mud or plants when you're cleaning up," he called back, brandishing a small flask, draining it and trudging on to fill it with water. "Sit yourself on that rock. I'll be right there.

She did as he said, climbing onto the boulder and looking up through the branches of the knotted tree. The twigs seemed to be reaching down to her, inviting her closer to the blue of the sky. The sun was high and hot, but the way the breeze cooled the sweat on her brow made up for it. Verenna slipped her feet into the stream. The water was surprisingly cold for that time of year, but infinitely welcome as it numbed her toes and the raw spots the shoes had worn on her heels.

Just beneath her reflection she could see the silver flicker of tiny minnows. One particularly brave one with a yellow streak on his side drifted close to her toe. Infinitesimally she reached to touch it, a fraction from its translucent fin. But the sloshing sound returned to break the calm and sent the many fish darting for the reeds like spilling marbles.

Verenna looked up to find Fabien slogging towards her with a brimming canteen and a dashing smile.

"Here we are. Hold out your arm now. Won't hurt a bit."

She held out the limb but refused to look. The shock of cold water made her wince. She dared a glance when she felt the last drips falling from her hand. The scrapes ran the length of her arm, elbow to wrist. Long, wrapping lines like claw marks, but not so deep.

"It'll be fine, no stitches. Just a bandage and it'll heal up like new. I'm sure Darius has some."

"He wouldn't be caught dead without one."

She looked down at the red swirls dissipating in the water and shuddered. Each drop bloomed and vanished with the current. Only then did she notice something out of place.

"Odd. Aren't river stones usually rounded? These are all rough at the edges." She could feel the jagged sides of the rocks with her toes. "They can't have been in the water long."

Fabien dipped a hand below the surface. It emerged clutching a palm sized stone, angular and unpolished.

"Hmm. Maybe someone was skipping 'em." Again he reached in and retrieved a rough stone. It went on and on. He waded out again to investigate. But by the time he'd checked a tenth or eleventh pebble it became clear they were all in the same state.

"There's not that many of them either. The bottom's mostly grasses here. And mud." Fabien put his hands on his hips, looking down and turning in a confused circle. "It's almost like it just got here. The river I mean. Nothing in it looks like it's been water worn. At all."

"There's fish and reeds. It can't have just got here. Can it?"

"Those could sprout up in a few weeks though. I'd guess it flooded, but in summer?" Fabien stopped short. A distant rumble sounded through the pines where the river dodged into the woods. "What was…"

Verenna sat bolt upright. The noise could have been mistaken for thunder had there been a single cloud in the sky. She stood up on the boulder for a better view.

Downstream the horse whinnied and flicked its head to free itself from Mortimer's lead.

"Did you hear that?" the old man shouted.

"We did! Thunder?" Fabien offered. Mortimer only shrugged, continuing his battle to calm the horse.

The current picked up. Quiet babbling had risen into splattering waves lapping at the rock.

"What's that now?" Fabien pointed to the woods. A strange, swooping gray rose above the distant forest.

"It's smoke," he said and scratched his head.

"No," Verenna muttered. She shaded her eyes for a better view. "Birds…"

Before she could lose herself in speculation Darius came screaming from the carriage at a full run.

"It's not on the map! Get out! It's not on the map!"

Verenna could hear him but the words themselves meant nothing. Gibberish. What did he mean *it's not on the map*? It was there in front of them.

A crash rang out again. This time louder. Closer. It drowned out Darius's cries. They trailed into obscurity, "Get out! Get…"

Following the flailing of his gestures she looked up stream. The trees danced violently. Old trees, well rooted and sixty feet tall, as if a great wind were rushing towards them down the path of the river. The motion rolled nearer and nearer, catching and swaying the pines until from their shade burst forth a massive, mound of seething water.

The foaming white crest leaped towards them, closing up the expanse so fast there was no time to flee. It raged high, three times as tall as Fabien who was still standing mid-river in shock.

"Move!" Verenna screamed and started for him, ignoring the stabbing pain of the rocks against the soles of her feet. He turned towards her and reached out a hand. They clasped just as the gnashing whitewater consumed them. They were ripped from the cacophony, thrown into blindness, into the growling world inside the wave. Fabien's vice grip on her hand strained the joint of her wrist as they tried to keep hold of each other, pelted by all manner of debris in the whirling darkness.

Chapter 14

Verenna's legs kicked hard without direction. There was no way to tell up from down in the spinning torrent. She put one arm up to guard her face, trying to keep the tumbling objects from knocking her senseless. Her shoulder shrieked from the pull of holding onto Fabien. Then, with a sudden wrenching motion, he was gone. Air fled her lungs in an explosion of panic. Her arms shot out in frenzy feeling for the surface, the bottom, anything to tell her the way up. After an eternity, her fingertips broke into the air. She followed, gasping in the day before going under the rapids again, swallowed by the chaos.

She barreled headlong into some underwater obstacle that smashed the air out of her. Clambering she found the surface again, each breath so desperate and deep she was sure her chest was too full to take in the next.

"Fabien! Sa-say something! Where ar-", she wailed between mouthfuls of water.

Ahead of her a bobbing figure. A weak hand splashed once and disappeared. Immediately she struck out for it, but was churned under by a dip in the path of the river.

She kicked off hard from the bottom, fighting against the weight of her waterlogged skirts. But something went wrong. Her overskirt caught on something, holding her from the surface by the hem.

Eyes still shut she followed the taught material with a hand until she found the problem. Whatever it was had hooked straight through. She pulled at it with everything she had. Hope surged within her as she felt it start to tear. Suddenly another tug. The dress had caught on the opposite side too. Feeling blindly for the cause, her lungs began to ache with the stretch of holding her breath. Her hand met something like winding grass. She wrenched it in an attempt to break it off and free herself.

A screech wrent the gurgling of the water. Instinctively she cracked open her eyes.

Through the murk her gaze found a blurred, grey face, formed in the whipping weeds and mud, it's eyes wide, white capsules of air. A mud pit of a mouth gaped to screech again.

A wash of bubbles escaped her, a curtain of encapsulated cries between her and the creature. She swung a blind fist through the haze. The water dragged at her sleeve, the blow gliding forward worthless and dreamlike only to be seized by something beyond her sight. As the bubbles cleared she saw strands of what looked like dead river grass winding up her arm. It wove itself between her fingers and cinched her wrist, towing her deeper. The weeds below opened to receive her. The mud at the base of them boiled with motion, reaching for her, clinging to the edge of her petticoats like scores of tiny hands.

Verenna's lungs filled with needles. She needed air. Her eyes burned from the murky water. Forcing them open again she wrenched the vines away from her arm. The face in the weeds rippled closer to throw out more tendrils of grass to rope her limbs.

The last of her air came flitting from her lips. She could hear her heart over the roar of the current. It thudded in her ears which were exploding with pain as the depth of water pressed in on her. Each beat wracked her and made her vision swim. Her fingers were going numb and cold from the constriction of the grasping weeds.

The cold of the water crept into her flesh and took hold of her muscles. Something in her was being dislodged, pulled from her, stolen. Verenna tried to force her hands to keep working but the world was closing in. The dim circle of light above her shrinking little by little, the thunder of the water overtaking the throb of her slowing pulse.

With the last of her fading consciousness she sensed a shadow above her. A dart of silver entered her slim field of vision. The grip of the vines went slack. Something warm encircled her waist and she felt herself rushing upwards. It wasn't until she burst through the surface that she could be sure the feeling wasn't death. Her weightlessness ended as her body took on its full sodden heft. The world tilted and left her staring at the sky, her back on solid ground. She tried to drink in the air that chilled her arms and legs but found herself too full. Mortimer's ragged voice called out from somewhere close. The sound muffled and buzzing through the water in her ears.

"Take her up the bank. Fabien's still gone."

A splash and the voice vanished, exchanged for another.

"Verenna! Answer damn it!" She tried to keep her eyes open, but a dim edge tinged the blue above her, closing in in the same drawstring circle as before. Smaller and smaller, until she might have been looking through a keyhole.

Darius's voice reappeared on top of her, along with a thud to her stomach that sent a rush of water gushing from her mouth and nose making way for an onslaught of coughing and gasping breaths. Sight and sound flooded in to fill the space the water left. Birds, the breeze, the bright of the sun, and over it all the sound of her own retching.

A careful touch turned her onto her side as a hand slipped behind her head to lift it from the flattened grass. Darius hovered above her. "Good God, you had me scared."

Verenna weakly grabbed his vest to make sure he was real. She blinked hard, trying to rid her stinging eyes of the muck she'd been immersed in. Darius was drenched as well. His clothes clung to his wiry form, his hair for once disheveled.

"I must be dead or something," Verenna panted. "You're a mess. You're never a mess."

His scoff turned into a smile, then into a laugh. It was surreal that a sound so full of genuine gladness and relief could come from someone ordinarily so sour. He looked up at the sky and back down to her. "You're a brat whatever weather."

The corner of her mouth perked slightly. "Maybe. But you deserve it."

Verenna let out a sigh. The summer heat had never been so welcome, sending life prickling back into her arms and legs. But her peace was soon replaced with a familiar cold fear. She tried to sit up, making it only as far as her elbows.

"Where's Fabien?"

The smile fell from Darius's face. "Mortimer went to look for him. We lost sight of him."

"What? You what?" She struggled upwards but he blocked her.

"Stay down. Your legs won't hold you now."

Verenna ignored him, wobbling to her knees, to her feet, only to collapse a few feet away. She swore and coughed more water.

"He's the one who got you into this, you know. If he hadn't been showing off in the water the two of you might not have been swept away. What are you doing? Again? Sit down."

"I'm going to help," Verenna informed him as she struggled to stand against a tree.

"You can't possibly. If a man who can't swim is stupid enough to put himself in the middle of a river there's no helping him."

"He can't swim? How are you not worried for him?"

"Worried for *him*? You were the one in danger and he's the one that put you there! Getting thrown around by a river is better than he deserves."

"How was he supposed to know the water was going to come up like that? He tried to save me."

Darius's voice rose an octave in indignation as he marched to follow her fumbling route downstream. "That's a load of tripe and you know it! You ran out to save him! He's not a hero!"

"He could be dead! How are you still this heartless?" She took another unsuccessful step and crumbled.

"Like Hell he's dead. We can't die, remember?"

His words caught her off guard. She'd forgotten about that facet of her traveling companions. However, the idea did not dampen her joy at seeing two men making their way up the bank. Fabien leaned heavily on Mortimer who waved with what looked like the case for the map.

"Look what we've got," he yelled as they drew closer.

Mortimer set Fabien in the grass next to Verenna and sank onto a stump to catch his breath.

"Give that here," Darius said, snatching the canister from Fabien's outreached hand. He fell upon the case, whipping it open to check on its contents.

The river had quieted. The rapids shrunk and allowed the hum of summer to resume.

"I thought you were done in," Verenna ventured to Fabien.

"Same for you. It doesn't really work like that for us. But I appreciate the concern."

"I forgot. I suppose you were safe the whole time."

"Well, I mean, I can still drown. Can't swim a stroke. I can feel the whole process. Filling up with water, lungs burning, going cold and all. It's just, after all that, I can get back up and keep walking around. It's what was in that river that had me worried."

Verenna paused to shudder, trying to remember the chapters

she'd read in the handbook. She certainly hadn't read about anything like what she'd seen. Her hand flew her pocket, sure the little book would be gone. Strangely enough it had stuck in her pocket. A small miracle. She pulled it out and feathered the pages, splaying it in the sun to dry.

"You saw it too, then. Do you know what it was?"

"A crossroads demon most likely," Fabien guessed.

"Most definitely." There was an inarguable tone in the way Darius said it. "A truly massive one. To be able to manipulate the flow of a river like that, to change its course, that kind of power is unheard of."

"What made it rise up like that? That wave?"

"Probably your blood," Mortimer grumbled. "You're a powerful one, Miss. Just a drop of you can make all manner of things happen."

Verenna looked down at her bare feet and wiggled her toes, remembering the tiny hands reaching for them. She turned to Fabien. "What would they, that thing, have done to you?"

"Don't know for sure. Drag us into whatever realm it's from. Hell, maybe? They may not be able to kill us but they can surely trap us somewhere unpleasant. Indefinitely."

The whole group gazed at the water, shifting uncomfortably. Fabien cleared his throat. "Hot out here."

"And it'll get hotter," Darius rolled the map and closed the canister with a click. "We have no sun serum."

"Quit complaining. I grabbed your bloody map, didn't I?"

"A nice gesture but it's not much good if we burn to a crisp. I'll have to make more when we reach Bronwell. We aren't far, but we'll be cutting things close. By the map, we'll be headed through the woods for the rest of the day. At least we'll have shade," Darius said as he rolled up the hide and replaced it in the canister.

Fabien sprang up and dusted himself off, shockingly agile after the ordeal. "Wait here. I've got to go back and get my sword. It'll only be a minute. I left it in that tree on the bank."

"It's gone," the doctor stated flatly.

"How do you know?"

"I saw it go."

"You're full of it. I hung it high."

"And I'm telling you the water was higher."

The corners of Fabien's mouth pinched in. He stared at Darius, unblinking, unbreathing, as if looking long enough might pry some other truth from him. None was offered.

Fabien gripped his hair and squatted down.

"Damn it! Gah!" he screamed at the ground. Rising to pace with his hands on his hips he rounded on Darius. "You're lying."

Mortimer interjected. "The water rose enough to take the whole horse and carriage. The sword is gone, boy. There's nothing can be done about it."

"You don't understand! It's important."

"I do understand," Darius corrected. "As I said, my bag is missing and so is every single vial of sun serum it contained. If we aren't somewhere by dawn you'll be saying goodbye to more than your blade."

"The horse is gone. How are we going to be anywhere by then?" Verenna chimed in.

"We start walking. Now. Every second talking is a second late doing," the doctor chided as he rose.

"We can worry about dawn when it comes. What we should be concerned about is a night in these woods," Mortimer reminded.

The old man's words sent a chill through Verenna that the heat of the sun could not prevent. In a wordless, shared agreement the group clambered up to the road and struck out northward.

Verenna found her legs stronger than she thought, but a firm handful of Mortimer's jacket was a comforting support. It billowed out around him in the breeze, as if it were still under water. As he moved an arm around her back to aid her, his coat opened, revealing the hilt of the dagger peaking from its sheath at his side. Verenna recognized it as the silver dart she'd seen just before she'd been rushed to the surface.

"Thanks by the way," she whispered. He smiled and nodded, his cheeks wrinkling into deep gorges on either side of his mouth.

"As promised, Miss."

They'd hardly walked five minutes when something large shifted in the deep green beside the road. Her breath went out of her. She pointed to the trees with her free hand, clutching fiercely to Mortimer with the other. "What was that?"

The stirring in the brush came closer. Heavy, heaving, breaths. The hair on the back of Verenna's neck went ridged. Mortimer tucked her behind him as all four braced for an attack. Images of the yawning mouth in the cathedral swam in her memory. If it was the beast, there would be nowhere to hide this time.

A soft, gray snout emerged, followed by two flicking ears, and the distinct thud of hooves.

Verenna laughed as the tension drained from her. "It's him!"

The horse's neck was ringed heavily in limp water plants like a shabby first place garland. Even sopping wet the animal still looked powdered by dust. Dragging at its sides, the remainders of its tack.

"Well, that's something," Mortimer left Verenna against a tree and set about pulling the weeds off the beast. Unlatching the buckles that held the frayed harness, he tossed the broken pieces into the river, leaving only the bridle.

"Can't get rid of the old thing, can we?" Darius mumbled.

"Seems we can't," Fabien shrugged, setting Verenna easily atop the animal. "We'll move faster if you ride. Hold on now," he warned, weaving her hand into the horse's damp mane. She took comfort in the warm, coarse hair, and how alive it felt compared to the slick, dark weeds that had wrapped her underwater. Mortimer took the reins and they set off at a more urgent pace.

Darius brought out the map again to study it as he walked. "If we keep a good pace we should reach the edge of the woods by nightfall."

"We'd better take the if out of that," Mortimer warned. "No carriage. No sword. We're a target for wolves."

"There are wolves?" Verenna gazed into the dark patches between the trees, imagining yellow eyes and hot breath acrid with meat.

"Maybe. I wouldn't be as worried about that as I would those hunters catching up. It'll be ugly if we've got to fight them unarmed," Fabien kicked a rock from his path. The puff of dirt it sent up matched his huffing sigh.

"Consider it that fair fight you're always looking for," Darius scoffed.

"Shut up," Fabien retorted, stepping to the edge of the path to collect a small branch. He tested its weight as a club.

The doctor laughed. "That for me or the wolves?"

"Why not both?"

"How is this getting us there faster? Save your anger for real trouble," Mortimer advised.

"There's going to be some if he…" Fabien stopped walking and pointed ahead with the branch. "What's that?"

"There's something in the road," Verenna whispered.

The group halted. "Stay back," Fabien urged them as he crept forward to investigate, club raised. He picked his way around rocks and twigs so that his footfalls landed soundlessly in the dirt. No one breathed.

About half way between them and the strange shape in the road, Fabien dropped his weapon to his side and rushed towards the object. "It's a woman! She's hurt!"

"Good God," Darius muttered and shouldered Mortimer out of the way as he ran to help.

"No, no, no," Verenna insisted as the old man directed the horse forward. "I'm not going over there."

"We need to stay together miss. The closer we are the harder it is for anything watching to pick us off."

"Don't you read? This is a trap," she hissed and tugged at the horse's mane to stop it walking. Both Mortimer and the horse ignored her. There was nothing to do but sit low and keep her eyes on the woods.

Darius knelt beside the woman. "Ma'am, can you hear me? Ma'am?" He touched her neck to feel for a pulse and immediately jolted and withdrew it.

What had appeared to be the flesh of her face collapsed in like the ash shell of a burned out log, revealing the fire darkened interior of her skull. The soot-like flakes fluttered into the air. Verenna gasped and covered her nose and mouth.

The whole group drew back except for Darius. "It's not dangerous. Not anymore."

"What happened? Did she..." Fabien trailed off in shock.

"She did. She was a husk," Mortimer murmured.

"A what?" Verenna said without removing her hand from her mouth.

"A husk," Darius echoed. "They happen when a demon, one strong enough to think and plan, takes up residence in a soul. Instead of consuming the soul quickly, as with Cold Fever, they sip it slowly. That way they keep the victim alive long enough to use them. The process is fatal, so the demon must find another before the life of the current one runs out. This is what happens when they don't."

"They just burn up? Insides and all?" Fabien stared at the

woman, jaw slack in disbelief.

"If the soul runs out and there is nothing else to feed on, yes. They'll consume muscle, organs, bone, until there is no more to take and the victim is just, well...a husk." Darius's explained, his matter of fact tone tinged with melancholy.

"Why didn't anyone help her?" Verenna worried as a few more flakes of ash took to the breeze.

"They couldn't. Even the one infected doesn't realize until it's too late. The demon allows them to go about their lives normally until it learns their behaviors, personality, where they go, and so on. Then it takes over. They're suddenly prisoners in their own bodies. They're consumed in plain sight and no one finds out until they drop dead. They can't seek help because their captor won't allow it. Anything out of the ordinary might scare the next potential host away."

"Poor thing," Mortimer sighed.

The group fell silent and gazed down at the woman. But a question nibbled at Verenna's nerves.

"But where is the demon now? Is it here?"

"Unlikely. Without a host they usually sink back to Hell fairly fast."

"How unlikely?" Verenna checked the trees, sure in her gut that the creature watched.

"Very. What I don't understand is why she's facing away from Bronwell. It's like she was leaving. The rich may have fled but there's still thousands of people there. Anything with enough intellect to control a host would be heading towards the city, not away from it." Darius straightened from his crouch and placed a hand on his chin to ponder.

"I don't like it. It makes no sense," Mortimer grumbled, joining Verenna in watching the trees.

Fabien shrugged. "Does it have to? Demons aren't always the

smartest lot. Maybe it got turned around or lost. What else could it possibly mean?"

"It means when we get to Bronwell, we can't trust anyone. The river, now this. If there are demons this strong in the area, we may be getting close to something even bigger."

"Souris?" Mortimer asked, anxiety overflowing into words.

"It did say she was supposed to wash the city clean. It would make sense if he was hiding in Bronwell. Or somewhere close," Darius interpreted.

Verenna felt herself go pale. The dream she'd had the night before bubbled to the forefront of her thoughts. The jeering invitation to come find what waited in Bronwell. "Already? But I - how? You haven't told me anything! What am I supposed to do?"

"We haven't told you because we don't know. Prophecy tends to be frustratingly nonspecific. We'll have to figure it out as we go," Darius snapped.

"That plan doesn't exactly reek of success," Mortimer jumped in on her side.

"Well, don't look at me like it was my idea," the doctor retorted.

Fabien broke into the conversation. "Won't matter whose idea it was or wasn't if we don't make it to Bronwell. Now, are we or are we not going to make it out of the woods by dark? Any insight on that?" he barked.

"Please say yes." Verenna begged.

Mortimer glanced back at her over his shoulder then cast his eyes down the road before them. Worry deepened the shadows under his eyes as he spoke. "We have to be."

Chapter 15

The heat of the day made drying clothes cling. Even in the shade the heat was a weight to drag with each forward step. The sun melted down from its zenith, dripping like honey through the gaps in the leaves. The world took a breath and cooled.

Verenna had been mulling over their path in her head. She tried to picture their route through the countryside to guess the distance home. She could see Canterford and Bronwell laid along a winding line on a map, the coast to the west, but she could not wrap her mind around any of the in between. The monsters drawn in the empty spaces of old charts made more sense than ever now.

"Where's Alma?" Her voice broke the hour long quiet streak, startling the group.

"Farthest West port on the coast. Why?" Darius grumbled.

"Trying to think how far we've come. And you mentioned it at the roadblock."

"Still don't know how you guessed that by the way," the doctor said and shot a glance at Mortimer.

The old man shrugged. "It's the port you came through. Thought if you were going to lie about where we'd come from you'd make it where you came from."

"You're from there?"

"I am absolutely not *from* there. But that is how I got here. Brought as a child on a ship to Alma. I lived there for a time."

"What's it like?"

"Like any other port. I'd rather not discuss it." Darius growled and unrolled the map once more. He sped up to head the group.

"Fine," Verenna huffed and swatted a fly away from her arm. The edge of her sleeve had gone brown with drying blood. Summoning a considerable amount of courage, she rolled it up for a look at her injury. The cuts from the tree were surprisingly free of clots and deeper than they'd seemed when she'd come by them. The long slender shape of the slices reminded her of the spindly fingers of the creature from her dream. They seemed to wrap her arm in a similar vine-like pattern. A tremor ran the length of her and she covered the gashes again.

"Mortimer?" she said in a hushed voice, stooping down to speak with him as he walked beside the horse.

"Yes?" he answered. His tone matched her quiet so that the other two would not hear.

"Can a demon- can they- come out of dreams?"

"No. But they can sometimes speak through them. Why?"

"It's just, I had a dream the other night that something came into the carriage while I was sleeping. It had hands that grew like vines. It choked me, crushed me, I couldn't breathe at all. Then it told me it could see me. Told me to come to Bronwell. To come fight. And lose."

Mortimer stopped walking as soon as her last words reached him. "You've been sent a message."

"By who?" Verenna whispered.

The old man scanned their surroundings before speaking low, "It's best not to say. What else did it tell you?"

"That was it really. It laughed. What do you mean it's best not to say?"

Mortimer looked up into her face with some mixture of heartbreak and desperation. But before she could press him for more information Darius interrupted them.

"Keep up! We're making good time. We should be there in a

mile or so," he called back.

Mortimer tugged at the reins and led the horse onward, leaving Verenna to her imagination.

Night would be upon them soon. True night, with only a wink of a moon left for light, if that. The thought of it turned every dip of the men's shoulders into a prowling roll. They'd be hungry. So would the wolves. Not to mention whatever else waited for the cover of dark.

"I hear something. Maybe we're closer than you think," Mortimer called in answer.

"Can't be. We only just passed this bend here."

"I could have sworn."

"What did you hear?" Verenna clutched the horse's mane tighter, ducking and gazing into the dim of encroaching evening.

"Don't humor him. You'll make it worse."

Mortimer let the subject go, though he kept his head up and alert, scanning the woods on either side of the road. Verenna followed suit. She'd almost reassured herself when the old man protested again.

"No. I hear something."

Fabien stopped to listen. "The breeze picked up. Might be that. At least, I can't hear anything else. Plus, there's still plenty of light. We shouldn't have to worry about demons for at least another hour," he offered.

The horse perked its ears and stared off into the trees. Verenna gripped the beast's sides with her thighs, ready to gallop should something appear. "Are you sure?" she squeaked.

"I mean, as sure as I can be." Fabien's honesty did nothing to comfort her.

"Don't you think we should be taking this a little more seriously? What if something's following us?"

"Speed up, then. No time to stop and investigate. If we look for trouble, we'll find it. We have to focus on getting out of the woods and into the city. We'll need real shelter tonight. Not just camp. Now…" Darius did not finish. He let the map sink to his side.

"Well? What? For god's sake, you can't just stop there." Verenna searched wildly for the cause of his silence. Looking ahead, she found it.

The group hurried to join him at a gap in the trees. The forest parted to reveal a vast stretch of floodplain glimmering gold in the dying light. The titanic walls of Bronwell erupted from it, ending the expanse in a gray line of stone. Even at such a distance Verenna could see the front gates. She'd heard stories that it had taken a hundred oaks to build each one.

She squinted. They hung open; lolling, lifeless jaws. And from them issued a smell that was at once sweet and putrescent. Sugar and rot. Verenna coughed and covered her nose only to find the scent on her tongue. She spat to try and rid herself of the taste. "What is that?"

"Death," Mortimer whispered. "We can't stay here." His warning went unheard as the men burst into bickering.

"We're supposed to be safe there? Look at it," Fabien grumbled and pointed to the citadel. But the doctor would not stand for complaints.

"I am looking at it. Clearly, there is something wrong. I got us out of the woods, didn't I?"

"Aye, and brought us here."

"So sorry. While I was distracted by Hunters, Hell Hounds and having all of my supplies washed away but a damned river demon, I must have forgotten to predict the future and see this problem coming."

"We need to move. I can hear something," Mortimer insisted.

"Quit, old man," Darius growled. "There's no time. Sun's

almost down. We've got to think."

"I'll make a fire. We'll need it for wolves."

The doctor immediately shot down the suggestion. "No fire. Our bigger concern is demons."

"The crickets have stopped," Mortimer could no longer hide his panic. Neither of the other seemed to notice. Verenna reached down for a handful of the old man's coat, breathless and wide eyed with speechless searching.

"What would you have us do then?" Fabien shouted.

"Shut up, is what I'd have you do. Keep your voice down," Darius snarled back.

"You know what? Give me that map. You got us into this, I'm getting us out. If Bronwell isn't safe there's got to be somewhere else around."

Fabien made a grab for the chart but Darius snatched it out of the way. "Over my dead body."

"Yeah? I'll see what I can do."

Verenna held tight as the horse stomped its unrest. Gazing back the way they'd come she saw something pass across the trail. "Look! There!"

A swish and thud, and Mortimer crumpled to his knees with an arrow through his shoulder. His groan silenced Fabien and Darius as another arrow struck at their feet. The horse reared. Verenna clung for her life, just managing to reach the swinging reins and hold the animal back from bolting. Another whizzing sound and red sprang from a graze mark across her knuckles. Another swish. She gasped as a searing pain wracked one side of her head. She clapped a hand to her ear to find a small chunk of it missing, a warm cascade of blood rushing down her neck.

"Don't shoot! Don't!" Darius held up his hands, circling to see where the attack came from. He wandered too close to the trees. A figure in dark rags leapt out, threw a burlap bag over his head and dragged him into the shadows. Another made an attempt on Fabien but he ducked and swung his club, striking the figure square in the stomach and throwing him off the road like a doll. Two more appeared behind him. Verenna screamed a warning but not before they'd seized his arms and knocked the club from his hand. By then the first attacker had recovered enough to throw a bag over the young man's head. Fabien landed a solid kick to the stranger's groin.

Mortimer had been overcome by another ragged figure, hauling him across the scraping, rocky dirt towards the bushes.

Verenna dug her heels into the horse's side, spurring it into a run. A hand caught her leg and brought her to the ground. All the air fled her lungs. She gasped like a fish for more but none came. Hooded forms stooped over her, one with a blade. She stretched to claw the hidden face, but before she could uncover it or draw blood, the figure flipped the blade and struck her with the hilt, plummeting her into nothingness.

❧

Pounding rippled Verenna's vision as she tried to get her eyelids apart. She could feel a muddy line going down the side of her face that she knew must be dried blood from her searing, arrow clipped ear. The smell of a hearth fire, cooking, earth and the dull scent of a shuttered house crept in, as well as the sensation of chafing rope around her wrists and arms. She was bound to something warm.

"Verenna?" Fabien's voice hushed behind her.

"What's going on?"

"Quiet," a low voice instructed.

Managing to crack an eye, the girl took a look around them. Human shapes lined walls made orange by firelight. As her focus returned, she found an unkempt gathering of men, women and children. Some had matching sets of crooked noses and stuck out ears marking them as family. Perhaps forty of them, all with dark, wild hair. Weapons leaned against the walls. Mostly farm tools and branches shaped into spears or clubs. The room seemed half pub, half parlor, with homemade tables and chairs crowded around a hearth and casks of ale stacked against the back wall behind a bar.

"I don't care about your names. No one comes here. Why have you?" a voice crooned, soft yet angry.

Verenna found Darius sitting across a table from a woman with fierce, dark eyes. She tapped her fingers on the wood, taking him in.

"I've been telling you for half an hour. I'm a doctor. We came to find the source of the disease. To stop it. And help whoever we can on the way."

The room chuckled.

"You have to believe me."

Smirking, the woman settled back in her seat. "I don't have to believe anything. These days people are out for themselves. They have to be. You could be anyone. No one." She took a knife from her belt and whittled the point under a nail to clean out the dark earth captured there. "If you are what you say, what makes you think you can stop all this, hm? It's taken three fourths of our people already. I count only four of you."

Darius swallowed and struggled for words. "I...I'm sorry to hear."

The woman's arm arched up and slammed a knife into the table between them. "I don't want your apologies. I want you to tell me the truth and help my people, or I want you to die. I'm just fine with either."

"I can treat them. I can make your people well."

"You say that so easily. That's why I don't believe you. If you had a chance in Hell of stopping this you'd know by now that it's not a disease, it's spirits. How can you heal that? The woods are infested with them at night. They get inside, eat you from the inside out. A family burned to death in their home rather than face them trying to escape. If you understood enough to help, you wouldn't offer us doctoring. You'd have a way to get rid of the spirits. Unless you can tell me that, I fail to see the use in you."

Eyes down, Darius sat speechless as the woman leaned in close over her knife.

"Know what happened to the last travelers who didn't make themselves useful? Bait. Tied up far from us to draw the spirits away. I'll tell you, it works. Gets to where you don't even mind the screaming. Makes me smile, in fact. Because it's not someone I know." The woman threw her pitiless gaze over Fabien and Verenna before settling on Mortimer, tied up alone a few feet away. "The old man. Take him and tie him."

"Wait!" Verenna heard herself shout as two men swooped in and took hold of Mortimer by his bindings They dragged him effortlessly towards the door. He grimaced as the ropes pulled his wounded shoulder. "Stop! We know about the spirits! We've escaped them before. We've made it all the way from Canterford alive."

The woman held up her hand. Verenna couldn't see the men over her shoulder, but the dragging noises halted at once. Pointing to the girl the woman gestured her towards a chair. Before so much as a sound could be made, the cords binding her to Fabien fell away, and Darius was shoved out of the chair to make way for her. Her head throbbed and spun as two sets of hands raised her from the floor into the seat.

"And what would you know about all of this?" the woman inquired.

"I know that the spirits like fire. They think the glow is a soul and they go to it instead. Candles are just as effective as people for distracting them." Verenna let the words tumble from her. Anything to keep the door closed with Mortimer inside. She could see Darius shaking his head but ignored his warning.

"And?"

"And sage. Burn sage if you have it. A lot of it."

"Anything else?"

"He really is a doctor. A good one. I was stabbed. I died. And he brought me back to life."

"Well," the woman stood and sauntered around the table to sit before her. She leaned in as if Verenna were a child. "What's to stop us getting rid of you now we know your secrets?"

Verenna suddenly understood Darius's warning. She hadn't thought so far ahead. Her hands went wet and clammy. She might have destroyed their only leverage. The time for talk was closing like a noose. With nothing else to say she blurted the only other impressive thing she could think of.

"You can't. They can't die."

The words wiped the room of noise. Even the children stopped playing.

"That so?"

"Yes. If anyone can help, wouldn't it be someone immune to the problem?"

The woman stalked from behind the table. She walked a measured pace around her prisoners, stopping in front of Fabien. She crouched and tousled his hair. It shone hay blond against the deep of her skin. "Seems like the perfect solution. If you're telling the truth."

Her blade plunged to the hilt into Fabien's chest. Verenna's shriek drowned under his cries. He wilted onto the floor and curled on his side groaning.

The woman stood and tugged her knife free, swaggering back to her desk with a disturbing nonchalance. "We'll see how right you are in a few minutes."

"Good God, there are children here!" Darius shouted, aghast at what the tiny watching faces had witnessed.

"You think this is the worst they've seen? They need to know there is someone left to protect them, and I'm here to do just that. Now if your friend dies, and he will, that means you lied to me. And if you lied to me, that means you're next."

"She's not next," Fabien croaked from the floor. He rolled to his back. The gash in his chest had stopped bleeding. The skin at the edges had already begun knitting itself back together. Gasps and clattering overtook the room as people jostled to get their families farther away from the incomprehensible sight.

The woman too had jumped back in shock, but it took only seconds for her to start barking orders.

"Cut them loose. All of them. Now! Bring water and bandages." The group scrambled to comply.

With a quick clip of a knife the ropes fell away from Verenna's wrists and knees, leaving her to massage the life back into her limbs. Fabien grunted in pain as a few rushed forward and sat him upright. He pressed his chin to his chest in an effort to assess the damage. Swearing he looked to Verenna.

"Darling, never just say someone's immortal. People tend to want to test it."

"I'm so sorry." Her voice wavered in vomitus horror as the last trails of blood slid down his torso. She could see the pain in his clenched jaw.

"Well meant but... I'm just going to be right here for a bit," he lowered himself haltingly back to the floor.

The woman turned to Darius with an outstretched hand to help him off the ground. He took it as if it might bite him.

"My apologies. We had no idea who you were. Our legends tell us ones like you would come this way in the end times, but it took so long. We thought you wouldn't come. My name is Enra Khal. What are yours?"

"Darius Defoe. These are-"

"Perfectly capable of introducing ourselves. Fabien, Gortheyrn Clan," he grunted from the floor.

"I am glad you've come. And I can't tell you how sorry I am for stabbing you."

"It's certainly unpleasant, but I'll be fine. Can't say I would have done differently if I still had my sword. Just protecting our people."

"Your sword?"

"Aye."

"What did it look like?"

"About half my height, silver hilt twisted into a falcon head, onyx eye."

"What happened to it?"

"The river took it. We got caught up in a flood. It's gone."

Enra nodded solemnly, then slid a hand behind the casks of ale against the wall. "Not anymore." She pulled from the crevice a long object wrapped in burlap. Its heft could be seen in the strain of her arm as she offered it to Fabien where he lay.

"Ordinarily I wouldn't give a guest a blade on the first night, but seeing we meet under special circumstances, it's yours. Consider it a peace offering."

Fabien peeled the fabric away from the falcon head hilt. "More than enough," he uttered, clearing his throat to relieve the tension of oncoming tears.

The woman nodded her respect and looked to Mortimer. "And you are? You look familiar."

"Oh. No. I couldn't be. Mortimer. Just Mortimer."

The woman turned to Verenna next. There were embers in her eyes, a smoldering, covetous belief. "You're the daughter then. From the legends." Her breathlessness seemed entirely out of place after the moments-old death threats. Incredulous expressions spread in every direction until the whole room looked on in awe. "I speak for everyone when I say we are so thankful to finally meet you. If I may make a more formal introduction," the woman took a knee before Verenna. "I am Enra Larine Khal, leader of the Sarzen. What is your name?"

She took Verenna's hand, clutching it as if she'd held some precious shell. Timid from the rapt attention of the room, the girl smiled weakly. "Erm, Verenna Dellins. If I'm honest, not really sure what you're thanking me for."

"For turning up. You're the answer to most of our prayers these days. When all else fails, we still have our legends. But, more of that later. First, medical supplies for the doctor. You'll probably want to patch up your friends. Adrinée, get the doctor whatever he requires. And someone get the rest of them a drink."

A girl stepped forward and gestured for Darius to follow her to the next room as the three others were helped to the bar. So many hands assisted they nearly floated into the chairs.

Verenna's blood pressure hammered at the inside of her skull as she rose and settled again. Her ears were full with the noise, muffling the commotion of the room with the whooshing throb. If she didn't know better she could have sworn the pulse whispered to her.

"Never touch the stuff," Mortimer protested from somewhere in the jumble of sound.

"You lie, old man. Sit down and have one. You can't tell me you don't want a drink after an arrow to the shoulder. Have you ever drank?"

She heard Fabien's voice as if they were under water. The

words did not make sense.

"I said did you ever drink? Miss?"

She put a hand to her forehead, staring down at the table trying to understand. When the spell broke she found Fabien leaning in close.

"Miss, are you alright?"

"Yeah. I guess. I think it's just the bump on the head. I'd love to know who did it. Give 'em one to match." She glanced around the room at the bustling people. They'd set the tables back in place and returned to their cooking, talking, cleaning, while trying not to gawk.

"No way of knowing. They're buying now, so let's call it the past."

"You're awfully trusting for someone freshly stabbed through the heart."

"I don't have to be trusting. They already tried to kill me and had no luck. It'd be pointless for 'em to try again. Does hurt quite a bit though." He dabbed at the semi-healed gash with his sleeve and flinched. "A lot."

A boy no more than ten took four misshapen cups from a shelf, their wood smooth with use. He filled them from one of the barrels and set them out.

"How'd they get all this ale anyhow? I thought this would be a fishing village." Fabien gestured to the barrels stacked ceiling high against two walls.

"It is, but they also brew ale to sell in the city. If there's still a city." Mortimer grumbled as he cradled his wounded arm. "My guess is this was all meant for Bronwell. But, no one's there to buy it now."

"You're telling me this place makes ale? Once we stop up the hole in my chest I think I'll quite like it here. Can't be all bad, aye boy?"

The child nodded to Fabien and ducked away with the fourth cup sloshing in his hand. Verenna watched him go, though he didn't get far. A man in ragged gray intercepted him, taking the cup. "Little young for that, aren't you? It'll kill ya."

The boy shot one wide eyed look around for anyone else who'd seen, and darted into the next room to hide from punishment. The gray man shook his head and smiled before taking a sip.

He alighted next to Verenna, saying nothing. It gave her time to notice the smell of him. It was strikingly like home. The rose garden and the breeze that carried it through her window, the bakery in the morning, the wet earth scent off the cobbles when it rained. It so possessed her that the next uncontrollable words from her lips were, "You're from Canterford."

"What would give you that idea?" He sipped again without looking at her.

"I don't know, I suppose. Just seemed like it," she lied, unwilling to admit she'd gotten lost in the scent of him.

"Not a bad assumption. It's a nice town."

"It is." She took a deep drink from her cup, filling her mouth faster than she could realize the bitter taste. She nearly spit it out but managed to choke it down under the pressure of watchful strangers. The gray man laughed. The sound of a friend.

"Like I said. It'll kill ya."

Verenna attempted a smile against the will of her flaring nostrils and reeling taste buds.

"Hurt your arm?" he asked.

"Yes, how did you…" A renewed maroon splotch had spread down her sleeve into the cuff of lace at its edge.

"Let's have a look?"

"It isn't pretty."

"Hardly anything is," the man shrugged.

She rolled her sleeve, taking deep breaths as she went to steady herself against the woozy feeling brought on by the thick stink of iron. She shut her eyes as the throbbing in her head stirred up again. Hot and cold flowed through her, making her shiver and sweat at once, sending her mind back to the frigid river.

"Careful with that," the stranger said, bringing her into the present. "Wash it and wrap it. No one here can afford to have you hurt."

"Darius will see about it whether I like it or not. Sir, if you don't mind me asking, how do you all know about the legend? About me?"

"Because people tend to like stories where those who wronged them get what's coming. Back when Bronwell had kings, one of them married a Sarzen woman from across the sea. In time they had children, a son and a daughter.

"Certain nobles did not approve that the heirs to the throne were of mixed origin. So the family was overthrown. Brutally overthrown. The prince survived and was banished from the city with the rest of the Sarzen. He swore revenge. Swore that one day Bronwell would be washed clean of those who betrayed them. He said he'd come back immortal and kill the one who took his family.

"Over generations tales change, though. Stories from travelers get mixed in. Now that hundreds of years have passed, they say the prince will send immortals to wash the city clean. If not the prince himself, his descendants will be undying. Until you showed up faith in that story was fading. It was becoming one of those tales you only believe when it's dark out. But then again, that's a full half of the time, isn't it?" He took a long pull of ale.

Verenna gazed around the room. Prying eyes turned away with quick birdlike reflex to avoid being caught staring. She rested her elbow on the table before her and pinched the bridge of her nose to relieve the merciless pressure knocking between her ears.

"Don't worry about that yet," the gray man's voice rang as if it were inside her head. "Worry about washing that cut out. Keep an eye on it. It could get worse if you let it."

"Thanks," she took another deep breath of the homey scent that hung about the stranger. Memories just beyond the reach of her thoughts told her she must know him. He looked something like the man in the gray suit she'd seen around the abbey. "I know you said you weren't from Canterford, but...didn't I see you in the tower at Falseman Inn?" She looked up to find an empty seat and an untouched cup of ale.

"Verenna?" Mortimer rested a hand on her shoulder. "Who are you talking to?"

"A man. He was just here. He must have gotten up." Even with her hazy vision she could tell the room held no one like him. "I don't know where he's gone."

The old man adjusted his new sling with an anxious hand and called the attention of the other two.

"Something's not right," she heard him whisper to Darius. He knotted the bandages around Fabien's chest and came to examine her.

"She was talking to no one."

"I can hear you and I was not. There was a man sitting there. He must have gone before you looked over."

Darius put a hand across her forehead, but she swatted it off. "What's the matter with you? Didn't you see him? If you're playing with me it's not funny." She could feel the heat of frustration rising to turn her ears red.

"No joke, Miss. No one sat down there. Not even for a second."

"Must be the crack on the head they gave you. I'll have a look at it. You'll need to be kept awake for a few hours until we're sure everything's fine." Darius announced, taking a drink from the fourth cup. In an instant his cheeks bulged and he spat the liquid back into the mug. "What is that?"

"I thought the same thing," Verenna grumbled.

"No, what is *that*?" He pointed to the bottom of the cup and slid it towards them. Two shining spots glimmered through the amber brew.

"Pennies?" Mortimer ventured.

Darius was the first to understand. "Dressed in gray, wasn't he?"

"Yes, why?"

"Damn it. Corvudeus."

"Who?"

"Death. He was here."

"As in he's a person?" Fabien set his cup aside to keep his trembling hands from spilling it.

"No. But he can be. Death can take any form, whatever comforts the dying into following him. He likes to drop by and leave two pennies laying around when someone's about to die. Enough to cross the River Styx. His way of mocking me when he thinks there's nothing I can do to save someone. Bastard thinks he's funny. Fabien, calm yourself, man. He can't take us."

"I know that," Fabien snapped, checking over his shoulder. "Call me superstitious, but I'm just not so keen on meeting Death incarnate."

"He warned me about this. He said it could be trouble." Verenna extended her arm.

"Good God, is that still bleeding? Pass me the rest of the bandages."

"I'm not the one who's going to die, am I?" she asked with a woozy slur in her words.

"Not if he leaves me a thousand of those damned pennies. Now quiet about it, they're coming over."

Enra approached with two of her number toting blankets. "It's not much, but it will have to do for the night. You can have the storage room. The whole lot of us have been sleeping in here at night for protection. This place is easy to defend."

"That's very kind of you. Verenna?" Mortimer's voice seemed a mile away.

The world blurred before her eyes, the same murk as the river. Firelight glinted off the teeth and eyes of everyone in the room, making her squint. Their faces and bodies moved like the reeds had, forming and unforming, nebulous and unraveling. She felt herself begin to float then fall.

She toppled against Fabien. He groaned as she leaned against his injury but he managed to keep her from the floor.

"Is she alright?" Enra rushed.

"She'll be fine. She just needs rest and quiet. Is there any other place we could stay?"

"I saw house on the way in here. Looked abandoned," Mortimer suggested.

"It's not safe. No one goes out at night here. If they make it back in the morning they're sick and dying. The spirits make disease."

"We've got quite an advantage I'd say," Fabien reminded her, tapping his chest.

"It would be better for her out there." Darius's confidence seemed to sooth some of Enra's nerves.

"If you think it's best."

The next thing Verenna knew was the sensation of being lifted and the touch of the night breeze, a cold caress after the heat of the packed room.

"Take this. Light the lantern when you're inside and safe," Enra instructed.

"Of course."

Her head lolled against the silk of Darius' vest, keeping time with the gentle bounce of his step. Two other sets of footsteps sounded close beside. She could not convince her eyes to open, but knew that the other two followed.

"Is that frost in her hair?" Mortimer brushed the cold away from her brow with a hand that felt like fire.

"Shh! They'll hear you."

"She's not alright, is she?" Fabien whispered.

Darius breathed a sigh, "No."

Chapter 16

Verenna vanished into a cold, dark sleep awash with nightmares. Quiet voices wormed through her mind. They tinkered inside her, muttering over their work. A wintery chill stiffened her joints, made her fingers and ears scream for warmth. Each breath she drew started hot at her lips, but chilled to ice water by the time it reached her lungs. When the terrors left her in darkness she thought she might awake in the river again, drowning. Part of her wondered if she'd made it out in the first place.

The dull scent of old timber and smoking sage called her upwards out of the cold. A welcoming heat moved up from her toes to her legs. Her eyelids pulsed. She could feel light just beyond them.

"Ah-ha, it's a straight. Better luck next time old man," Fabien boasted somewhere nearby.

Mortimer grumbled just above the sound of shuffling. "That's just what it was. Luck."

"No, no, no," the young man argued. "I've never known Fortune to favor anyone for longer than a day. It's skill and you know it."

"She's waking up."

Chairs scratched against floorboards as both men rose and rushed to her.

Blinking against the jarring bright of a fire she could make out their furrowed brows and troubled expressions. Verenna parted her lips to ask where they were but only a feeble, cracking noise came out.

"Water," Mortimer commanded.

Fabien hurried to a carafe in the corner as Mortimer took a seat on the bed. "Just relax. Don't try to talk. We're in a cabin at the edge of the Sarzen village. I don't know how much you remember, but we're safe here. At least now we are."

Fabien extended a sloshing cup to her. She went to reach for it but the weight of the blankets proved too much. Her hand hardly moved despite her strain.

"Give it here," Mortimer took the cup and lifted her head to feed her a sip.

She barely managed to choke it down without coughing. As soon as she could gulp air she tried words again. "What...happened?" The sound raked her throat.

Both men shifted awkwardly, glancing at each other to explain. Finally Fabien took up the tale. "At the river. Those things that took hold of you. One of them must have come in contact with that cut you've got on your arm and made you sick. That's the best guess we've got."

Verenna shivered both at the memory and the unbearable cold that lay siege to her bones. It made the warmth of Mortimer's hand against her cheek burn like a brand. She turned her head away and shut her eyes as the voices rose up again. Something whispered right behind her ear though she could not make out what it said.

"Rest up. We'll be right here if you need anything." Mortimer's hand slid away and with it all semblance of time. The next hours could have been days or just a matter of minutes. It was impossible to tell. Eventually night sealed up the cracks in the shutters, caging the scampering firelight. The door to the cabin came open, appearing as a black hole in the wall through the mirage of fever. A figure stepped inside.

"Good God, these people," he sighed, shutting the door with a clap.

"Unhappy customers?" Fabien asked.

"No. They love me. That's the problem. Everyone wants to be seen. And of course, examinations need good lighting, which means sitting near windows, which means sunlight. It's murder. I will say, though, I didn't know a group could be this injured and sick and still hold out. Especially this close to Bronwell." He lowered himself into a decaying armchair next to Verenna's bed with a groan. "The sooner we have the ingredients for sun serum the better."

"I still can't find silver nettle. It's one of the only things we still need," Mortimer pointed to a collection of herbs on the table.

"Keep looking," Darius let out an exhausted sign. "If the hunters track us down we'll have to run, whatever time of day or night it is."

"We stand a chance fighting now that I have my sword back." Fabien offered.

Darius stared into the fire. His words were more for himself than the others. "Maybe. We'll have to try anyway. If they find us, we'll send the girl off on the horse. Hold them off while she rides. If she can ride by then...How is she?"

Verenna tried answering, but it came out as a wheeze too soft for the men to hear.

"She woke up once. Asked what happened. Fabien tried to explain, but there's no telling if she understood. She's weak. It's getting worse."

Darius let out a breath and put his head in his hands. The crackling fire lent an empty cheer to the room. The space had been hollowed by unspoken dread between them.

"You better hope this turns out," Fabien settled back in his seat snapping the cards as he shuffled for the next round.

"Is that a threat?" Darius growled.

"I'm just saying, you're the doctor. If she doesn't get well it's certainly not our fault."

Darius burst out of his chair and stormed towards the table. "If you don't think I'm trying…"

"I think you're not trying hard enough." Fabien stood and braced for a fight. "You spend all your time on these strangers when she obviously needs you more."

"I can't be everywhere at once," Darius fumed.

"Well, be where it counts."

"This is the only safe shelter for who knows how many miles. If I don't earn our keep we lose it. And I don't see you jumping to help."

"And how does this help her?" Mortimer thundered to put a halt to the row. "Darius, don't you think you should change her bandages? Fabien, go hunt. The moon is nearly dark. It's no good having the two of you cooped up in here hungry. Go."

Neither moved, staring as if they could see the brawl play out on the surface of each other's eyes. Darius broke the standoff.

"I've got better things to do."

"Like your job?"

"Leave," Mortimer gave Fabien a push towards the exit.

He shouldered his sword, grumbling, and paused halfway out the door. Verenna could feel him looking at her even though her failing vision blurred his face. "Take care of her, and we'll have no problem."

Darius whirled, but Fabien had already dipped into the night. Mortimer shut the door with a sigh. He gathered a bundle of bandages in a bowl and brought them to the doctor.

Verenna felt the heft of the blankets come away from her injured arm and the pull of dried blood as the wrappings were peeled away. The whispering in her mind grew louder. It seemed the voices in her head now poured forth from the opening in her flesh. Even in her thin field of vision, the wound looked angry, her arm wet with blood and seepage. She winced as a cold rush of water poured over the injury. Somewhere her body found the strength to moan.

"Almost over," Darius' voice broke through the hubbub of murmurs, scattering them for a single peaceful moment. He bound it again with clean cloth and replaced it under the blanket. Though as far as she could tell, she produced no body heat to warm the covers.

"Well?" Mortimer's words came breathless with worry.

"She's colder. Gone completely white. Given, there isn't far to go but...makes those freckles stand out like ants."

"Think she'll see morning?"

"With luck."

Mortimer scoffed, "Luck doesn't last that long."

℘

The gray morning came hushed with rain. Verenna blinked at the ashen line of daylight peeking under the door. Her vision had cleared somewhat overnight. The cold and the pain of her arm were now only a skin-deep buzzing.

Mortimer curled against sacks of grain in one corner. Fabien had his boots on the table, arms crossed, head drooping. Even Darius had his head thrown back, mouth open, letting out a faint snore in the rundown armchair.

Verenna smiled and spoke, this time without the clawing feeling in her neck. "I thought you lot didn't need much sleep."

Mortimer startled and sat up. His face was drawn and covered with wisps of incoming facial hair, the bags beneath his eyes heavy with what looked like grief. He pushed his hair from his eyes. It seemed longer than she remembered it. He gazed at the bed but made no answer.

"I'm up! Glad to see me?" she tried again, but he did not hear.

Rising, he came and reached to lay a hand across her forehead. At the last moment he jerked his hand away, dashing to Darius to shake him awake.

"Her eyes, there's something wrong."

The doctor half stumbled, half crawled to her side, weariness replaced by alarm as soon as he saw her face.

"What's going on? Are you even listening to me?" She went to sit up. Nothing happened.

Fabien had woken with the commotion and joined them. "What is that? What's happening to her?"

"Go get rocks. Throw them in the fire. We need to get her warm again." Darius had hardly finished the command before Fabien sprinted out into the rain to do as he said.

"Verenna can you hear me?" Mortimer looked on the edge of tears saying it.

"Yes of course I can! I'm awake! Listen, you idiots!" No response came. Darius tucked the blankets tight around her. "I'm not cold anymore. Stop!" She felt herself kicking but her legs would not move. She demanded motion from them, straining to force her arms loose from the sheets.

"Frost," the old man said, sweeping his fingers across her hairline and showing Darius the glittering crystals. "And her tears are black."

Fabien burst into the cabin with an armful of stones, tossing them into the fire so that the logs buckled and crashed, letting out a plume of sparks. "I'll get more wood. Is she breathing?"

"I can't tell."

"You've been a healer for centuries and you can't tell?!"

"Firewood," Mortimer barked. The young man ducked outside

again.

Verenna looked on in horror as they tried to bring the life back to her limbs. The stones were pulled from the fire, wrapped, and stacked beneath her blankets. She felt none of them, even as she watched them placed.

Darius held out his other hand to Mortimer. "That dagger you carry with you. Give it here."

"What are you going to do?"

"Just give it here!"

Mortimer slid the blade from its sheath. It seemed new and bright and alive, even in the dark of the cabin. Darius snatched it and held silver blade an inch from Verenna's lips. "Steam. She's still breathing, but barely. Get more of those stones near her. We've got to keep what little heat she has left."

Mortimer replaced the blade in its sheath. "They're all in the bed already."

"We'll send Fabien out for more as soon as he's back. Help me pull the bed closer to the fire."

Wood groaned against wood as they slid the bed along the floorboards. Verenna's head fell to one side, giving her a glimpse of the rest of the room. There was something in the corner, a coagulating mass of smoke and dust motes. She tried to point, but her arm remained limp and useless under the covers.

The door banged open and Fabien hurried through it, soaking from the rain with an armful of firewood. Panting, he dashed to the hearth and began stacking the logs inside, oblivious to the formation across the room.

"Took you long enough. Get more stones," Darius instructed.

"Already?"

"Yes. She's dying."

"Don't say that," Mortimer wailed and stood to pace.

Verenna shrieked inside her head, hoping it might propel some warning from her lips about the presence in the corner. Still, her demands would not reach her body. The creature grew darker, denser, larger until the oddity finally caught Mortimer's eye.

"There!" he shouted and pulled his knife.

Fabien took up his sword from the hearth while Darius shielded Verenna.

"No need." The words reverberated through the room, familiar, as if she'd been hearing them her whole life. The captivating sound quelled their panic as the dust and darkness settled into the shape of a face and body, resting lightly in the corner chair.

The figure rose and the dust fell away, sliding off like sand to reveal a strikingly tall, lean man with sleek hair and a dapper gray suit. If it weren't for his immaculate grooming, Verenna would have guessed he was the man she'd seen the night they arrived.

"I know you. How?" Mortimer breathed in awe.

The stranger's head turned, gliding on his shoulders. "Through your sister."

Mortimer's jaw dropped and his knife hit the ground. Fabien loosened his grip on his sword as the tension drained from his arm. "I've seen you too. But that was…"

"The last battle you saw with that sword. About eight hundred years ago, if I remember. You know me. All of you do."

Verenna felt a name on the tip of her tongue, a sound just beyond memory. Each word the man spoke was soft with comfort, the shush of wheat. She trusted his voice the way she'd trusted the warmth of afternoon calling her to sleep.

Darius was not as impressed. "So we do," the words came through clenched teeth and a sour smile.

"It's nice to see you, doctor. It's been quite some time."

"It has."

"I suppose it upsets you to see me."

"Oh no, I'm honored that Death would stop by to check in on us. What's the occasion? No one here is dying."

"Death," the man let out a single huff of laughter. "I think we've known each other long enough for you to call me Corvudeus. Even Corvus if you like."

"Little arrogant calling oneself Raven God, isn't it? You're not a god, you're a clean-up crew."

The man's body stretched like shadows at sundown, swelling in height until his shoulders met the ceiling. He loomed over the four of them. "I said we were familiar. I did not say friends. Let's not overstep any boundaries. You have something that is mine."

"And what would that be? We can't die. Unless you've found a way to sew up that loophole you created with the Merlin girls."

Corvudeus expanded again, taking up nearly half the cabin. Mortimer and Fabien stumbled back to make room, their jaws slack in disbelief. Verenna wanted desperately to join them, to hide from the otherworldly anger that seethed below the surface of the man's placid face. Even Darius leaned away, still careful to keep himself between the newcomer and Verenna.

"I am aware of the mishap," Corvus explained. "I signed away my free will because of it. That makes this situation non-negotiable. I'm here for the girl." His form shrank as he calmed until his back no longer slouched against the ceiling.

Verenna worked furiously to undo whatever kept her body from the commands of her mind. Her eyelids were ten ton weights and each lip a mountain to move. Still she fought. She must speak.

"No. Please," Mortimer rushed forward to plead. "She's so young. She's all we've got to put things right. We'll do anything. I'll do anything."

"It may not seem fair but this is how it has to be. She's not your sister, Mortimer. Saving her will not change the past."

Corvus settled a hand on Mortimer's shoulder and looked long into his face. "She comes with me."

Mortimer crumpled to the floor, his head in his hands, rocking. Verenna wanted to reach for him, to help him stand, to stop his gasping sobs, to tell him she was still there, that she wasn't going. But tethered in her own immobile body she could do nothing.

Fabien pulled Mortimer up from the floor and seated him on the end of the bed before turning to Corvus. "I'll go instead."

"It's a valiant offer, but you don't really have a life to give. Even if I were still allowed to take bribes, it's hardly a balanced trade."

"Then you have my services." Fabien drew his sword, kneeling to offer the glinting falcon hilt. "You will have a thousand lives for hers. Mortal lives. Real ones. I swear to you. We need her."

"My boy, I am bound by the Laws of Neutrality now. Gods, Forces, Powers That Be, we can't strike deals anymore. That's the sort of thing that lead to the creation of your kind. You're a world of trouble we can't afford to repeat."

"Our kind was your mistake. Why should we have to pay for that?" Darius spat.

Corvudeus craned his elegant neck to an abnormal length to stare directly down into the doctor's raging face. "Oh trust me when I say I'd erase you if I could. You have no room to ask for favors. Not then, not now."

No one dared speak. Time seemed to lock up around them, constricting the air, leaving no room for breathing. "You can put that sword away, boy. I do not want one thousand lives. I'm here for the girl. She's suffering, you know. It's time for that to end. You forget in your age that mortals are not meant to last. They share the fate of smoke. They vanish when their fire burns out. I'm sorry, but I cannot change it."

"Bullshit," Darius snarled again. "You're bloodthirsty. Wars, sickness, it all boils down to you in the end. I've lived long enough to see that. Don't pretend you give a damn about anyone's suffering."

"I am only one of four, doctor. Malagrir brings famine. Marhasim brings war. Souris brings disease. My task is simply to sort out the aftermath. I believe you called it 'clean up'? What does that make you, I wonder. You take those who should be mine and keep them on this plain far longer than my ledgers dictate. I can see your meddling in medicine in my books. A trail of unbalanced numbers. You steal from me."

"No one can take anything that truly belongs to Death. He hasn't stolen anything," Mortimer cried in the doctor's defense.

"Debatable. That doesn't change the fact that the girl must come with me. If she doesn't it will upset every list I've got. She's not just anyone. If I leave her in this realm everything will change and it may not be for the better. If she survives, there will be war. I guarantee you." Death's voice grew as he spoke, filling the whole room with palpable frustration. "Do you think I want that? I am tired of riding. Endlessly, endlessly, riding. No one wants to see the other Horsemen halted more than I do. There is no rest for me until they're stopped. They destroy the balance of my records, upend natural order. All because of these mortals and their mistakes; filth, distrust, greed, war…" Corvus trailed off shaking his head. "When mankind's darker natures run rampant, that's what allows the Horsemen to rise. And I come dragging along after." He sighed and the entire room cooled.

Fabien pointed back to the bed where Verenna lay with desperation etched across his face. "Then how can you take her? She's the one supposed to stop the other three Horsemen. If you want to put an end to this you can't take her away!"

"As much as I want things to return to balance, I will not go against my ledgers. That's how your kind was created. Imbalance incarnate. Life without death. Abominations. If my books say she comes with me, the girl will come with me.

Exhaustion set upon Verenna's thoughts. Still no words. No motion. It was getting harder and harder to feel the bed beneath her.

Death reached a slim arm upwards and held out an open hand. Again the dust motes turned to sliding sand that streamed through his fingers, leaving a massive book in his palm. He threw it open. "Here. Her name."

In swirling red ink the page condemned her, listed with a thousand others passing that hour. She didn't want to go back to the cold, feeble house that her body had become, to the aches and whispers in her head. The letters of her name scrolled across that parchment said she'd never have to.

Corvus flipped forward through the pages, each painted with countless names. He stopped and let his thin finger run the length of the paper.

"And here, ten thousand more. Perhaps now you understand why I have no use for your offer of a thousand lives. I'll have ten times the number in a year or so."

"What if we refuse?" Darius smarted.

"Makes no difference to me. Your friend has almost left her body already." He turned and looked directly at Verenna. Not at her withering form, but into her mind. She felt a pull in her chest, drawing her towards him, a fish on a line, slowly reeled out of the physical.

"But she's got your protection," Mortimer blurted frantically. "All the heirs of Merlin are only children. They have Death's protection until they have a child of their own. If she dies there will be no heir."

"My protection will return to her mother. She is still young enough to produce another child. Perhaps even well enough to serve as the heir herself," Corvudeus corrected.

Fabien pointed to the book with a shaking hand. "But her mother's name… it's there."

Dread swept through Verenna. She felt as if her eyes overflowed with tears though she could not feel the wet against her cheeks.

Death tugged the line he'd cast again, shaking her out of what small grip on life she had left. Verenna tried to cling to the blankets as she felt herself lifted from her body. She wanted life. Even in her sickly form, if she went on living there would be a chance at getting home, perhaps a chance to see her mother again, or save her. She might see the rose garden and the green door, might watch the smoke from the inn rise against the clouds, smell her father's tobacco or her mother's perfume. Each instant she drifted farther from it all.

"Her mother is weak or ill more days than not," Darius berated. "She'd never have made it even this far with everything we've had to face, much less give birth to another healthy child. If we wait for that all Hell will have time to crawl onto earth and start consuming our plane. I am not about to sit out the rest of my immortality watching that happen."

"It's a gamble, yes. But it's in my ledger. I'm afraid there's nothing you can do."

"Oh, there is." The doctor's voice dropped to a rasping whisper. "I'll make her one of us."

"Don't test me, Darius," Corvudeus hissed. Again he grew, rapid and wild like a vine, consuming half the cabin with his mass.

"Don't come any closer." Darius held out a warning hand. "You move and I'll do it. I'll bite her again. I'm sure you saw in your book that I've done it before to save her life. This time will turn her."

"You would dare defy me?" Death howled.

Inside Verenna clambered to speak. A life as one of them was no better than death. Eternity could not be worth watching her family wither from a distance, living as an outcast while all the things she thought beautiful about the world died out around her. She tried to press herself away from her body in an attempt to hurry towards oblivion before the choice was made for her.

"Darius, you can't," Mortimer insisted throwing himself between the doctor and the girl, his tears spattering the wool of the blanket. "She won't be the same. No one's ever the same. You don't know what will happen."

"Mortimer's right," Fabien urged. "Her being alive and mortal is the only thing stopping all Hell coming up to meet us. There's no way to know what will happen if you bite her. The whole Prophecy could come crashing in on us right now."

Darius snarled, "Either that or it buys us time. If we don't, this world ends and you know it."

Verenna saw Fabien's expression shift from defiance to sorrow. A solemn nod and she no longer had his protection. She fought to rend herself from life before they could pull her back.

"You have no idea what you're doing to this world!" Corvudeus boomed and reached an ever-expanding hand for Darius.

"I'll take the odds." The doctor tore Mortimer from the girl's empty form, tossing him to Fabien for restraint. Before Death could grasp him, Verenna felt two tiny pins of pain pierce her neck. Sensation gushed through them, infusing her world with all the senses that had abandoned her. She had weight again, and the distant feeling of arms and legs.

Then the cold returned, biting her everywhere. It sent burning spines through her veins, her whole body searing with sudden warmth. She could smell the metal of her own blood. The voices that had whispered to her were sent shrieking from their champers in her mind. She followed them, violently thrown back to life.

Gasping and coughing she met Darius's gaze, his mouth still

red with her blood. Behind him loomed Death. Holding aloft his book he clenched his fist and let the sand it became rush through his fingers.

"Get gone then," Darius growled over his shoulder.

Corvudeus struck at him like a viper. He wrapped Darius's neck entirely with a single hand. He choked as he tried pry it from this throat. Stooping his ten-foot form to meet the doctor face to face, Corvus spoke with a soft venom. "I would love nothing more than to rip you out of life. Put you where you belong, where everyone belongs after two hundred years. I cannot. But know this. Your sad bunch here has only made it this far because of my protection. And I renounce it. Over her, and especially over you. See what you can manage without my cooperation. I am done with you."

He released Darius with a shove, knocking him to the ground. Corvudeus shrank like draining water until he was just higher than the door frame. He moved to go but Mortimer broke free of Fabien and scrambled to block his path.

"Don't renounce her. It's our fault. She doesn't want this. She needs your protection."

"Oh? Because it seems you think you can keep her safer than I can. We'll see, won't we?"

Corvudeus reached out a hand. This time he landed it on Mortimer's chest. At once the old man clutched at his heart and crumbled to the ground.

Then he rounded on Fabien, pointing and freezing him on the spot before he could move to help Mortimer. "Keep that blade sharp, boy. Heaven help you now." With that he ducked and vanished through the door. Fabien fell to the floor gasping as Death's hold released him. He struggled up to follow but halted in the doorway, looking around wildly. Corvus had already gone. He slammed to door closed. Fabien sank down with his back against the boards and his head in his hands.

Darius peeled himself up from the ground with the help of the bedpost. "Doesn't seem the world's ended."

Mortimer rolled to his back but kept a hand over his heart. "Never mind that. How's our girl?" he panted, his brow still furrowed with the pain in his chest. Forcing himself to his feet, Mortimer shuffled to her side.

Verenna stared blankly at the ceiling. Perhaps it had all been a dream, whispered to her by the voices that had taken up residence inside her skull. But they had gone. She was silent inside, alone again with her own mind.

The touch of Mortimer's hand on her shoulder made her wince. "Verenna? Can you hear me, dear? How are you?" Despite the kindness of the old man's coaxing she did not answer. It felt as if it would take years to sort out what to say.

Two more shadows fell across her bed as Fabien and Darius joined him. She winced again as Fabien's heavy hand found hers.

"Miss? It's over now," he offered. "It's just us."

"Verenna, we need you to speak. We need to know you're there. You're safe now." Darius's worry was the most striking of all. It disgusted her that such concern could come from a mouth still smeared with her blood.

"When was the first time you bit me?" She rasped, her copper gaze finding the doctor.

"Is that really a question for now?"

"You wanted talk. When did you do this before?"

Darius stared back blankly, mouth forming words without sound. Fabien shifted and fiddled with the rough edge of the top most blanket guilty like a child. Mortimer let out a single nervous hum and went to fetch water from the opposite side of the room.

"You're tired. You should rest," Darius began tucking her in. Verenna took hold of the blanket from beneath and stopped him.

"No. When?"

Mortimer returned with the water but she pushed it away, sloping half the cup onto the floorboards.

"The night you left home," Darius answered with his eyes down.

"I was chased," she croaked against her dry throat.

"The night you were chased out of your home, you crossed paths with a man in the street. He came after you. He caught up to you, and he stabbed you. You were dying on the ground. The only choice I had was to bite you." The doctor wrung his hands, his words coming fast.

"The first bite doesn't change a person. It just gives a human our ability to heal for a time. I didn't think I'd have to do it again. You would have died right there if I hadn't. Verenna, I was just trying to save you."

Verenna could feel her eyes growing glassy with tears. Her ire colored her ears blushing red. "You knew it wasn't the first time. You knew what would happen to me with the second bite."

"I did." He nodded, his voice the meekest she'd heard it yet.

"And you did it anyway? You did it and now I won't ever go home."

"You might still," Fabien encouraged and went to adjust her pillow.

"Don't touch me!" She crowed and fell into a fit of coughs she feared might break a rib. She took the offer of water from Mortimer for the sole purpose of continuing her tirade. "Fabien, how could you help him. Mortimer was going to stop him biting me. You kept him back."

"I didn't think-"

"No! You didn't! Might as well have done it yourself."

She slapped the cup that Mortimer held to the floor as hard as her newly mobile arm would allow. She wanted to hear something shatter, to hear something come apart irreplaceably, to be lost forever. Alas, the cup was wooden, and yielded only a hollow clacking and the wash of spilling water.

"None of this had to happen! Where was the guard?"

"I don't know what you mean," Darius muttered.

"I mean Mortimer. You said it in the tower. That you were the one sent to guard my house. If you were really watching to keep me safe, why didn't you stop the man who ran after me? Why didn't you keep him from hurting me? Darius wouldn't have had to bite me the first time if, if you'd just...Where were you?" Verenna seethed through clenched teeth. She struggled to prop herself up on one elbow. She wanted to look right into his face when he answered her, but the old man refused to meet her eyes.

The doctor gathered a reply, but a sharp word halted him.

"Don't," Mortimer whimpered and moved for the corner like a kicked dog. "Don't tell her. Please."

"Don't tell me what?" No one spoke, but the truth had come to close to the surface to keep it from her. "Don't tell me what?!" she raged against her cracking voice.

The cabin went dead of sound, allowing the wash of the rain to murmur what must be the only answer. The quiet allowed memory to seep back in. The old man carried a knife. The silver dart of metal that had freed her from the river bore an uncanny resemblance to the one that had slid between her ribs that night in the rain. She hadn't thought much of it at the time, but she'd seen him. He had been sleeping in the street when she'd glanced out the window in her mother's room.

Nearly choking on his name she wheezed, "Mortimer?"

He turned away, fixating on the sliver of gray daylight intruding through a crack in the shutters.

"You didn't- did you?"

At once the man burst into pleading. "Please, Verenna,

understand me. I wasn't myself. I never meant to hurt you."

"Why?" Verenna uttered, the word slipping nearly soundless from her lips.

"It was an accident. Things got out of control. It was dark, the creature, I couldn't see."

"It was a full moon," she challenged.

"I know. That's just the thing. I'm sorry," he knelt weeping at the end of her bed.

Verenna fell back onto her pillow and shut her eyes, squeezing the tears from them. They steamed onto her cheeks only to go cold, tracing shivering lines into her hair.

"Get out. All of you!"

The three men rose as if at the close of a funeral. "Verenna, I'm…" Mortimer started.

"Don't you dare say it again. You're not sorry. None of you are. Just leave!" She took up handfuls of blanket though her grip was too weak to crown her knuckles white. She gritted her teeth to restrain an outburst. She couldn't look at them.

From the corner of her eye she watched Fabien put a hand on Mortimer's back and guide him to the porch. The doctor lingered. She could feel in the prickling of her neck that he wanted to say something. She filled her lungs to scream, ready to drown his words if he dared. There was nothing to say that could mend any of it. It took him only a moment to realize as much.

Darius slid from the cabin with no more than the tap of his shoes to announce his departing. The door closed with a moan, leaving her alone with her wrath and the sound of the rain.

Chapter 17

It had been two days since Verenna had spoken a word. Most of her time had been spent brooding on the porch with a cup of broth in her hand. It smelled like a spice market but tasted like nothing; one of the unfortunate side effects of becoming one of them. It was the only notable change so far, though they assured her there would be more.

She had no appetite. Yet the others insisted she eat and wouldn't leave her in peace until she did. They kept saying she'd have to gain enough strength to run if they were discovered. It seemed laughable. She'd mastered at best a hobbling walk that heavily depended on walls for support.

The only things that appealed to her were watching the steam roll from her cup, and glowering at the men every time one of them came in or out of the cabin.

It bothered Mortimer most. He always nodded and said hello, but guilt wouldn't let him look at her long. She liked it that way.

Having a remarkable tolerance for the sun, the old man had been put in charge of gathering herbs from the woods for more sun draught. She'd been assured that as soon as Darius had the potion ready they'd be on their way. Verenna smirked at the irony of their hurry. Now none of them could die, yet there they were trying to rush off somewhere new. There didn't seem to be anywhere worth going anymore. Only to the shade of the sagging porch to watch the day pass by. Her third day in the same spot.

She looked up from her cup for a moment to the tree-sheltered place where Fabien chopped wood. Now and again he'd flick a glance her way, uncomfortable under her blatant glare. His shoulders glistened with work in the glow of late afternoon. But his looks no longer called to her. He'd had a hand in her situation just as much as the others. If she'd kept walking for home without him that night how things might be different. She might not be set on the creaking porch, sipping broth she'd never taste, outside the ramshackle semblance of a building, in the woods beside a dead city serving as a hive for demons. She let herself get lost in the hypnotic swing of Fabien's axe. The steady swish, crack and thud of it, over and over and over. Life would quickly become a nightmare if this was all there was.

Darius hadn't been forgiven either. Luckily, he was out most of the day healing the whole village in exchange for what they'd need to travel. He'd be back when the sun went down, red in the face with sun sickness, his nose burnt and peeling. She felt no twinge of sympathy for him, and certainly didn't bother to hide her staring. She hated him and let him know in every silent way she could; knocking over his cup at the table, locking him out of the cabin, sending blistering glances that would have burnt him up just as well if the sun hadn't gotten to him first. After all, he'd been the one to deliver the bite.

Verenna jumped as the groan of a step brought her back from her thoughts. The doctor had returned and passed without greeting. Sour that she'd missed her chance to glare at him, she tossed the tasteless broth onto the dirt and watched the hungry ground soak it away.

Fabien noted Darius' return, gathered some of what he'd chopped under an arm and headed inside. He wiped the back of his hand across his brow, both to keep the sweat from his eyes and avoid looking at Verenna. She heard the clatter of the wood as he let it fall by the door. A conversation had started up. She leaned against the wall under the window to hear.

"No one else with Cold Fever so far," Darius sighed.

A chair scraped across the floor and she heard Fabien's boots go up on the table. "Maybe it's already killed everyone it's going to."

"Not at all," the doctor informed. "Cold Fever doesn't stop until everyone's dead."

She heard the map unfurl.

"How soon can we leave? Those hunters will be on to us soon if they aren't already. We can't hide forever." Mortimer's pacing nearly drowned out his words. "I looked around for miles today. We've got everything we need except silver nettle."

"Search harder," Darius demanded. "From what I've gathered, we'll need to make a move soon. I found out a bit more today."

The old man's pacing crossed the window now, keeping any more of the conversation from her ears. As much as her defiant quiet pleased her, she was too curious not to go inside. Wobbling to her feet with the help of the wall she made her way to the threshold.

They stopped talking the moment she rounded the corner, unsure of what to expect. Verenna eyed them warily as she took the few faltering steps up to the table with the map laid across it.

"Continue," she commanded.

Darius shrugged and went on. "They told me about one particular creature they've seen on the road. They think it's living in Bronwell. Apparently, it has roots like a tree and grows to move."

"Sounds like Souris, from what I've heard," Fabien shuddered. "The quicker we get this done with the better."

"Agreed," Mortimer grumbled.

Darius held up a finger. "Not before we wash the city clean. Somehow."

"*I'm* supposed to wash the city clean, you mean," Verenna griped.

"Well, yes."

"Still no information on doing that, I suppose?"

"We just have to work out what 'wash clean' means. And we'd better hurry." Darius leaned in to study the map, tracing the route they'd come with a steady hand. Mortimer took a seat and joined him.

Verenna slapped a hand to the table. "I don't like it. Seems like we're missing too much."

"No one likes it," Fabien said from under his hand as he held his chin to consider the marks on the page.

Not to be left out Verenna cast an eye over the depiction of Bronwell. It seemed so large on the map in comparison to the shrunken shell she'd seen through the trees. The river ran right up to its walls. Then, thankfully, out to sea. She couldn't imagine what rancid water would be gushing into it from the decaying city.

They studied the page for a moment, each alone with their own thoughts, until Mortimer bounded from his seat, upsetting his chair as he backed up against the wall.

"What is it?" Fabien pried.

"The three roads. The two on either side of us. There's disease along them. Only the one we took is clear."

"I'd call that lucky. And I'd call you over dramatic," the doctor dismissed and returned to his investigation.

"No. Look." Mortimer came forward with tentative hands and traced the shape of the roads in the air above the marks, as if he were afraid to touch them. "We're in the center."

Verenna pushed Fabien aside for a better view, leaning in to follow his fingers. Her stomach churned. The marks Darius had drawn seemed to form a mile-wide mouth poised to engulf them.

"A pincer move," Fabien gasped.

"For a disease?" Verenna looked to Darius hoping to see a

smirk, but found no such mirth. His furrowed brow and gently shaking head only confirmed her fears.

"Good God…" he hushed. He braced himself against the table to hold himself steady under the weight of his words. "It's not a disease. It's an army."

About the Author

Alisar Eido's debut novel, Fate of Smoke, is the first book of three in The Soulfire Series. Her works span multiple genres including science fiction, psychological thrillers, dark fantasy, and historical fiction. The author's inspiration stems from her many experiences with strange coincidences and unexplainable events, as well as battles with mental illness. She currently resides in Austin, Texas, with her pens and pencils.

www.ingramcontent.com/pod-product-compliance
Lightning Source LLC
Chambersburg PA
CBHW030255200626
46816CB00002BA/648